RED BIRDS

ALSO BY MOHAMMED HANIF

A Case of Exploding Mangoes
Our Lady of Alice Bhatti

RED BIRDS

MOHAMMED HANIF

BLOOMSBURY PUBLISHING
LONDON · OXFORD · NEW YORK · NEW DELHI · SYDNEY

BLOOMSBURY PUBLISHING
Bloomsbury Publishing Plc
50 Bedford Square, London, WC1B 3DP, UK

BLOOMSBURY, BLOOMSBURY PUBLISHING and the Diana logo are trademarks of
Bloomsbury Publishing Plc

First published in Great Britain 2018

A catalogue record for this book is available from the British Library

ISBN: HB: 978-1-4088-9718-8; TPB: 978-1-4088-9719-5; EBOOK: 978-1-4088-9721-8

2 4 6 8 10 9 7 5 3 1

Typeset by Integra Software Services Pvt. Ltd.
Printed and bound in Great Britain by CPI Group (UK) Ltd, Croydon CR0 4YY

To find out more about our authors and books visit www.bloomsbury.com
and sign up for our newsletters

For Nimra & Poppy

لال تاں پہ ھولاں جاں

And when I look through it, it's red.
    Shah Hussain (Madhu Lal Hussain)

'Something has happened to everyone and if
it hasn't happened yet, it will happen. Only a
matter of time.'

'Please take your seats and don't forget to
switch off your phones. We are about to
begin.'
                    Sabeen Mahmud (1975–2015)

In the Desert

Chapter 1

Ellie

On the third day, I find the plane. I'd been looking for something to eat or drink, anything of nutritional value really. I know that I can't survive for long on the measly rations in my survival kit. A ripped parachute and regulation sunglasses were all I had found on my bruised ass when I came to. Roving Angels would be on their way to rescue me, but sometimes Angels can take their time and in order for this rescue to be successful I need to stay alive.

I unzip my survival kit again to inspect its contents, the things that will keep me alive.

Four energy biscuits.

Two vitamin smoothies.

A roll of surgical cotton.

A roll of surgical gauze.

Needle and thread.

They give you a 65-million-dollar machine to fly, with the smartest bomb that some beam rider in Salt Lake City took years to design, you burn fuel at the rate of fifteen gallons per second and if you get screwed they expect you to survive on four energy biscuits and an organic smoothie. And look, a mini pack of After Eight. Somebody's really spent a lot of time trying to provide the comforts of a three-star hotel. Here, have another towel. Now go die.

I look down and notice that my left boot, my flying boot, is smeared with blood. I pat myself on the forehead, move my limbs about: nothing broken. I wriggle my toes in my boots: all fine, nothing bleeding. A perfect landing. Now if I could only find some part of the plane, more like some remains from that 65-million-dollar machine, my chances of survival might increase. Chin up. Check pockets for any clues. Nothing. Standard maps. A ballpoint pen. A couple of rivets. Always carry them, just in case. A bunch of rivets have never harmed anyone lost in a desert.

Sand in my breast pocket. A half-finished, in fact just-begun, letter. *Dearest Cath, I write this with the heaviest of hearts...*

I am in shock, it will come back to me. Right now, to preserve the clues, to make a positive location ID...

My nametag says *Ellie* and there's an oxygen mask around my neck. There are no ranks on my flying suits, there never are in combat situations. A captain would be too junior to be flying without a formation, most colonels are too elevated and sensible to end up in a desert without a map. So, yes, say hi to Major Ellie.

It started with a meeting with Colonel Slatter. I remember a cup of black coffee, a glazed doughnut and an informal meeting for my annual appraisal.

I wondered what the fuck they were evaluating me for. Everyone was shedding their load in the designated zone, so was I. Did they think that I worked in the household appliances department at Sears? Have I sold enough bed linen? Am I a team player? Do I respect the sanctity of fire exits?

But there are forms to be filled out, even in the middle of a war. And, for Colonel Slatter, filling out the forms for a three-sixty-degree peer evaluation is the war.

Look around, the horizon is clear, the sky as blue as the colour of Cath's eyes. Perfect day for one last mission. Not too far ahead of me the sky dips and merges into the sand. I can't see a single leaf of grass, not even dried-up bush. Earth is a hotplate that doesn't even allow for reptile tracks, even the scorpions seem to have abandoned this godforsaken desolation. Nothing even pretending to be food. I should have eaten that doughnut.

The appraisal had been going well, I thought, I had earned the respect of my juniors and seniors. I had completed my Advanced Desert Survival course. I had completed my Cultural Sensitivity course with distinction though I'd failed to enrol in the compulsory foreign language course, preferably from a high-intensity conflict area. I had not missed a single PTSD session with the squadron's designated therapist. When we got to next year's objectives, I'd mumbled that I wanted a position on the Staff and Command course. 'Not enough points to make the cut,' the Colonel told me. 'Drone operators are running the show now. Zoomies are going out of fashion. We are just museum pieces they keep for old times' sake.'

Great, I thought. They're going to retire me and replace me with a geek in Houston who remote controls drones, someone who can fight a one-handed war while dipping his fries in barbeque sauce.

Colonel Slatter politely suggested that I work towards raising my profile before this happened.

Profile? And I thought we were no-show and all go.

My career had been a bit of a straight line, he said, all bottom-line competence but there were no acts of extraordinary valour, no courage-under-fire-type citations.

But, but, went the Colonel, 'There is a war on and what is a war if not an opportunity, an opportunity to make up those extra points.' Under the Colonel's shaved, shiny head, his eyes were icy blue pools of certainty, the kind that eighteen years of implementing distant wars brings.

I wonder if there is a special medal for pilots who went out on a mission and found themselves lost in the desert. People only talk about being lost in the desert in Sunday school, or in air force folklore. They put GPS chips in pets and migratory birds now, I mean who the hell gets lost these days? And how can someone flying around in a 65-million-dollar machine get lost.

Say hi to Major Ellie.

I scan the horizon, turn around and look at the endless sea of sand surrounding me. I pour a drop of water on my parched tongue.

In the distance I can see the sun reflected in a giant, blurred mirror. If I look long enough, I can see the little ripples running through it, like the sweet waters of a natural lake, like an infinity pool made specially for me. But you can bet your dog tags that there isn't a drop of water to be found there, it's just your mind playing tricks on you.

Desert Survival Rule Number One: Seen something nice? Forget it. It's a mirage.

That reminds me of Desert Survival Rule Number Seven and I slowly start taking off my flying overalls. My suit is olive green with the head of a shrieking bird stuck to my chest and can probably be detected from miles off. I turn it inside out and put it back on. I've blended in now. I can lie down in the sand and wait for the Angels to come and take me away in a helicopter. I can roam around without being detected. I can probably go and search for the camp that was in my cross hair for a second, my thumb ready to push the drop button. Had I pushed it or not? Was the world a little bit safer now or had I fucked up?

There is a Hangar, and there is a Camp. The Colonel had pulled out a map. The Colonel still liked his printed maps and coloured thumbtacks and pointers and cross hairs on targets. Before he could send us off to wipe out a bit of earth, he liked doing his thing with the pointer. In a world of uncertainty, if you can nail them down on a paper map, the enemy's existence becomes much more real.

'You take this out and we are done. One last sortie and you can go home, make babies, and take care of them for the rest of your happy life.' I knew they were offering a little extra to save on long hires. I didn't know they were also dishing out advice on how to spend it. The best pilots of the best air force in the world being treated like cabbies: *Hey, need an extra fare? Here's another bombing run.*

The Colonel had resisted a lot of things in the force. He had resisted the induction of priests in the combat units (*They screw little boys*), when don't ask, don't tell protocol came into effect for homosexuals (*They'll want to ass-rape rather than fight*) and in the end the induction of women into combat units (*Now we are all truly screwed*).

But the Colonel had never resisted a good war, or for that matter any war which had an aerial component to it.

He had earned medals on the battlefield and a stack of warnings for opening his mouth at the wrong time; in the presence of generals he was not above calling them accountants in uniform. Passed over many times for promotion now, his mission briefs had become a bit of street theatre.

'So this camp at the end of the world, hideout for some of the worst human scum, we have positive ID, there is some talk of sending the SEALs in, like one of those night raids that they can film and then jerk off to. I say we take it out first and say it was all a happy mistake.'

A target at the end of the world? By mistake? Is that even legal? Am I to start obeying blatantly unlawful commands? The Colonel considers my silence a declaration of mutiny.

'What do you think I run here? The Salvation Army? It's a combat unit. We are pilots, not fucking monks. You go, you take it out, you take your Purple Heart and get the hell out of here before they start reassigning us to polish the silver in the officers' mess. Do it then you can go and serve your lady love. Ladies are going to bury us all one day anyway.'

Fine, Sir. Fine. But. . .

'Get the goat-fuckers but watch out for our own. Here is us,' he stabbed the map at a random point. 'You'll get the coordinates. Fairly basic. On one side is our Hangar. A refuelling facility. Actually a bit more than that, a rest stop. R&R for those who don't deserve it. You can't miss it. It's massive, air traffic tower, landing strip, the whole works. And on your port side is the compound. It used to be a refugee camp but they downgraded it. Basically a real bad place full of bad bad people. You can smell the evil from the skies. Nobody is going to miss this lot. Trust me on that.'

'What's wrong with the boots on the ground, Sir?'

'Should I have you court martialled for insubordination?'

'Just trying to understand, Sir,' I said.

'The Hangar was my boots on the ground. Their locals started fiddling with our comms and they shut it down. I'm walking blind in there. So get this. My Hangar is shut. But the refugee camp that's the source of all this trouble still exists. And they tell me not to take it personally. Routine. Restructuring. I think we need to take care of that bit of Mother Earth.'

And while I was still thinking whether to report him to High Command or not, the Colonel embarked on his crazy-ass mission to bomb the camp himself and basically went Elvis on us.

I should have learnt. Now say that again.

The 'Desert Survival Rules' emergency procedures section states that if your fellow zoomie crashes during a mission, you don't wait for orders. You hear your man is down, you take off and fly the same route, complete the mission. It used to be about fighting off fear, telling enemies that maybe they can bring you down but you'll still scorch their miserable lives. So they flew after Colonel Slatter and found the debris but no remains. None. Colonel Slatter had crashed his plane and evaporated into thin air. No zero-zero ejection for him. He was the most open man I knew. Now he is mission-briefing-room gossip.

In the beginning of my career there was some argument about Central Command for country, or country for Central Command. It was dropped after Central Command denied any role in running the day-to-day war and claimed it existed only to provide a sort of spiritual underpinning for the war effort. But there are no arguments in the briefing room anymore; you get your mission brief, you inspect your survival kit hoping you won't need to use it. And if it is one of these missions you pop your pill, take a swig of black coffee and hope for the best.

There was a rumour that the Central Command have been reading too many Sufi texts. That they are copying whole sections of SOPs from foreign libraries transported to the States and translated diligently by tenured professors of obscure languages. Central Command insert them into your emergency procedures, into your survival guides. But while they've probably already found nirvana, you get blisters and dysentery. And if you veer too far away from the Path of Oneness, you might get suspended from flying. And what is a pilot who can't fly? No better than a broken-winged shrieking bird.

Fuck Oneness, I need another drop of water.

I walk and walk; I walk past dancing monsters made of sand, past a gutted road, a runway-sized road with a bright yellow line painted in the middle, a big crater which may have been the result of a thousand-pound bomb or a natural water reservoir that has dried up. I come across a mud hut, which might have been a military barrack at some point or a nomads' camel stop. There is a pile of ash in a corner. I sift through it to see if there is anything of nutritional value. There is nothing. I am about to turn back but I decide to walk a bit more, my hand in my pocket, fingering and contemplating the pair of rivets like prayer beads.

I climb over a little sandy hill and see the plane sticking out of the sand. *I found the fucker*, I shout and run towards it.

This is a bad idea. When you see something shiny in the desert, you shall not run towards it; most likely it's something useless like a mirage, or a mirage of something that's useless, like a wrecked plane. While I am running and remembering Desert Survival Level 6B, it occurs to me that my mission here is to rescue the plane. And if you go by the logic of love, and peace and Oneness and everything else that is fucked up about our Central Command's new philosophy of war and advanced survival, then the plane is there to rescue me. As I said, Central Command with their obsession with Oneness have been teaching us 'Moral Enigma, Modern Wars' in the morning, and lecturing us on 'How to Conquer Yourself Before You Conquer Your Enemy' in the afternoon.

Survival courses are all about restating the obvious: What is the temperature at which you lose your sense of direction? It depends on your sense of direction. Does sand have any nutritional value? No, but your own urine filtered through it will keep you alive for an afternoon. Central Command also emphasizes ethical survival. It's not just about staying alive, losing a few pounds, promising yourself to love your wife more, no, you don't just have to get out alive, which you can do if you employ some basic skills, but a better person, a more ethical person.

No guts, no glory, I tell myself and plunge to the task. The plane's nose and the upper part of its canopy jut out of the sand, shining hopefully. I start shovelling the sand with both my hands and realize within a few minutes that it is futile. The more I shovel, the more the sand shifts; the rest of the plane stays out of sight. The sand is very hot and it singes my hands. But I remove my flying jacket and, using that as a shovel, find a way of shifting it. I focus on a small area and start to use my hands again. Underneath the sand isn't so hot. It is cold and moist; it might even have some nutritional value.

The job is done in four to five hours during which I eat another energy biscuit and take three sips of my passion fruit smoothie. Less than half the fucker is here. The plane has broken off neatly just behind the canopy, part of its port wing peeled off, the back half of the fuselage gone, the rear end a jumble of coloured wires, chewed-up shiny pipes, guts exposed. So this is what I have; the front half of an F15 Strike Eagle with two 500-pound laser-guided bombs, one marked YES, the other marked OH YESS in grey stencilled letters. Where did the other half go?

I gently wipe the sand off the canopy. Inside, the cockpit looks familiar. It's like being locked out of your own house, looking in through the window and finding everything in its place, sofa warm and welcoming, dog napping in front of the fireplace, Cath absent-mindedly flicking through *The World of Interiors* in slow motion. How I long to get in and take off. I go over the controls carefully, looking for any signs of life. But the gyros are stuck, radar screen blank, not a single peep from any of the dozens of shiny lifesavers. How did it get here? And, more importantly, how will it get me out of here? There has to be another half of the plane somewhere in this desert. If I can somehow open it, the radio on this thing may still be working. Radios in these things sometimes go on working when everything else stops working. Even when these things catch fire and everything including the pilot burns to a cinder, the radio keeps going. When rescue teams arrive they find lumps of coal and still-intact fireproof bits like helmets and oxygen masks. These lumps of charred material sit here ignoring desperate messages from a very desperate control tower. On paper your flying jacket is also fireproof but the papers don't tell you it can't protect your eyes from melting in their sockets.

Chapter 2

Momo

This place is full of thieves. I know what you gonna say. You're gonna say what's there to steal? And I'm gonna tell you: look with care, there is nothing to steal because everything has already been stolen. You're gonna think maybe you can have a camp without water taps, a camp with road tax, a camp without a road, a camp with electric poles, a camp without electricity, but surely you can't have a camp without a boundary wall? So where is that boundary wall, you gonna ask? Stolen.

You're gonna say how can anyone steal an entire boundary wall? And I'm gonna say you don't know these people, my people.

When it comes to stealing, they are artists.

They stole it brick by brick. Foundations were dug up and every single bit of concrete, mortar was taken away, steel wires were pulled with bare hands. There are those who're gonna blame me for prying the first brick loose, but I did that to keep an eye on the comings and goings of the international-aid types, nice-smelling do-gooders who obviously were the biggest thieves of them all. But they did their paperwork. You see that crater there? That was gonna be a dam for a water reservoir. You see that pile of shining steel poles tied down with chains and locks? That was gonna be electricity. You see that shack with two buffaloes in it? That's my alma mater. For every wad of cash being pocketed, for every sack of grain or sugar being stolen there is a pile of paperwork to prove that it's not being stolen. There was a complaints register where you could report this kind of thing, it had a ball-pen tied to it with a piece of nylon string.

Yes, you guessed that right, it was stolen along with the ball-pen.

There was a waterfall here, yes a proper waterfall, it had shrunk to three feet and the fall was only basketball-hoop high. Bro Ali and I used to bathe under it when I was a child. And that was not a very long time ago. Some people're gonna say that if I was only a child back then how would I know? How can there be a waterfall in the middle of the desert, they're gonna ask. And I'm gonna say you know nothing about this place, my place.

Take a little walk and you'll see the main attractions of our Camp; Allah's Servant's Fresh Chicken and Vegetable Shop, that man is a smuggler and a hoarder and a black marketer. Escape the swarm of flies around this slaughterhouse and you come to the Royal Hardware Depot run by a pair of teenaged thieves who used to steal from the Hangar, and now forage from the desert and sell it on the open market, random piles of scrap metal. The corner shop is occupied by Doctor and his chair rescued from an ambulance, yes there was a time when the Camp had its own ambulance. It ran up and down the streets, blaring a faulty siren, announcing new deaths, promising maybe you're not gonna die and only lose a limb. Where is it now? A pile at the junk shop, you can buy it by the kilo. No wonder Doctor has given up emergency medical care. Everybody saw how he became a doctor, through trial and error because there was no other doctor. But he isn't happy being one. Some people are never gonna like moving up in life. Doctor's all-encompassing attitude to health care is simple; don't worry about your wounds, or your wasting organs, worry about Mother Earth because she really is gonna die.

The blue plastic sheets that serve as the roofs of all the camp houses are joined together. When Mutt is in a good mood he can run from one corner of the Camp to the other just by jumping from one roof to another and comes back within three minutes. Sometimes children chase him, sometimes he chases children. Children are increasingly bored with him.

You can't be a child in this place for long. Blame it on the heat, or buffalo milk or camp food but you are expected to grow up fast. Big bro Ali was two years older than me when he was sold. People tell me now that I am the real boss and every bit of respect I get I have earned, but I know he was the original boss. He didn't even have to try. At school, he was the only one who would read all his books on the very first day of the academic year. His notebooks were full of gold stars.

We woke one morning and instead of his school uniform he put on black overalls, with a golden wing on his chest. It seemed as if he had gone to sleep a normal big brother – who slaps the older boy who fingers you in the street and then comes home and slaps you for having got into trouble in the first place – but woken up with wings. As if the night had turned him into an angel. The day Ali was sold, he was dressed in black overalls but underneath he didn't forget to wear his Boss T-shirt. Of course Bro Ali had no idea he was being sold. He thought he was being offered contractual employment at the Hangar with guaranteed overtime; most bright school graduates think life is contractual employment. I think life is a business opportunity.

Father Dear still insists that he got his son a job at the Hangar.

Mother Dear was still trying to start a fire, tears in her eyes, when he sat on Father Dear's motorbike and went away. *They are powerful because they are never late. They work like clockwork.* I ran after him to give him the omelette roll she had made. But they were a little whirlwind in the distance. He turned around and waved as if telling me he'll be back before I know it. I took a bite from the omelette roll. It turned into sand in my mouth. I threw it to Mutt who had followed me in a state of excitement. He sniffed it for a very long time before gulping it down. I think I like Mutt because he knows how to exercise controlled greed.

How're you gonna keep your integrity in a place where thievery is not only accepted but also expected? If you are not a petty thief, if you are not gonna steal bricks and paper and sugar then surely you are a bigger thief, you are probably gonna steal truckloads of sugar and buy all the bricks and copper wire that all the petty thieves stole. What you gonna do when wading through a morass of moral corruption?

Education, they said. *Education gonna solve all our problems.* There was art education. Art teacher said draw a pitcher, with a crow drinking water from it. There was science education. Newton, science teacher said, sat under an apple tree. I drew pitchers, I thought about Newton. But the real education was on TV. It doesn't always work but when the signal is good you catch bits of Nat Geo Xtra and *Capital Talk*. And Father brought back an old copy of a book called *Fortune 500* from the Hangar. There are men in that book got their own personal yachts. They've got uniformed waiters serving them food in the middle of an ocean. You tell me how drawing pictures of pitchers and crows and sitting under an apple tree gonna help you acquire that yacht? How you gonna pay those waiters' salaries? Maybe you can get all your science and all your art education and then become a waiter on one of those boats.

I focused on my business education and I became an entrepreneur. No, it doesn't mean that since you can't beat them you join them, because they wouldn't let you. And you definitely don't fight with them because you'll lose.

I became a businessman. I buy and I sell. I provide services and I charge. I make deals and I take my percentage. While people discuss problems of growing up, I find solutions to the problems that grown-ups have.

Some might say that I am an evil entrepreneur, a post-war profiteer, a petty black marketer, and I am gonna tell you that is jealousy speak. That's basically petty thieves telling you how petty they are. Show me another fifteen-year-old businessman in this Camp, even all the other camps, who owns his own Jeep Cherokee 3600 CC. It's vintage. It's sky blue. And when we are on our way to make a deal it floats above the sand as if it's being carried on angels' wings. I got plans to acquire a Land Cruiser Vogue which is gonna be more suited to these climes, but even when I have acquired my Vogue I am not gonna abandon my Cherokee. You never get over your first car and your first love. I don't know about love yet (it will come when it comes but I don't intend to fall in love until I have made my first million), but even when I have made a few millions I am gonna keep this princess. How I ever gonna get over a beauty like my Cherokee? Never. It's Momo's promise.

Like every successful businessman I have other assets, some tangible some not, I treasure both equally. After all, what is business? It's the process through which you turn ideas into hard cash, you take positions on futures and you see what bits of the past are gonna do well in the markets.

But sometimes the past is very costly merchandise.

I have to admit that Bro Ali going away like this was a blow we are still recovering from. I was forced to take on the responsibility of running the household; drying Mother Dear's tears, pressing Father Dear's pants. I am not going to school either. And if I am not gonna go to school, then school is gonna remain shut. Buffaloes needed their shelter back, now they have it.

I want those overalls too. People say kid brothers always gonna follow in the footsteps of their older brothers. They are wrong. I want to do better than him. Also what footsteps do you follow when there are no tracks in the sand? We have looked and looked for him, not a sign anywhere. Not even a rumour about him being seen on moonlit nights at the edge of the desert. Sometimes families stand there calling out to their boys and they swear they can see them, they wave their hands and sing lullabies, and shout their annoying nick-names: Moon, Flower, Abdul. . . And then they run towards them and find only shadows on the sand. I stood there with them once and I got to confess, I felt stupid. I didn't see Bro Ali and I didn't see any of the other boys either. When you perform certain actions because everyone else is performing them and then feel stupid, you probably are stupid. I have to admit we have reached a plateau. With the Hangar shut down, no planes coming, no planes going, it seems the whole war thing was started just to take Bro Ali away from us.

But I also hear the call. I can't live here and enjoy the comforts of the Camp while Bro Ali remains missing, living in some hellhole and God knows what they are gonna do with him. There were boys who didn't come back before, but they were not Bro Ali. When you are pushed to the wall you have to go to war because there's nowhere else to go.

When I am stuck for ideas I take my Mutt for a hunt. Sometimes he catches a few lizards, sometimes I have to pull live scorpions from his mouth. Mutt is not suicidal, just plain stupid. Sometimes he gets into a sulk, and runs away to the desert and pretends he is about to die. He always goes to the same spot, the place where we were gonna breed our racing scorpions. He wants me to come looking for him and find him and persuade him to not die.

When Bro Ali didn't come back for a whole week after starting his contractual employment it became clear that contractual employment was code for kidnapping. Around the same time Mutt started seeing things after his brains got fried. I knew that business was gonna have to be put on hold. You can say that it's a mid-career break. But sometimes you need to tend to the family business first.

Did I tell you about the real family business? Father Dear worked at the Hangar, Supplies and Logistics, and ran the occasional workshop on youth affairs, mostly sex education. And his employment and his love for his employers is the source of all our troubles.

I intend to change that. We're gonna become people of independent means. My personal business model is about saving lives and making money while doing it. Rescue and rehabilitation. Bigger risks, bigger returns. They can't have soldiers everywhere. You can't afford to be sentimental about these things. Have you ever seen a fireman cry after he rescues a kitten? He is just doing his job. It's for the kitten owner to cry, or for that small curious crowd with their mouths open as if they are not watching a man in a uniform climbing down a ladder holding a dumb kitten but God himself descending to save his creation.

These people; my people, they are nothing but thieves with tears. Doctor comes over and cries about the dying planet and the sun and the moon. Scrap-dealing brothers cry over not finding more redundant military hardware and falling scrap prices. Others come to Father Dear asking for his help to bring their boys back. These people are rude, they have no shame, asking someone who can't even bring his own boy back.

This is no room for sentiment in my line of work. You look at your liabilities. You look at your assets. You take a position on small, safe investments like my Falcons for Ethical Hunting project. You take a bet on the long-term prospects like I have done with Sands Global.

But a rescue mission is a different kind of business. You need motivation. And, trust me, with Mother Dear's sighs and her laments I have enough motivation. You would think that Father Dear would provide the logistics. If not a car and a gun and a map, at least he should find a way to get us into the Hangar. I can score fuel for the car, I can get my own gun, but can't he get us some ammo and a map? Definitely a map. He ran the Hangar's logistics and all their local purchases for three years and now claims there is nothing in there. All he has to say is that they have moved to a secret base and he doesn't have the security clearance anyway. I can tell that he knows more than he tells us. He behaves like Mutt when he steals a bone but then hides it somewhere because he is afraid of being caught. Father Dear thought we were all set to become rich and powerful. *My boy has a job at the Hangar, it's not like the menial jobs that other boys get. Maybe they'll give him a rank, give him a uniform. If not that, then maybe witness protection programme, because after my Ali is inside the Hangar he gonna know all about the operational stuff.* Let's just say Father Dear got greedy, and now he pretends he's just another hapless dad and honest worker.

Incompetent thieves call themselves honest workers.

He is that kind of dad. I am gonna tell you a story about the guy who cut his finger to help you understand Father Dear better. So the guy cuts his finger accidentally and he asks his friend to piss on his finger so that it might help in speedy recovery or at least save the cut finger from festering. This friend looks at the cut finger, then looks down at his own crotch and says *I can't do that, it's humiliating.* The man with the cut finger begs and pleads and says *I know you respect me and you respect our friendship but what's a few drops of piss between friends?* But the friend says it's all dried up down there.

Sometimes that's how loyalties are tested. Don't get me wrong, Father Dear's moral rectitude is all-encompassing: Father Dear is the kind of person who is not gonna piss on his own cut finger. He is not gonna help me bring Bro Ali home. He is hiding something. How does a person sign up for a job and disappear just like that? I wonder what if a lady cuts her finger would she ask her friend for the same favour? I suspect ladies are gonna be cunning about this. In the first place they are not gonna cut their finger. And if that does happen, they are gonna find a more cunning way of curing the cut finger before resorting to piss remedies.

But Father Dear is also chronically depressed. He is going through a phase of unrequited love for his American employers. This is the problem we suffer from. Not only are we thieves, we are chronic lovers too. Thieves can give up. Lovers can't.

Mutt is also a chronic lover. Mutt is dumb but reliable. He needs appreciation like we all do. Sometimes he needs appreciation when there is nothing to appreciate. Recently he has been seeing things on the rooftops. He raises his mouth and growls as if he has seen a ghost. But you indulge him; you look up towards the roof and assure him that whatever it is he is seeing, you are seeing it too. I indulge him because I am gonna need him. Mutt is essential to the mission.

Also when you love someone you try and train them.

The first step is to acclimatize them to the conditions. I have taken Mutt on long walks and left him in the desert to find his way home. He is a veritable commando now. He can survive in the desert without water for three days and he is never gonna betray my trust. His brain might be fried but his heart is gold.

I am still testing him though, toughening him up. Just the other day I was practising my special free kick on him. The ball hit him, maybe broke something in his fit but brittle body. And he went into a sulk. He is probably waiting near the scorpions' pit in the desert for me to go and find him.

I know he only considers it a game but sometimes it hurts: as if Bro Ali going away wasn't bad enough, now Mutt is also gone. People who leave you of their own accord, without any external pressure, that is always gonna hurt more. Mutt will get over his sulk and little injury and head home.

With Bro Ali, we'll have to go and bring him back.

Mutt will come back himself. He always does.

CHAPTER 3

Mutt

There's a big difference between biters and lickers but the human race is not given to subtleties and most people can't spot the difference. They see the bared teeth, they don't see the lolling tongue. They see the curled-up, shivering tail and not the intellect at work. They hear the growl and not the whine that says *give me some love, oh please give me some love.*

Sometimes it's good to have a bad reputation. It's a matter of utmost satisfaction when you see a pair of feet approaching and although you are only smelling a glacial indifference, or I-am-late-for-work-type thoughts and suddenly they spot you and you can smell rotting apples, the smell of fear of death. The wise ones don't only imagine being bitten, they imagine catching rabies and being drowned in freezing water and then buried in wet earth where the angels who turn up to ask questions will also be dog-faced. The feet take a quick turn as if they have remembered something very important or cross the street as if the angel of death can't do a quick hop and get them across the road. I watch with amusement, stay put and let out a low, prolonged growl, just to reassure the lowlife that his instincts for self-preservation are appreciated. Well done wise man, you can go on living a bit longer. This Mutt appreciates a bit of fear, a modicum of respect even if it's won through deception.

I don't bite. I lick sometimes when I am not sure if it's a friend or an enemy and sometimes I snap at a random shin when I can't reach a conclusion, but really, paw on my heart, I don't bite. Not that I don't know how to, not that I haven't when duty has called, but mostly I can get the job done without resorting to digging my teeth into actual, real flesh.

Mostly I sniff. If one has the reputation of a sage it's because of the olfactory senses and not the sharpness of one's molars.

I can tell what things smell of. Today, for example, my existence smells of an empty-headed, unloved cat. Not that I am complaining. Although I have reason to. Nothing to sniff here but my own broken and bloodied leg. Nobody comes to this part of the desert on a picnic. You come here to die of shame.

I am what they call stoic of nature but sometimes I bark and howl. But do these people listen? This place is in shambles because nobody believes in premonitions anymore, nobody listens to clear and well-articulated warnings.

The day Momo's older sibling was sent away with much fanfare I howled myself hoarse. I begged, I pleaded, I yelped and I barked as if the Camp was about to be overrun by a bunch of foul-smelling cats.

If you prefer cats, I congratulate you; you can put this aside and go play with your grooming kit. I have dealt with many in my time, I have nothing to say on the subject. I congratulate you, you have made a life-positive choice, you have made a choice that will make the world a safer place.

Well done and woof off.

Leave me alone to contemplate my miserable existence.

When they took him away I refused to cry. Crying is for sissies. I refused to behave like a heartbroken princess. I refused to be part of the send-off for Momo's brother when they dressed him up in a white shirt and black overalls in the hope that he'll become a man and bring home a washing machine and a microwave. All they got was tears. Everyone in their own corner with their own tears. An entire United Nations of the teary-eyed.

You would think those touched by tragedy would become kind-hearted. No. They become teary-eyed and cruel.

It was difficult to leave home but I decided to withdraw from that heartless household, where they hark on about your loyalty but never appreciate your intellect. What am I doing here? In the middle of this desert, not a leaf to shade me, neither human nor canine company, just the occasional scorpion consumed by its own quest for invincibility. Did I lose my way? Did I want a bit of solitude? Did I get tired of being best friends with folks who not only call me Mutt but have finally started to treat me like one? What is the point of looking for a single catalytic incident when, as the poet says (I respect poetry but it's not for me, so I am always paraphrasing), an accident doesn't happen in the moment it happens, for years before the accident Father Time is nudging you towards it. And what happened to me was not an accident by any stretch of the imagination, it was an assault, simple and brutal. By my own mentor and best friend and self-styled, so-called owner, Momo.

It's a well-known fact that those under assault from outsiders take it out on their own. The opium eater gets kicked in the bazaar and since he can't hit back, he comes home and kicks his kids. Big, rich nations get a bloody nose in far-off countries and start slashing the milk money for poor babies at home. You can't bring an enemy plane down with a stone, but you can smash your neighbour's window.

There was something about the unexpectedness of the assault, the sheer viciousness of it that shook me. I have taken a few beatings in my life so let's not write me down as a quitter. But when you take a brutal blow to the back, you say, excuse my foul language, forgive my bad breath, but woof this Camp. A curse on this already cursed house. Let's take to the desert. What is the worst that can happen? I'll starve to death. I'll roast under the sun. Better than limping in these desolate streets for the rest of my life. Are these streets desolate, you ask? You haven't seen desolation. When good citizens like me, sons of the soil, start abandoning their ancestral abodes, you should know there is no hope left.

God left this place a long time ago, and I don't harbour any delusions about my own role on this earth but I can imagine what he must have felt. He had had enough. I have had a bit more than that.

On my way out I looked at the desolation one last time. With its plastic blue roofs huddled together the place looks and smells like a giant Portaloo. That servant of God sells deceased chicken, he steals from people and saves it for Allah. Those scrap dealers with their lust for all things shiny, the pillars of the local economy, are a pair of morons. Doctor sits in his own wasteland, he believes everyone should grow their own vegetables. Nobody ever asks him where the proteins will come from.

I am from the times when there were houses instead of this Camp, when there was no war and Doctor wasn't a doctor, only a farmer with an interest in herbs. He could grow stuff with a few drops of water. When the bombs began to fall and the first ambulance arrived I dragged

Doctor right into it, I looked for the survivors and Doctor hauled them into the ambulance. He started to travel in the ambulance with real doctors and nurses and maybe learnt a thing or two: how to stop people from choking on their own blood or tying that knot on a limb that might just save it. And after the real medics went back everyone started calling him Doctor. He can deliver babies and set bones but he is not happy being a doctor. He wants to go back to being a farmer. It could only happen in this Camp: a farmer becomes a doctor but is not happy. He can rid people of their pains but he would rather grow turnips.

Others loitering around the square are drunks and concubines, men pimping their wives for half a bottle of moonshine, wives smashing those same bottles on their buyers' heads and then everyone threatening everyone else with hellfire. We were the only tightly knit, upright family in the Camp and look what happened to us. OK, the older boy did a bit of target spotting for those people in the Hangar who smell like boiled cabbage, but you don't get to own a big jeep by being pacifists.

The jeep was leading a small convoy of Americans on their way to get their water supply. Apparently they had everything they needed in the Hangar except water. The jeep was followed by an armoured car with a gun mounted on the top and a very alert American soldier standing behind it. The jeep broke down in the middle of the square and the Americans had got all kinds of helmets and guns and radios but they hadn't got the one thing they needed: a technician to fix the broken jeep. Urgent messages crackled on their wireless sets, their antennae quivered like an excited Mutt tail. Bro Ali stepped forward and said *may I?* They had three guns pointed at him, as if he was not a teenager offering to help but a highway robber. Bro Ali pointed to the bonnet of the jeep and moved forward carefully. His head and upper body disappeared into the jeep's engine, his legs dangling in the air. After a few moments he shouted, *OK try now*. The jeep shuddered for a moment and then the engine was running. The guns were lowered, Bro Ali emerged trying to suppress a smile of utter satisfaction.

'Thank you, young man,' the tall guy in the helmet said. 'How'd you like to drive one of these babies?'

Bro Ali was shy, he mumbled something about school. Father Dear stepped forward and sealed our fate. 'But he can work after school, he is very good with machines.'

Father Dear became Mr Fix It for the people at the Hangar, their logistics man, their local guy. He procured goats for them, and when they asked for local help, he got them boy labourers, boys on daily wages who were sent off to do small jobs, fixing broken barbed wires and filling up sandbags to make more bunkers. Sometimes the boys didn't come back, but those were busy times and nobody took much notice.

This place was something back then. Life had some meaning. Don't get me wrong, I am an out and out pacifist, but I miss the time when those white cabbages in uniform from the Hangar used to drive through the Camp and we used to have falling bombs. Those whistles, those sirens, those blasts, all that whoosh, whoosh, whoosh used to scare the Mutt-shit out of me. It was terrifying. But later, after everything that could explode had exploded, there would be calm. And much rubble to jump over, burnt flesh to be sniffed; there were search parties to be led to the people under the rubble who would be cursing everyone on this earth. One saved lives. One got a biscuit as a reward. Life was good. It had a purpose. There was terror but after that there was life to be sniffed out and saved or funerals to hang out at, where you could smell rose water over the freshly dug earth and feel sad. The smell of rose water is the smell of sudden death after a well-lived life.

Have they run out of bombs?

There has not been a bomb since Momo's older sibling wore the black overall and his mother hugged him about a hundred times and he was sent off. The Americans say he went missing. They used to say he went up into the mountains on a mission and is still there. Now they say nothing. Momo says his father sold him to the Americans at the Hangar because he was very good at sending signals to the planes telling them where to bomb. If you are cooperating with the people who destroy your houses, it can have tragic results. But one has to say that he was good at that, our Bro Ali. But what if he refused to tell them where to bomb after they hired him? He would have had his reasons. And Bro Ali was stubborn as a Mutt's tail. Once he stole Father Dear's files just for fun and when Father Dear beat him black and blue he refused to say a word. How is a Mutt supposed to know the truth about these things? But you don't sell your sons even if you are being paid in dollars. Even if your son is a brat. Even if your son is asking for it.

But they believe in big theories. They can't believe that someone might go off of their own accord and then might not want to come back. Whatever modest intelligence I had I shared with Momo and look where it got me. A mangled leg. The desert. Distant sounds of metal cracking in the sky. What is going on up there? There was such a din last night that for a moment I thought those happy days of night raids were back. But it lasted only for a few seconds and then there was silence.

And it's the middle of the day now. Not a leaf for shade. Even the lizards have gone into hiding. My only companions here are stupid scorpions looking for other scorpions to fight or make scorpion love to.

So maybe I lost my way. Maybe I decided that there is only so much that this Mutt can take. But here I am missing that desolate place that I have left behind forever. It always irritated me when Momo called me a drama queen. It implied lack of intelligence on my part, as if I had let my emotional self override my rational being, or as if I was creating a scene to get attention. And here I am feeling nostalgic about falling bombs. And about those who call you their best friend ever and then plunge a dagger in your back.

Yes, you can call me sentimental.

Is it possible they really have run out of bombs?

Like they ran out of salt.

Before the second worst day of my life, before the worst day of my life, there were the best days of my life.

Sometimes between dropping bombs they used to drop these slabs of salt, pink hewn and white, and they floated down tied to little umbrellas. The good thing about them was they didn't make any noise, no alarms went off, nothing burnt, no houses collapsed, there was nothing to sniff, nothing to save. Only a lot of excited cattle to deal with. This salt bombing was supposed to be some humanitarian plot to help us animals. Apparently if animals lick salt they don't catch all those nasty diseases that spread because of the rotting human flesh. And all the so-called animals rushed to this falling manna. Nobody obviously considers Mutts animals or that we might also need a dose of salt; I never thought I had that need. But then curiosity is essential for the brainy dog, I also needed to know what the ruckus was about, so I would sneak in. Trust me, I have been there: when goats or cows were licking salt they were so absorbed that they would not kick or head butt you. So I could sneak in between their legs and take a lick. But more than licking I loved looking at those salt slabs, they seemed to hide pink treasures, as if somebody had mined jewel-laden rocks and thrown them around the desert. After every three licks a cow would look up to check if there was more falling from the sky or maybe just to make sure that no one up there was looking down. And then they'd look down at their hoofs and in this heavenly salt-induced kindness they would lick me too. Oh that breath. It was horrible and smelled of the memory of calves forcibly taken away when still suckling and the foul smell of all that milk stolen by humans. You can't tell them, *listen big mama, hold your tongue, it's my job to lick.*

As I ran out of the Camp one last time I could smell grief wafting out of the stoves in people's houses. Someone was sent, someone didn't come back. There is a school uniform shirt, pressed and waiting in the cupboard, a deflated football, half-finished drawings of pitchers and crows on the walls. The boys who have gone for a bit, the boys who will come back soon.

There is no going back for me. There is nothing to lick but sand. I can smell hunger approaching me. Yes, someone even hungrier than me is walking towards me. Imagine. I try to bury my head in the sand. It's not possible. The atrocities they have committed with the language. My head is on the sand. My fractured leg hurts.

But what is really broken here is my heart.

Chapter 4

Ellie

On the sixth day I come across the first signs of habitation. I find a copper bowl half buried in what must have once been a stream. It is caked in mud. I clean it carefully with the sleeve of my flying suit, at the bottom it reveals some oriental calligraphy. I wish I had taken that basic Arabic or Persian or modern Pashto course they were offering instead of the guerrilla gardening module that I went for.

I look up and look around with renewed hope.

In six days I haven't seen one sign of life. If the goat-fuckers had shot me down they would be all over the place trying to hunt me down. Or maybe they just like shooting people down and have no interest in capturing and torturing them, they see no point in getting information from them or making their videos. Nihilistic resistance is the worst kind of enemy; it was all the rage, we were taught in our Cultural Sensitivity 101. Colonel Slatter had laid out the foundations: We used to have art for art's sake; now we have war for the sake of war. No lands captured, no slaves taken, no mass rapes, fuck their oil wells, ignore their mineral deposits. You can outsource mass rape. War has been condensed to carpet-bombing followed by dry rations and craft classes for the refugees. People who had not left their little hamlets for centuries, goatherds who believed in nothing but grassy fields and folk music, women who had never walked beyond the village well, now they could all go and live in UN tents, eat exotic food donated by USAID and burp after drinking fizzy drinks.

The progress, the old kind, was too slow; you couldn't make a modern civilization out of screwing sheep. You couldn't wait for the roads to arrive, for tourist resorts to be built. If the world has to end, as it must – there are no exceptions now, everyone from the Jesus-is-knocking-on-your-front-door nuts to the earth-is-hotting-up-and-we-are-all-going-to-get-roasted freaks agrees – things must quicken, interventions must take place. You can't give them drip irrigation and tent schools and hope for them to become civilized and accomplish the next millennium goals. Where's the thrill in that? What is the point of denying human nature when it will always be about taking over your neighbour's house and screwing his young wife. Give these men on camelbacks rocket launchers and see them arrive in the new millennium with a bang. They don't even need an ideology. Or any elaborate training. A rocket launcher doesn't require you to have the ability to aim. Get it on your shoulder and shoot.

It's Colonel Slatter speaking in my head. The Colonel had taken off after I had dithered and never came back. Still listed as Missing in Action. MIA my ass. Now here I am living up to the tradition. Your zoomie goes down, you follow his path. I wonder if maybe Colonel Slatter survived his crash and now roams the desert, terrorizing goatherds. When you start talking to your dead comrades, you are about to join them.

Wake up.

The wind picks up speed, sand around me slowly starts to lift and hover; the beginning of a storm, or just a gentle breeze, I can't tell. There is a lot that I can't tell about this place. It had all made sense on the Desert Survival Course, you can mark your escape route by picking out the direction in which the sand swirls. I pick up my binoculars and take a look. I see a flag fluttering in the distance. Maybe I've got something in my eye, I rub them, open them again and see a red blur. I can't tell if the red patch is in my eye or is out there in the desert.

The desert fills your eyes. Your eyes become desert. I've got used to it by now. A bird. No, it isn't a bird. Depending on the time of day I keep seeing things that turn out to not be what they were. Mirages. We had discussed them in our 'Introduction to Cultural Sensitivity' module in Advanced Desert Survival. At first I had thought they were talking about the Mirage fighters, those French contraptions that were handsome beasts, like most things French, but completely useless in a real war, like most things French. But this mirage, Colonel Slatter, said was like sand blinging, sand pretending to be not sand, sand playing its oldest tricks, sand which from a distance looks like water and you motherfuckers run towards it and by the time you get there, there is no water, just some more sand. And you have already wasted a lot of water within your body and now you are dying just because you saw sand that you thought was a water body.

Don't do that. Don't. Even if you are sure that what you are seeing is not just a body of water but a proper oasis, with those Arab trees and a lush pond, and topless chicks in transparent veils and shimmering pants beckoning you. Even if you can count those ladies, even if you can see through their harem pants, don't run. Wait and contemplate. Your water-starved little brain is playing tricks on you. But if you find the spectacle too real, then walk slowly.

Shut your eyes and open them again. Think of the children. Think of all the dying children in all the wars in the world. If you are not careful, if you don't watch your step, you are about to become one of them. And nobody is going to feel sorry for you because you are not really a child. If you get closer and still believe in what you see then either you are already a zombie or on the way to becoming one. You should be glad if you are already a zombie, because you are not going to like what comes next. You are going to wish that you were dead. Not dead in the whining I-wish-I-was-dead sense but, like, for real, because you are going to get so much pain from those shimmering beauties that don't exist and that you insist on running towards. It's called a mirage; there's a fucking reason. It's a French word, what good can come of it.

Colonel Slatter had continued as the rookies in our workshop covered their mouths and giggled. 'Because if you are lucky, sure there is a pond full of warm piss and some shrub too. Well as far as you and your starving ass is concerned it is paradise on earth, a little gated community with canals full of milk and honey, a valley of sex-starved girls and eternal erections.

'And your mother's name is sweet Mary and your father is Joseph who never ever touched her.

'What you'll find is a goatherd. If you're lucky you find a camel-herd, because they tend to be a bit aloof, like their herd they are well fed and patient – maybe occasionally vicious but patient – also, whatever their reputation, screwing camels is a major inconvenience. Also camels have long memories. No camel-herder messes with their camel. It says so in their book. Their ancient poetry is full of how you shall not mess with your camel. And definitely not with someone else's camel.

'So with your luck, you'll meet a goatherd with a flute, playing some stupid sad-ass melody that'll make you homesick. And he'll welcome you because he is bored of the fucking goats and bored of the constant whine of his own flute. He is an artist without an audience and hates himself for playing that flute. In the end he'll butcher you like he butchers one of his goats every few weeks, but before that he'll bugger you. And although the first thing you are thinking is that our great nation's honour is getting soiled at the hands of some sad-ass, flute-playing goatherd, it will be more personal. It will hurt. He'll not give you any water after that first cup he gave you. He'll just encourage you to bend down and slurp it from the pond, to be one with the blasted nature. And he does it not because he is a nature lover, no he hates nature, he wants to escape nature and live in that porn movie that he once saw, with the foam mattress and two Russian women; no, he has asked you to slurp the water from the pond so that he can check out the thing that he has been waiting to bugger, that pale, grateful butt of yours.

'You'll be wondering, where did those dancing girls disappear to? Maybe they're preparing a feast for you or maybe their culture doesn't allow them to prance semi-naked in front of a starving white zoomie. And the shepherd will start playing his flute again to get himself in the mood while you'll be slurping that piss-coloured water, and you'll think you are somewhere safe. You are finally about to taste the legendary hospitality of the desert folks. You know what this hospitality business is, right?

'You are about to find out.

'There's a ninety-nine per cent chance he'll slaughter you. The remaining one per cent chance is that he'll want to invite his friends over, have a little party and the last one to bugger you gets to decide if they should slaughter you now or gift you to some other fellow goatherds.'

Colonel Slatter would announce a coffee break at this point, so that we could contemplate these images for another fifteen minutes over decaf and cookies.

This was the core module of Cultural Sensitivity.

I look through my binoculars once again. The sand is still floating around my knees; no storm, but at the edge of my sight sand is swirling. I can't see any red smudges anymore, I can only see a whirl of sand moving slowly, determinedly towards me, as if a bit of desert is looking for an oasis and has found it in me. From this swirl emerges Cath, in a white shimmering kaftan, her arms open and inviting. She has finally come to take me away. I try to run towards her and then she isn't there anymore. Things appear and disappear. Like Cath was once here, on the sofa, in the bed, on the phone, across the restaurant table, choosing baby names, looking at adverts for properties near good schools; then in the ambulance, in the hospital and gone but still here, everywhere. The most common myth amongst unhappily married people is that one day their spouse will die a not-very-horrible death and they will come back to an empty home from the funeral with a grieving heart, aching to start a new life. But when they do come home they usually find their partner sitting on the sofa, asking them where they've been.

You believe in this mirage, you believe in anything.

Chapter 5

Momo

I've been dreaming of a man falling from the sky. He's not falling as a man thrown from the sky would fall, like a stone hurled by a furious god. He is floating down, like a flower petal plucked and dropped by a god in a good mood. As he approaches the earth, his eyes widen; he's falling to an earth that he recognizes from a bad dream. I have got my hands up in the air to catch him, or at least to steady his fall. His weightless body floats into my hands, the earth beneath my bed shudders and I wake up.

Mutt is trying to drag me out of the bed even though it's still dark, his wet nose in my ear, his paws tugging at my chest. It's days before he takes a hit during our training and disappears into the desert.

I give him a sleepy hug and wonder if that's what's gonna happen to me now? Am I gonna go back to God? When I was twelve and a half I turned into a proper God's man. I had my hand on his pulse (or whatever God has in place of a pulse). I could pray with such intensity that I'd get proper fever. I would borrow Mother Dear's rosary and speed-read all His names: the creator, the destroyer, the forgiver. . . Mother Dear would look at me with pride and give me an extra biscuit with my glass of milk as Bro Ali looked at me with disdain. 'Look at you using God's name to get an extra biscuit.' But I was beyond his taunts. I would go to sleep shivering with His fear and wake up in His warm embrace and, despite my morning erection, feel His holy presence. Now I know that everyone goes through that phase in their early teens. The pleasures of the spirit visit us before the pleasures of the body. The awakening of the soul occurs just before we can learn the ecstasies of rubbing our own flesh.

Am I gonna become a relapsed teenage fanatic? I don't think so. Because He ruled himself out of the game one day. That day.

Let's say God was kind to me and I was His humble servant, but then Bro Ali didn't come back from the Hangar. I prayed with extra care, appealed to His sense of fairness – *O solver of all problems, O revealer of all those who are missing, O the most merciful, please, please, please* – and then I said what the hell. No Bro Ali, no God. Simple as that. No deal. There are others who're still at it, reciting His names and hoping that He's gonna bring back their sons and fix the electricity. I hope one day they're gonna meet Him up there in the sky, then they can ask Him if He had a plan or was just having some fun with his favourite people, the people of the desert.

Bro Ali was prepared to go. I have to admit that he was a bit bored with life around here. He didn't see any potential in this place. He had no business acumen. When I started my Sands Global project he went all patriotic on me. 'This sand is the earth you walk on, it's like selling your mother,' he would taunt me. And I would say what about all those countries that sell oil? 'Are they selling their mother's milk?' I would ask him why was he going around giving them targets. 'Did you ask them to bomb our house so that you could prove your loyalty and get a job with them? Is that your idea of being patriotic?' And he would pull that *you are too young to understand* face and walk away. Some people are born to be slaves. He had to become a corporate slave. And slaves, by the very nature of their profession, are not supposed to be very good at bargaining.

What do you want to do in life? I asked him.

I want to see the world.

What does he wanna see the world for? It's the same everywhere. Mothers, fathers, junk shops, schools, Hangars. You know what I wanna do with the world? I wanna own it. Or at least I wanna own some nice chunk of it.

I was in class and after I had drawn a pitcher and written an essay on the topic 'The Happiest Day of My Life' I raised my hand and asked the teacher: 'How do you build a supply chain?' I read in *Fortune 500 Annual* that what makes a business great is not production, not distribution, not HR, but a great supply chain. Teacher was surprised.

'If I need to own a yacht, I need to have my own business and a business gonna need a solid supply chain. Can you teach me how to build it?'

Science teacher, of course, had never had any ambition. 'What do you need a yacht for? Have you even seen an ocean?' He is not even gonna become a Newton because he thinks there are no apple trees around here. I have seen the ocean in *Jaws 2* but there was no point telling him that. Later I asked Bro Ali the same question and he was no help either. He thinks I lack morals.

'Why don't you say you are going to grow up and become a thief, like the rest of them,' he said.

It seems he disappeared in the middle of our argument.

Here, Mother Dear is gonna correct me and say *your father sold him like sheep.* Let me correct her. Father Dear has never sold sheep. Father Dear has never sold anything. Father Dear has no entrepreneurial skills. Father Dear is a mere accountant and not a very good one at that. He also thinks he is a social worker, a sex-education professional. He thinks he is the best. Nobody laughs at his jokes.

I am still trying to calm Mutt down, still trying to remember the features of the man descending from the sky, his fear still infecting me. What am I gonna be afraid of? A man falling from the sky? The sky itself could fall and I'm gonna stay right here; I would figure out a way to turn it into part of my business portfolio.

In the morning Father Dear brings home Lady Flowerbody.

Let me clarify that I have no interest in insulting nicely dressed working ladies who I assume also must smell nice and do nice things and have nice manners. It's Mother Dear who calls her Flowerbody, her way of saying that the early-morning visitor is no more than a common slut. And her proof is that Father Dear presents her as a co-worker of sorts. That's the kind of father Father Dear is, he has no work but he claims to have co-workers. Nobody ever answers his petitions but he carries his files around as if they contain all the answers to all the mysteries of our universe.

Mother insists on calling her *this* Flowerbody even after she is introduced as the new Coordinating Officer for the Families Rehabilitation Programme. I hate to insult a woman based on her character, let alone her looks, after all they are born with their faces and bodies and everybody needs a job, but Mother Dear is certain that we have a dubious character in the house. *Look at that hair, look at that make-up, what is she doing here anyway?* Mother

Dear's fingers are frozen around her rosary. 'Shouldn't she be taking care of her own family rather than trying to wreck other people's families?' she says.

We've had researchers before. They were these nice-smelling do-gooders who would give us powdered milk and ask about our feelings then note them down in lovely, leather-bound notebooks.

'She is the new Coordination Officer for. . .' Father Dear clears his throat. He has spent a lifetime clearing that throat only to realize that he has nothing to say.

He also coughs gently, as if coughing gently makes him the voice of reason. They disappear into the kitchen. Yes, that same kitchen where Mother had a last chat with Bro Ali and shoved me out. She never told me what they talked about. I am not gonna ask because that'll bring more tears and she'll start spitting God's names at me. Mutt sneaked in and, although you can rely on him to find long-lost items, he doesn't know much about how family works. He came out howling. I am the only family he has ever had, and I am the only family he is ever gonna have.

There is a whispered argument in the kitchen, escalating into a whispered fight that nobody is supposed to hear but everyone does. Mother Dear's trademark whack to Father Dear's shoulder followed by his threats of divorce and murder. It's all audible from where Lady Flowerbody is sitting outside in the courtyard on a plastic chair, eyeing up dried-up plants in clay pots, admiring the green glass shards covering our boundary wall. It's obvious that she can hear it but she is looking into the distance as if she has nothing to do with this raging domestic squabble. I try to distract her by introducing her to Mutt who seems to be saying yes, alright, your mother might be pre-judging her character but this woman is trouble.

It's quite obvious that part of her training is to ignore conversations about her role in this world. I myself appreciate good training; if my schedule was not so packed I would start training Mutt all over again. Nothing can replace good, old-fashioned training. But it's useless here; Mutt's brains are fried. This whole nation's brains are fried. You live in this compound, your brains are fried. We can train them all their life and then when it comes time to put it into practice they gonna forget their training and go back to God. When it's time to run to the trenches or evacuate in case of a fire or even form a simple queue to get their rations, half of them start shouting God is great, the other half starts cursing each other's ancestors. Their sons keep going away and they keep waiting for them hoping they will return one day bearing goody bags from a better world.

'Who is that woman?' Mother Dear has dragged Father Dear out and is interrogating him in front of Lady Flowerbody. 'And what in God's name is she doing in my house?'

Father Dear is unfazed, as if giving a job interview on her behalf. 'She is a USAID consultant. She works with the families affected by raids and is conducting a survey on post-conflict conflict resolution strategies that involve local histories and folklore.' Father Dear is cradling his stack of files that contain all the petitions he has ever sent.

'Why is she calling us names, why is she saying families affected by this and that? Why doesn't she say his name? How has she come here? Can she walk in the desert with those shoes?'

I was beginning to appreciate her taste in shoes. Those could double as weapons in hand-to-hand combat situations. I was thinking her blue-tinged, shoulder-length hair and the pulsating mole on her upper lip were a welcome change in our drab household. Three parallel wrinkles on her forehead speak of an intelligent mind. The ones who came before her never smelt this nice. And they stopped coming anyway when the Hangar shut down. It was simple, they bombed us and then sent us well-educated people to look into our mental health needs. There were workshops called 'Living With Trauma' for parents, there was a survey about 'Traditional Cures in a Time of Distress and Disorder'. Our Camp was the tourist destination for foreign people with good intentions. I tried some of my business ideas on them. They were hopeless.

'I am here to work with teenagers,' she says, trying to spare Father Dear some embarrassment. The mole on her lip turns into a red dot.

'He is not a teenager, he might act like one but he is no teenager. He is a good-for-nothing old man. That black hair is dyed.' Mother Dear is not done with Father Dear yet.

Lady Flowerbody smiles an understanding smile, as if she gets paid per insult.

'My PhD thesis is on the Teenage Muslim Mind, their hopes, their desires; it might come out as a book called *The Children of the Desert*. But I am trying to extend my academic work, I want to put my ideas into practice,' she says. 'I intend to use this community as a laboratory for testing my hypothesis about how our collective memories are actually our cultural capital. . .'

You need to be careful about what you read. Bro Ali read many books and it made his mind a place of trouble. If this lady writes a book about my mind who is gonna read it? Not me. Whenever I have the urge to read I go back to my copy of *Fortune 500* or turn on the TV and hope there's a signal and *Secret Millionaires* is on. . .

And now I am thinking is there money in this? Is this lady gonna provide another revenue stream? Can I get her to be part of my very own rehabilitation plan?

Mutt gives her a sniff and comes back shaking his head. He has marked her as a spy. As far as Mutt is concerned anybody who doesn't kiss his wet snout is a spy. But if she is a spy, then better to have her under one's own roof, get her to see what you want her to see. I am never gonna be a spy myself but I know how it works. It's spirituality for people who are otherwise completely, hopelessly practical.

Tea is served. More tears are shed. Many more of God's names are uttered. The argument has moved on. It's about sleeping arrangements.

'Can you have a single, unattached woman sleeping under your roof when we have a young man in the house?' Mother Dear is talking about me. Mother Dear is talking about our house, the house I built. Bro Ali was the lead builder but my input was more than substantial. We built it with the rubble from our old house and a little help from USAID. It may not seem much to Lady Flowerbody but it's a palace as compared to the other houses in the Camp. It's a combination of standard-issue prefab and what survived of the old house. When they gave us the same blue plastic corrugated sheets for the roof I protested – *can't we have another colour at least* – but the prefabs came in the same blue for everyone. Bro Ali felt responsible so he worked extra hard. Bro Ali rescued the tiles from our bathroom, the solid wooden doors were pulled from their hinges and sawed off and recycled as windows. The kitchen is a chrome cooking hob, a gas cylinder and an open-fronted cupboard for Mother Dear's brass crockery from her dowry. The master bedroom has a carpet and a real spring mattress. In the corner of the living room there's a TV that Mother Dear

45

covers with a bed sheet as if it was a chick who needed to do purdah because of young men in the house. The courtyard is massive and Father Dear had the bright idea of lining the boundary wall with shards of broken glass, remnants of a container of empty J&B whisky bottles from the Hangar. Two cabins are installed at the other end of the courtyard for guests. A rainbow of nylon washing lines stretches across the courtyard. One day there will be drawing and dining rooms, a gaming room, a boardroom for business meetings, a four-car garage for my personal fleet of vehicles – but right now it is what it is. And it's not a dump. It's gonna change soon, but as Mother Dear reminds us, I am still a young man.

I approve of being referred to as a young man, but nobody is gonna cast aspersions on my character. This young man is not gonna fall for a honey trap. When you are aiming high, nice-smelling tits are not gonna pull you down. I know how to prioritize. My aims are much higher than nice-smelling tits.

'She is a consultant. She has been sent to assess the psychological effects of post-war adjustments that young people have to make to integrate with the changing world and their own evolving bodily needs.' Father Dear knows he wants to slip in his philosophy about the importance of sex education.

I shake my head in enthusiastic agreement.

The plan you don't fully understand is a revelation about to happen.

Mother Dear doesn't need consultants in this house. She doesn't need psychological assistance to get a grip on her life. She doesn't need folklore or any such sad-ass lectures to get her life–work balance right. She wants her son back. She wants to go to sleep watching him snore gently. She wants to pile more butter, more sugar on his bread. She wants to give a gentle tug on his trousers to hoist them up before he goes out. She wants to hear him banging at the door, barging in and shouting *I am hungry*. She wants to collect his shirts strewn on the floor and smell them before throwing them on the laundry pile.

Father Dear does the only thing he knows will work with her. 'She has contacts,' he says. 'She'll help find information about him. The Hangar might be shut but she knows people in the Headquarters.' I find it strange that he doesn't mention Bro Ali by his name. Mutt raises his face to the sky and gives a long yelp, which is his idea of calling out an overdose of bullshit. He is not a very good observer of the human condition. He doesn't understand human longings. He used to have some manners but he lost them all in the accident when his brains got fried. Now he is never gonna learn.

'Of course, the process of rehabilitation can't start till we recognize our losses,' says Lady Flowerbody, showing her professional side, which means *I'll say anything you want to hear.*

Mother Dear is not impressed. 'I refuse to recognize my loss. It will never be my loss. If you don't give my son back, you'll learn the meaning of the word loss. Your do-gooder families will burn. Your fragrant world will rot.'

Flowerbody is frazzled and makes a noise. 'I don't want to be misunderstood. Managing expectations is part of my job.'

Mother Dear is in no mood for misunderstandings or clearing them up.

'So you mean that you don't have anything to do with the people who took my son now? You work for them but you don't know what they really do? You mean to say that there is one department that picks them up and then another department that is sent out to make us forget them? Are you here to make us feel heroic for losing our son?'

'I am trying to help.'

'How?' Mother Dear demands. 'First they bomb our house, then they take away my son and now you are here to make us feel alright.'

'I know people who work specifically on cases where people disappear. Let's admit that things happen on both sides. It's very tragic of course, the loss of a loved one. I have access to some data. We can make a beginning.'

Mother Dear approves of this beginning. 'You'll sleep out in the shack next to the main gate and you'll not leave the Camp until my son is back.'

CHAPTER 6

Mutt

The second worst day of my life started unremarkably. I woke Momo up early as we needed to begin our work on his Falcons for Ethical Hunting project. We were still in the training phase. Momo is big on capacity building. Momo had been training a kite to hunt. He thought that since a kite already looks and acts like a falcon, all it needed was a nudge, some motivation and some on-the-job training. He had been starving the kite to motivate her. Starving a scavenging bird for business purposes is something only humans can think of. And Momo goes around saying that *my* brains are fried.

Momo sleeps in Bro Ali's bed now, although I am not sure if he gets any sleep anymore. One gentle lick on his ear and he jumped out of the bed. When Bro Ali was around I had to wrestle Momo out of that bed.

Momo thinks that I had a moral compass before the accident with the electricity pole in which my brains got fried. In his book – and I say that figuratively, as the boy has no interest in books of any persuasion – I was a morally upright Mutt before the accident. Now I am just another depraved beast. He also thinks I have become a thief. A laughable allegation. Why would I steal? I take what I need. That's all there is to it. I don't own safe houses and lockers, I don't borrow and I don't lend. Do I have a godown full of bones somewhere? Momo has turned an embarrassing incident into a justification for my continuing character assassination. The same Momo who used to say his Mutt has more guts than any warrior who walked this land. The same Momo who used to say not only am I his best friend but his *only* friend. That I am better than family because he had not chosen his family. He might have wanted to say brother but couldn't because that might spark off a conversation about his real brother and people would ask *Did your dad really sell your brother? For how much? What if he decides to sell you one day?*

On a still, dusty day when the sun couldn't decide if it wanted to shine bright or sulk all day, the kite arrived. A slightly injured kite, not in any critical danger I must say, with one broken wing, landed in the courtyard. She was obviously looking for something to steal but Momo was all over her as if she was a long-lost lover. Mother Dear ignored it. He is a good boy, learning to take care of the injured. If a boy can care for a stray injured bird, that boy might one day learn to care for his long-suffering mother as well. Sad mothers are made of compulsive, reckless optimism.

But oh, the human duplicity. Whenever I hear the word 'care' or 'compassion' on Momo's lips, I can see dollar signs in his eyes.

I can tell when Momo has a business plan. I circled around the little filth-eating scoundrel with a broken wing from the avian world. I tried to tell Momo that maybe it looks like a falcon from a distance, but it's no falcon at close quarters. It's a sad specimen of scavenger, something that you'd get if your average crow spent a few amorous moments with a below-average vulture, a falcon's poor cousin. But Momo already had a plan. And you can't tell Momo anything when he has got a plan.

He once saw a convoy of Arab sheikhs with six Range Rovers and a hooded falcon. They had come for a hunt, and although they didn't find anything to hunt Momo says he saw with his own eyes that they fed their falcons minced beef and, he swears, chocolate bars too. So Momo got this idea that if he could train this kite to hunt, he could sell it to the sheikhs when they come around next hunting season. Momo was thinking that he would trade this misery on wings for a Range Rover Vogue. Because Momo remembered that two of the Range Rovers in the convoy were empty. He is at that tender age where he doesn't understand the concept of backup vehicles. He doesn't understand the concept of backup anything.

Not that Momo cares. Not that he listens. He went rummaging through his mother's closet looking for things that he could use as hoods for the kite's eyes. He was convinced that all it takes to turn a scavenging filthy bird into a royal falcon is a pair of hoods. His mother's under-garments were too big for the kite's tiny, hungry eyes so he decided to use his I Heart NY cap.

I have said this before and I'll say it again. Momo is Momo and he'll do what he wants to do. Momo is quite attached to his cap. He is attached to me too but a boy this age can be attached to more than one thing. When he wears this cap he feels that he is the king of the Camp. As far as I am concerned, cap or no cap, he is the king of everything he surveys. As soon as he puts it on he starts to smell like cherry blossoms, which is the smell of conquering-the-world-then-on-to-Mars type of overconfidence.

So I pissed on that cap.

I am not the kind of Mutt who will do his business everywhere. This is my house and you don't go around pissing in your own house. But I was sitting there keeping an eye on this nasty little piece of shit from the birdie world. It was squirming under Momo's cap, trying to get out, whimpering like a sick puppy. What was I supposed to do? I did it to prove to Momo that this kite was no falcon, if it couldn't even defend itself against a Mutt's piss, how was it going to hunt other birds? Also the kite was practically asking for it. Really it was not the I Heart NY cap that I pissed on, I have the highest regard for the cap, the cap is crucial to maintaining our status in the Camp, but that stupid kite wanted to be pissed on.

It was almost an act of mercy.

Having fulfilled her sick desire, I panicked. I was forced to hide the cap, like an amateur criminal who thinks that he can just wipe off surfaces and nobody will notice that there is a body on the floor.

And now Momo thinks I am a thief.

You hide a soiled cap because you are slightly embarrassed after a compulsive act of compassion, and you are called a thief. You think you can turn scavengers into hunters by keeping their eyes hooded and you are a genius.

As I said, Momo is Momo and he is a genius.

I had every intention of sticking by him. If he says there is an enemy army on the other side of the mountain I yelp, *yes people, listen up people, there is a huge army on the other side of the mountain*. I say it with conviction even when there is no army, not even a single soldier, not even a mountain in sight.

I hid the cap because I wanted to avoid a mega Momo tantrum. And I believed then, and I believe now, that hiding things doesn't make you a thief. Here's a list of things that

I have hidden and you decide if it makes this humble Mutt a thief.

The carcass of a cat who died accidentally.

A bullet pouch from the now defunct Central Ammunition Depot at the Hangar, from when natives were allowed in.

A key ring with a compass and two rusted keys.

Lady Flowerbody's nail-polish remover.

And, of course, our beloved I Heart NY cap.

Momo went ballistic. Called me a Mutt.

I am not the type to get upset when called a son of a bitch. But Momo had forgotten his manners. All over a stupid cap. I was only trying to save him from his silly plans. Arab sheikhs wouldn't be sheikhs if they started giving away their backup Range Rovers in exchange for a half-blind kite with a fetish for golden showers. This is not how distribution of wealth works in post-war economies.

For a few moments it seemed Momo had seen the folly of his ways as he reached for his football. Whenever Momo's business plans come apart he reaches for his football. And he kicks the ball so hard, and straight to the sky, that it disappears for a long time and only comes back to earth when everybody has forgotten that there was a ball kicked towards the sky. It always comes back of course because whosoever lives up there in the sky is not into catching balls lobbed at them. But you have to pretend that the kicked ball is not returning to this earth and when it does you have to rejoice, act completely, crazily, surprised. You also have to try to get to the ball before Momo does and after a little bit of dribbling let him take it.

This is how Momo deals with the trauma of losing his dream. This is how most grown-up men deal with their grief: by shoving a ball into a hole or hitting it hard. It was quite obvious to me that the nasty little bird was out of a job. With Momo's peak soiled, there was going to be no hood for her eyes, she was not transforming into a royal hunter, she was about to return to a life of scavenging from garbage dumps.

And our Momo was not getting a shiny Range Rover anytime soon. I was fine with that. There is nothing wrong with our Jeep Cherokee. The boy needs to resist his unreasonable, consumerist urges.

But I underestimated Momo's love for his cap and his lust for that vehicle.

It's a regular enough cap with a red little heart on it, nothing that one should get sentimental about. Momo has taken a beating from Dad Dear for wearing it backwards, a scolding from his mother for putting that filthy thing on his head and taunts from his former school mates for wearing the headgear left behind by dead white men, but Momo has never parted with his cap.

And then he found the hidden cap while the ugly little bird sat there fluttering its one good wing and sharpening its beak on the floor. Momo sniffed the cap. He is not a good sniffer but even he couldn't miss my stamp on it. And if there was any doubt, the ugly bird fluttered its wings again and sprayed Momo's face with my nectar.

'Mutt,' Momo spat out the word like it was a bitter almond.

I watched as the ugly bird lifted off the ground and hovered for a bit as if testing its injured wing, then took a slow, lazy flight. Ugly bird, clumsy flight. Out of our lives, good riddance. I looked towards Momo, expecting some appreciation for having exposed this fraud on wings.

Momo picked up the ball and went into the courtyard. I followed him, looking up at the sky, encouraging him, yes, that is the positive attitude we need around here, kick that ball into the sky and let's forget that stinky little cap, Mother will wash it like she washes everything that's soiled or smells of grief.

He was standing there, daring me to come and get the ball. *Let's put it all behind us*, he seemed to be saying; *let's play*. He wasn't in a hurry to kick the ball, he was holding it in one outstretched hand, as if kicking the ball would be the final proof that Falcons for Ethical Hunting had gone kaput. I could smell danger in the air (which smells like tea about to boil over), but what possible danger could lurk in our own courtyard? There was me, there was Momo and there was the football. I looked towards the sky, clear and blue and waiting to receive the ball. And then it happened.

If he had kicked that ball in an actual football match Momo might have become some kind of champion foot-baller, the kind who have shirts and shoes with their names on them. But this was our own courtyard, the silly kite was hovering in the sky, Mother Dear was cooking in the kitchen and working her rosary. I was still looking skywards when the ball hit my hind leg. All the air went out of my lungs and not even a little yelp came out of my mouth. There was no time for any evasive action. I jumped after the ball hit my hind leg with the force of a cannonball tearing through a state traitor. I heard the crack, but my Mutt instincts and my eternal love for Momo made me jump. I was too slow to respond and I landed on the same leg that had just snapped. That's double stupid.

I smell blood. My own. I don't feel any panic, I am not thinking of my future life as a lame Mutt. I am not thinking of houseflies and cats tormenting me for the rest of my life. I am thinking of Momo.

Yes, my leg is fractured and I am dying of hunger and thirst and shame but if someone was to walk up to me and ask me Mutt, what happened, did you break your leg? I'll tell them, yes but what's really broken is my heart.

Chapter 7

Ellie

The wind howls around me. It seems a million dead soldiers are cursing their enemies, their enemies' mothers. There is Colonel Slatter cupping his balls and giving the sky a finger. There's that other Purple Heart, hero of Kandahar, doing somersaults on the sand as if it was his local park. Here's an army of dead fellow soldiers come back to claim their medals and back pay from Mother Nature. Their dead faces have never been seen on TV, only their cuddly family pictures, not their torn limbs, not their ghoulish demented grins from battles won and lost far far away; here they have come back for one last group photo with me. Or maybe they are missing their own mothers, their lovely fiancées. I am way past missing Cath. I can barely remember Cath, her little taunts, her whispers.

I listen to the howling wind and try to decipher its message. I can hear voices, tribes on the march, yelping their war cries and trying to scare me. I can hear my own dead comrades shouting at me, giving me directions, warning me not to take the route I am taking. As if I am following a fucking map. As if I am scared of the enemy. I am beyond fear. Not in a soldierly, slogan-raising kind of way but because I have already drunk the contents of my bladder and discovered there is no nourishment under that sand. What is there to be scared of when you have consumed the contents of your own bladder and you are still thirsty? I have chewed wires from my Strike Eagle's fuselage and only got stomach cramps. I have sniffed the empty fuel tank and got no high.

The wind dies down for a bit, like a fever subsiding for a few minutes and then coming back. It reminds me of my Cath, who had tormented me but waited for me to return from missions; my Cath with her shiny hair, who had loved me and held me when I screamed *Mors Ab Alto* in my sleep. Between that moment of calm remembrance and the wind going apeshit again, I hear a distinct yelp. It isn't the whining of the desert wind, nor an imaginary crackle of more things tearing off my plane, nor the muted sounds of my rockets exploding in Mosul, Kabul, and cities that I am likely to mispronounce even when I am questioned about them in the afterlife. It's an almost human cry. Almost. A short burst of anguish and then a wail which promises to go on but is drowned out by the howling of the wind. I stand up in the wind, my hands clutching my stomach, my flying suit zipped up to my neck, sand grinding in the remotest parts of my cranium.

I try to figure out which direction the sound has come from.

The desert yelps at me again and this time there is no mistake, it isn't human anguish expressing itself, but nor is it the elements in the desert sympathizing with my condition. My dead colleagues may live forever in their loved ones' hearts but they are dead for every other purpose. I prick up my ears, I start to walk. The wind has slowed down and is whispering now.

I remember a half-forgotten fact from somewhere, from my high-school geography or from some TV channel: Arabs have ninety-nine names for their god and one-hundred-eighty-eight names for desert sand. But I can't come up with even one. Were these Arabs whispering their god's name? I hear a weak moaning from behind the mound of sand and start to walk. I am halfway up the hillock when my legs collapse.

The wind brings louder moans. I go down on my elbows and start to crawl up. It's good to crawl anyway, I tell myself. Soldiers faced with hidden enemies always crawl. I don't know what awaits me on the other side of the hill.

I reach for my dagger and am quite surprised to find out that my hand is fully functional and steady. I can feel no life below my torso though. Is this how people die, from the toes up? Lower half lifeless and upper half wielding a dagger, raring for one last fight. The brain is the last thing to die, I remember. Probably better to crash and burn, where your skull explodes first. What good is the brain if your legs and pecker aren't working? I am not really worried about my pecker. It was a potential water tap which has dried up, I am not going to get any sustenance from down there. I hold the dagger steady with both hands and I crawl up and up where lurks either a saviour who will deliver me of my misery or an enemy who will deliver me of my misery.

'Fucking mutt,' I say when I reach the top and spot a medium-sized poodle lying on its side with her face turned to the sky. She is howling at the sky.

I look up in the sky to see what is troubling this mutt; there is nothing but the mad bloody Arab in the sky being his furious self. And although I have never really seen an Arab, let alone an Arab god, and I have also never seen anyone in labour (except for women in the movies, with their parted legs, pushing, screaming), for some reason I believe that the mutt is going through labour; its agony not caused by heat and homelessness but something more primal. I am about to witness a birth. I look at my dagger and think this should come in handy. I know that you have to cut a cord after birth. This is my purpose. This is why I have been wandering the desert for such a long time. I move closer and the mutt recoils, a typical sign of a wild animal in birth pangs. She has probably walked away from her community to give birth in the desert, like those women who wandered into the desert and gave birth to ancient Arab prophets. Women are forced out into the desert so that they can give birth to prophets. That was the history, that was how civilization was born. At least, Arab civilization. I can't remember anything useful about this from my 'Cultural Sensitivity Towards Tribals' module.

I bend down to have a closer look at her. She looks into my eyes and, failing to understand my friendly intentions, yelps at me again, but this time a subdued, helpless protest, maybe tinkered with the hope that this tall creature who is bending over her and smelling of rotting beef jerky might be here to help her. I wish someone would take a picture: 'Lost American officer helping a lost mutt give birth'. I have seen one on the homepage of *Stars and Stripes* where a marine was putting a bandage on a baby donkey. I put my right hand under her head and she lets me, but as I move my other hand towards her belly she yelps violently and tries to drag herself away from me. *This monster is here to steal my babies*, she is probably thinking.

But then I notice two things: one of her hind legs is twisted at an odd angle; also that she's a male. I see a smear of blood on the sand and realize that this unfortunate creature isn't here to give birth but has broken a leg.

'Lost American officer helping a puppy with broken leg'; not like helping a lost bitch give birth but still a compelling headline.

I can't decide for a few moments whether this is a good sign or another curse. Is this pretty mutt with a broken leg my saviour angel or has he been sent to test my resolve? Am I supposed to nurture him back to health and then look for a way to escape this desert, or just eat him up bit by bit while looking for a way to escape this desert? I look into his eyes again and feel a surge of energy. Your chances of survival increase substantially if you find a fellow traveller. Although, when they came up with the fellow traveller theory, they probably meant a fellow soldier, a native guide, a casual acquaintance from a wrecked ship, a native informer who has been found out and expelled from the community by the other natives; they probably didn't devote much thinking to how a lame stray dog could come to lighten your burden.

I have already made too many educated guesses and every single one of them has left me more famished. I put my right hand under the mutt's head and look at its moist eyes, its dried-up little tongue, a little wet patch that it has made on the sand during our introductions, a clear sign that this injured little animal still contains fluids, soft flesh, still moist, innards brimming with juices, a promise of life in short. An injured promise but a promise nevertheless. I hold his head firmly and pin it to the sand, and with my other hand reach for my dagger, which is secure and ready in a leather sheath just above my boot.

I find myself on my knees clutching onto sand for support. There was no warning: one minute I am plodding up the hillock, like a determined warrior (admittedly, with heavy feet and tongue hanging out, but I was walking with a purpose); next moment I am on my knees panting. I see a dab of red colour spreading on the sand. I am bleeding, hell I am bleeding, I think, and then a flutter of wings and a shiny little bird emerges from the sands and takes flight. My hands flail in the air to capture it but it shoots like an arrow into the air and is soon a little red dot on the horizon, dissolving into nothingness in the sky.

Chapter 8

Momo

The bombs stopped falling soon after Bro Ali went to the Hangar and never came back. Did he refuse to give them any more targets? Did he single-handedly end the war? It's unlikely, but if anybody could, it was him. Some people think a bit of peace and quiet is a good thing, others wonder where their salary has gone. Bro Ali taught me many things. You're gonna ask what kind of skill set you need to live in a fugee camp. You need a ration card and of course you need some serviceable English to convince the foreign do-gooders who used to run the Camp that you are at least half human. If you are well off you might need to learn how to milk a goat or at least have the ability to tell when a goat doesn't want to be milked. Bro Ali was a man of science, just like I am a man of commerce. He tried to teach me to build a transistor radio with shiny components and copper wires he brought from the Hangar.

The only transmission we could receive was crackly boleros from some country on the other side of the earth. I had no interest in home-made transistors and volunteer informers. I told him I love transistors, I love boleros; I promised that I was gonna grow up and set up a transistor-making factory, that I was gonna import a guitar from Argentina and learn to sing boleros.

He would disappear at night with his transistor, *just going for a walk to clear my head*. Every time he went out to clear his head, a plane would appear in the sky. He was sending them signals. He was on a mission to clear our area of evil guys. You can't mix business with politics. He was doing it because he believed in his cause. First he was helping the people in the Hangar clear the area of our own bad guys. And then he decided to clear the area of the bad guys who were taking out the bad guys. He never thought all this clearing out was gonna leave a big hole in our lives.

What I really wanted him to teach me was how to pick locks. It took some convincing on my part but he relented. Yes, you do need that little crooked wire, but more than that you need steady hands. Your heartbeat needs to sync with the movement of your fingers and yes, steady breathing always helps.

'If you are going to grow up and become a thief just like them, you better learn to pick a lock properly.' Bro Ali was joking of course but it hurt. He went around picking targets for the people at the Hangar but I never called him a traitor. And I want to pick a little lock to take what's rightfully mine and I become a thief.

Lady Flowerbody's locker is a basic job. Sometimes you pick a lock just because it's there. To stay in practice. You never know when you might need to pick your own handcuffs. Right now I just need a cursory look at her credentials, a background check on where she comes from, what she'll bring to my team.

She has also called me for a preliminary interview or an assessment as she puts it. I should know about what she wants to know.

We shall see who is gonna interview who.

Holiday pictures. A safari, a demented-looking elephant trying too hard to please the visitors who seem quite pleased with themselves in a cage mounted on a jeep. Some invoices. She is on a $120-per-day contract. Five-day working week. Expenses must be filed with receipts. She's a service provider like me but she pretends she has been doing God's work. A full box of nail-polish remover. I suspect she abuses her stash. There is a pouch of tobacco, large rolling papers, a lump of brown gooey stuff, a stack of dark chocolates in shiny gold wrappers. She is the one with a teenager's drawer and she wants to study *my* teenage mind.

By the time my first session with her comes up, I am ready for her. She is here to research my trauma. I intend to take her into the very heart of trauma and do some research of my own.

There is no reason to take along a professional junke-teer on my mission, but she has the power to distract and I am gonna need someone like her in my team. We are not planning a traditional raid, we cannot afford to start open warfare, and all the talk of guerrilla warfare may sound romantic – hit and run, a thousand little cuts, poke them in the eye and hide – but where you gonna hide in a desert? Also this place may look poorer than Afghanistan, and more violent than Sudan, but thank God there is no ideology at stake. Not for them, not for us. They bomb us because they assume we are related to bad Arabs. We steal from them because that's all we can do. They take our boys because they think that's all we have. And to lure the boys they sent out their tallest soldiers, their shiniest vehicles.

It looked awesome, the way they came out of the Hangar, an armoured car in front, a soldier standing on it, gun cocked, visor on the helmet lowered, their radio crackling. They always looked straight ahead, as if nothing on their left or right interested them. Behind the armoured car came a water tanker, and behind the water tanker another armoured car, another soldier standing behind a gun talking on the radio to Headquarters. That's Americans going to get their water supply from the pond at the edge of the desert. And they flew two flags on every vehicle as if they were not getting three thousand litres of contaminated water but conquering some big castle. And the children would run after them, waving, wanting to shake hands, hoping to get a joyride. Not gonna lie, I also joined the idiots in the chase the first time I saw the awesome convoy. Bro Ali spotted me and thrashed me proper. 'I can understand the urge to ride in a big vehicle but we have our own jeep,' Bro Ali whacked me as soon as the convoy was out of sight. 'But you never let me drive,' I managed some tears. If you make Bro Ali feel bad, he is gonna let you do what you want. He started to teach me to drive and I never chased the convoy with the idiots again.

It was jobs, jobs, jobs after that. The boy who sat on my left and the boy who sat on my right in my class, both got work. Cleaning up, clearing kitchens and bathrooms; they got rubber gloves, they got to keep those rubber gloves. They got paid in new crisp notes. Sometimes they were sent off into the desert to lay mines, they got extra money for that.

Making some moolah and thanking our creator is the only ideology that works here.

We gonna go in like debt collectors. And in that kind of situation it's good to have a well-dressed, nice-smelling, vaguely European-accented lady on your team.

The lady in question has set up her shop in a little tent, an iron table covered with newspapers, notebook ready. She is in business.

I pour water from a red plastic jug into a white paper cup, look at the time on my watch only to make a guess about how long it takes her to roll out the letters PTSD. Post Traumatic Stress Disorder. First they bomb us from the skies, then they work hard to cure our stress. But when she finally mentions it she abbreviates, and rolls it around her tongue and makes it sound like a promise I made a long time ago and that I must not forget.

But right now we are going through the pleasantries that every researcher scholar who comes this way goes through with his or her subject. I have been the subject of many studies since I was eleven. 'Growing Pains in Conflict Zones'. 'Tribal Cultures Get IT'. Even 'Reiki For War Survivors'. I am a good subject. She is the doctor in the white coat, I am the lab rat quivering in my cage but showing healthy curiosity towards my tormentor. I have done this before. They all come from somewhere. I am gonna ask her before she asks me.

'How was Tanzania?' I ask, taking a non-sip from the paper cup. In two years of do-gooders having come and gone I have learnt that it helps to hold on to something while listening to their fairy tales. She lifts her head from the file and I notice that the bluish tint in her hair is not so shiny, her thin lips are made slightly fuller with the creative use of lipstick, and the mole above her upper lip seems to change colour according to her mood. I remind myself to look into her eyes or keep my eyes on the mole – you look below the neck and they start thinking you are just another horny teenager. I am not gonna fall for that old tit trap.

I have heard they have nice spas in Tanzania, where you can eat and drink all you want and then get three men to massage you simultaneously. Always good for the skin. Soul benefits too. It's an all-inclusive package. One day I'll build one here too. We'll throw in a goat milk detox and they'll all come rushing. But right now there is other business to take care of.

'It was nice, relaxing. I like being close to nature.' She doesn't consider this place nature, maybe because there is no spa.

She is businesslike, making it clear that we are here to discuss my issues, like how I am coping with peace after years of conflict. I am the Young Muslim Mind that will pay for her six-handed massages and her toned skin. She is here to learn from me, as she has said.

I get PTSD, she gets a per diem in US dollars.

'Safari?' I take a sip of water and it doesn't taste of metal like the water at home. She has a stash of bottled water somewhere. *I am gonna save the world but let me first ensure there is enough Perrier.*

She lifts her head from her file and I imagine she is trying to decipher her own handwritten questions. 'I started out as a family therapist but my focus is on conflict areas. I have worked with real soldiers coming back from real battles but I can tell you that domestic battlefields are so much nastier, everyone comes out a loser. And all you have is kiddie pictures to show for it. And that's my current focus.'

I have Bro Ali's pictures but I am not gonna show her. I am not giving my family secrets to some visiting surveyor.

I want to tell her about the technicolour happy dreams that I have been having. Bro Ali and me jump from a tall building on gliders, we land softly, we walk on the streets with white fluffy angel wings; there is snow but we don't feel cold. There is something about her glowing skin that makes me think about wild animals in Tanzania, where she was probably asking teenage waiters about their inner lives. She is the type who would demand socio-political insights in return for generous tips.

'Sometimes I think this is what we have achieved,' I hold up my paper cup. 'We used to drink wine from our enemy's skull. Now we drink purified water from paper cups made by cutting down trees.' She looks relieved. I think I have given her a glimpse into my young, troubled Muslim mind. She closes her file and bends forward to listen. I am a student of history. Linking up my own condition with some imagined medieval trivia helps you live in these parts. It makes my mild depression feel like a part of the great march of the humanity through millennia. Here is a cheerful thought: one in every two hundred men is linked to Genghis Khan through a direct bloodline. I am probably his great-great-grandson. Would Grandfather Genghis submit to questions about his mental health?

History can wait, I'm gonna address the economy first. You know how much she is getting paid, $120 dollars for a day. OK, I am probably myself getting four dollars in subsidized food, but I am a survivor of the most useless war in the history of wars. Even our conquerors have abandoned us. What has she done for the country? Gone on a safari and spa holiday to Tanzania? As a businessman you always have to see if you are gonna get your money's worth. I could use $120 as seed money for setting up my Scorpions Racing Circuit. I can feel jealousy creeping up. It's never a good thing in business meetings.

'This is good,' she says. 'Go on, tell me more about what you have been thinking about civilization. Let's start with what's on your mind.' My young Muslim mind is wondering what kind of noise she makes when she reaches the point of sexual gratification. Father once brought home an old copy of a book called *Cosmopolitan*. It had nothing about how to build supply chains but a very long essay on 60 Paths to Orgasm. My mind is capable of thinking many things at the same time. I am never gonna be that single-track-mind kind of guy who thinks of girls while driving and vice versa.

I can think of countries where one could get three seventeen-year-olds, keep them all night, and buy them all a hamburger and a beer for $120. Late nights on Nat Geo are more educational than you think. If you can't tell a girl who gets $120 a day to find out how you feel, who can you tell? But I am not gonna tell her about my true feelings.

'Was there a real safari?' I ask. She seems dismayed, as if she was still in Tanzania and I was a native refusing to give her directions to the nearest lions' sanctuary.

I notice her patient, benevolent demeanour, ballpoint in her left hand moving in short bursts. I suspect she is doing her expense accounts.

'I am not sure if I asked you but why did you choose Tanzania?'

She explains patiently: she likes the wild, she likes being close to nature, she has read a Scottish writer who has set a very moving detective story in Tanzania.

I try to imagine a world where people read a book by a writer about a place where the writer has never been and then decide to go there to study young minds. We live in that world. Not much different from the white men (and women, but mostly men) who flew halfway around the world to bomb us because they believe even if we are not bad Arabs we must be up to something.

'I think we should talk about you.'

'But it's related. I've been having these dreams about wild animals walking around in my courtyard. There is always a fox stuck to the windowsill, not really wanting to come in but not going away either. I wonder what that says about my mental state. But first tell me how close did you get to the lions?'

She looks up, startled, amused and then stern again as if this kind of intimate conversation is not part of our arrangement.

But then she relents. 'We were on this safari,' she says in a grave tone. 'We were in these vehicles, very well protected, with iron bars that could be electrified if they came too close and a guard with a shotgun on every van. But it was nice to be close to nature, miles and miles of shrub, real caves. It was all very relaxing.'

Maybe that should be your natural habitat, I think, still resentful of her per diem. Maybe you should live behind iron bars, which can be electrified with the flick of a switch and a man with a shotgun should stand behind you all your life. I imagine a hungry lioness chewing her shoulder-length hair. I imagine someone throwing twenty-dollar bills at her. I drink from the paper cup and imagine a lioness smacking her lips.

She is still scribbling in her file. She ignores me. 'We didn't really see any lions, only footprints and a half-eaten buffalo that the lioness had supposedly killed. You never know if these safari guides are telling the truth. But it was wonderful. You need to get away from all this,' she vaguely moves her hand. I'm not sure what exactly she wants me to get away from.

'I think my father sold my brother.'

'Why would you think that?'

'Father took him to the Hangar and then he never came back,' I say.

'Did he go against his will?'

'No, he was willing, he wanted to, he insisted. But Father Dear should have known better. There were boys before him who went and never came back. Father Dear believed he had a special relationship with the people at the Hangar. Why did he trust them?'

'Did your father bring home any money? What is your proof of the transactional nature of this incident?'

'Haven't you heard of fraudulent deals? What makes you think white people always gonna keep their promises?'

'Maybe you are right. And how do you feel about this?'

'I think they should have given us compensation for our house they destroyed. But all we got was some blue plastic sheets and a job in the Hangar. I think Bro Ali should have been given a medal or something. I think he single-handedly ended the war. He went to the Hangar and all the bombings stopped. They even shut down the Hangar but my brother didn't come back.'

She scribbles in her notebook. 'Your brother is not the only one missing.'

'Yes, yes I know, many boys in my class have gone too. The boy who sat on my left, he used to draw for me in my art class. The boy who sat on my right, he used to help me with maths,' I say impatiently.

'How many boys?' she asks.

'Many,' I say. 'Why should I count? I have only one brother.'

She ignores my answer. 'Some of their people have also gone missing,' she says. 'I've heard rumours that many of the people who worked in the Hangar are not there anymore. Some disappeared in the desert. But these are military matters. I assure you there are processes in place which work by and large. They have categories for the disappeared, there are those who are jet black, there are greys and there are white. Whites always come back; some even get compensation.'

She is obviously not gonna tell me the whole truth, however many times I remind her that Bro Ali hasn't come back and he is whiter than white.

'All I can say is that when the world shifts, when the tectonic plates of history readjust, some people fall through the cracks,' she continues. 'We only focus on death and destruction but it's a basic fact about life that in these circumstances people go missing. You can help me study the phenomenon. Please tell me how you feel about this?'

'I feel I'm gonna have to fix that. I am gonna have to bring him back. I am gonna have to abduct him from his abductors if I have to.'

'And where are you going to find these abductors if they have all gone and disappeared as well?'

'Well they sent you, didn't they? We're gonna find them together,' I say.

'You are not the only one grieving, there are others missing, and their families. Have you asked them how they feel about it?'

'I have only one bro and his name is Ali. I am not gonna let anyone's feelings get in the way of what I have to do.' She wants me to go on. I tell her about Mutt and his broken leg. She accuses me of cruelty to animals. 'That's one classic symptom of PTSD,' she says. 'Soldiers traumatized in conflict areas go home and take it out on their pets. Sometimes on their fiancées. Sometimes on other people's pets. But mostly on their own pets.'

I terminate the session. 'You have no idea,' I say. 'You don't know my Mutt. He's the one who has been cruel to me.'

I better go and get Mutt before the scorpions devour him. I better prove to her who is being cruel to whom.

I better show her who is the real heartbreaker in this place.

CHAPTER 9

Ellie

The Jeep Cherokee with the fat, fading USAID logo and a limp white flag stops a few metres away from me. I am on my knees now, not quite dead but fading fast. Is this driverless vehicle another mirage? Has my mind gone so far that it is remote controlling vehicles for my own rescue? It is so close I can see the diesel fumes evaporating in the background, I can feel the reverberation of its engine under my feet; hell, I can inhale the diesel fumes. I shudder in hope and collapse on the sand.

At some point even hope gives up on itself. I have blisters all over my body and my insides feel like they've been scrubbed with sandpaper; parched and cleansed of any residues of fear.

Extreme dehydration can cause pleasant delusions. I have been to some nice places in my head since I stumbled upon the mutt. I have been inside a pristine marble-floored bathroom with running water; I have almost opened glass-fronted fridges full of cold beer; I have seen my dead comrades, they are kind but distant, they have fed me fries dipped in gravy; many a helicopter has scooped me up and flown me back to the base; I have even had a change of clothes, gotten into my Nissan Sunny and driven home, knocked at the door and waited for Cath to come and take me into her arms. She has scolded me for being late.

I am beyond dreaming now. A driverless vehicle driving in to rescue you sounds like a third-world militia member's idea of the good life. Not even a soldier, only an enemy combatant surrounded on all sides, out of ammo, could dream up such a miracle. Or an American zoomie lost in a desert.

I am a mid-ranking officer. I am not falling for it.

I don't open my eyes when I hear the door of the jeep creak open, it sounds as if someone is kicking it from inside. I hug the whimpering mutt and let my mind drift to a place where children on a see-saw urge each other to go higher. I might comfort a helpless creature in my last moments. I hear Cath laugh somewhere in the past. *Suit yourself, here, take my pillow too.* At last, a faint smile spreads across my lips. Cath might have occasionally been sarcastic about my weakness for small comforts, hogging the duvet, scooping up the last bit of dessert for myself, pouring myself the last drops of wine from the bottle, pretending to be asleep when the doorbell rang in the morning; she knew me and I miss her knowing me. But she'll have to forgive me now. We were petty to each other in life. In death we can be magnanimous. I'll never miss her again, I'll never be scolded again; all will be oblivion soon.

Goodbye earth. Goodbye war. Goodbye peace. Goodbye frozen margaritas.

First comes a kick in my ribs, then another. A small figure hovers over me, bends down and snatches the mutt away from me. Then another kick, this time with less force but more contempt. I hear English. 'You were gonna steal my dog. You dog thief.' I have been accused of many things in life but stealing stray dogs isn't one of them. But the boy standing over me has made up his mind. He is caressing, kissing the mutt and periodically prodding me in my ribs. 'You steal my dog. Can't you see he is injured? You brute. Rot in hell. You are already rotting in hell. God has punished you.'

Slowly it dawns on me that this boy standing over my head has driven over looking for his dog and now believes that I tried to steal his dog. Finally, after eight days of wandering in the desert my saviour has arrived and he is a very angry teenager.

I raise my hand in the air to refute the charge. I almost faint again with the sheer effort.

'If you are not gonna steal the dog, what are you gonna do so far away from Camp? Only mad men wander around in the desert dressed like that.'

The boy is possessed by the certainty of a fifteen-year-old who can drive. He is wearing a soccer shirt, white shorts and spikey boots. I am glad that he hasn't used the spiked sole of his shoe on my ribs to convey his displeasure. He seems like someone dressed for a soccer game rather than someone looking for his beloved dog in the desert.

'What is this uniform? Are you a scorpion hunter? Lizard lover?'

The boy, it seems, has just noticed my flying suit and is now accusing me of being a scavenger in uniform, with a sideline in stealing dogs.

'Did they leave you behind? Because they have all gone.' The boy gives me one last kick, this time in my buttocks, spits on the sand, picks up the mutt with one hand, kisses the mutt's face and starts to walk off.

I am alert now and fully awake. This is no mirage. You don't get kicked in the ribs in a mirage. I look at the boy and now I can tell that he is no more than fourteen or fifteen years old at most. He is opening the door of the Cherokee and settling his mutt on the passenger seat. He goes around the jeep, opens the door and disappears into the driver's seat. How is he even allowed to drive? Where are his parents? How can they let this little kid drive around in an SUV in the middle of the desert? I have heard stories about rich Arabs' love for luxury vehicles, gold-plated Lamborghinis and Range Rovers fitted with Gucci seat covers and matching prayer mats. But even by their silly standards this is absolutely bonkers. And I'm not even sure if he is an Arab.

'Hey,' I scream, and realize that it comes out as a puff of hot dry air. I raise myself on my knees and wave both my hands.

'You can't leave me here.'

I can't see my saviour. He has disappeared into his seat.

The boy starts the engine, it coughs, a blast from the silencer, the jeep shudders and the engine refuses to start. Another attempt at starting the jeep, the sullen sound of the engine not giving a shit about the ignition. The boy comes out now, his eyebrows arched in irritation, someone not used to an engine not obeying him. He thumps the bonnet with both his hands and then with some effort manages to lift it and dives into the engine.

I see it as a sign. Still startled with the boy's arrival and then his determination to drive away with his injured dog, his insistence on acknowledging my existence as nothing more than a petty criminal, and then the jeep's refusal to start; is it the divine intervention I have been waiting for?

Sometimes God can manifest himself as a mechanical failure.

I manage to drag myself up and hobble towards the Cherokee with the footballer boy half hanging out of the bonnet. I almost fall over the bonnet, my face next to the boy who is cleaning a plug with a toothpick. I finally see his face clearly. The boy has wide brown eyes, a hint of hair on his upper lip, and dark brown hair that keeps falling over his eyes. The boy ignores me and goes on cleaning the plug till I can't take it anymore and say in a hissing voice: *Have you got some water?*

'I have checked the water. It's full. No problem.'

I lunge towards the carburettor as the boy watches me. With trembling hands I manage to remove the cover; the water is boiling hot and it singes my tongue as I try to lap it up with my tongue through the tiny opening.

'Don't be an animal,' the boy says, putting the plug back and wiping his hands with an oily rag. 'Drinking water is inside the jeep.'

I can't decide whether I want to hug the boy or slap him. I also realize that the boy had no plans to leave me here. He's just trying to fuck with my mind. Everything is trying to fuck with my mind. Gingerly I move towards the Cherokee, open its rear door and see a rubber flask, a standard UN Food Programme rubber flask. I pick it up, the water sloshes inside it. The flask is ice cold.

CHAPTER 10

Mutt

I saw a red bird shoot up from the sand before the white man in green overalls rose out of the sand. I am not scared of ghosts but I don't like to hang out with them either. He came over and cuddled me. It was awkward. He was one of those men who don't know how to pick up a baby, how to pet a dog, how to be a man. He handled me as if I was a precious vase.

And I can't smell this man. He doesn't smell of boiled cabbage like the ones at Hangar used to smell. What kind of man has no smell? Or have I lost my one remaining talent? To smell is to survive. I don't smell anything on this man. Only ghosts and spies don't smell. I don't believe in ghosts, they're something invented by my human companions to console themselves that when you die you don't really die. When humans die, and it doesn't matter if they choke on their own vomit, or die while trying to rescue a kitten, they go to heaven or hell. When Mutts die they just stay dead. As for the spies, they have already left this place – there is nothing left to spy on.

Not being able to smell gives me a throbbing headache. And why is he still trying to cuddle me?

I don't need your clumsy love, I want to tell him. *I need some aspirin.*

These red birds worry me. They are everywhere. What worries me even more is that nobody seems to be able to do anything about them.

I saw the first red bird on the rooftop the day Mother Dear went on a cooking strike. Her stated position, just like that of any professional agitator, was only a front: she said there was no salt and so she wouldn't cook. But it was a deceptive little game. What she was really saying was *bring me my son or go die, starve yourselves to death or go eat flour and raw meat. Or learn to cook your own food.*

She is good that way. Not wearing her depression like a badge of honour, but turning it into a subtle form of resistance. If she had been born in another place she would be a socialist leader ruling a mid-sized nation with an iron hand. But here she is just a mother with a plastic rosary.

I can usually smell birds before I see them, most birds smell like mischief, most of them except crows, who smell like other people's dirty secrets. But that day I didn't smell anything. I was surveying the sky, and trust me, when you live here you learn to survey the skies without thinking, because here things fall from skies. I saw a smudge of red on the rooftop as my eyes focused. I became aware of its presence. It was no bigger than a house sparrow, but unlike house sparrows that can't sit still and believe that life is a series of festivities, the red bird was very, very still. And it had no smell. I snivelled, suddenly scared that maybe I had lost my mojo, my olfactory capabilities, and caught only a faint whiff of sorrow but that, not surprisingly, emanated from the kitchen. That's a laughable notion – this house is drowning in the stench of sorrows. When Mother Dear does her daily laundry you can smell despair wafting through the washing line. She pours tears in her curry, so sad is that woman. Why does she need salt, she could just cook with her tears? Sadness doesn't worry me. Sadness is practically my sibling in this household.

I don't want to be an alarmist, but one has duties as a son of the soil and as a responsible family member, so I did what one does when one is puzzled by a presence and has to tell the others to watch out; I raised my head and let out a quick succession of warnings. Mother Dear looked up at the sky, shook her head and got busy with her sad enterprise. In order to appear useful we sometimes invent work when no work is needed. She was ironing bed sheets with an unplugged iron.

I gave a long whiny woof which, in this household, is generally considered a sign that one is serious and not fooling around – the world is coming to an end, the bombs are going to start falling again, or the cat is eyeing the milk pot. Mother Dear threw her slipper at me. I managed to barely avoid it. Any bird, even the stubborn kites, would have fled after this little commotion. Most birds in these parts are safety-first-type creatures who don't trust the human race – a wise policy one must add, but a privilege not available to me. But this red little beauty sat there without a care, not fluttering, not even opening its wings to take flight, just in case. One felt one was losing one's powers of persuasion.

Then Momo came in and I gave another yelp and implored him to look up, and he did look up and shook his head, went out and disappeared under his Cherokee.

I was a bit slow to get this at first: eventually I realized that not everybody can see the birds. There are things that I see that others don't because they are not observant like me. My brains might have gone a bit woozy after that horrible accident, but it hasn't affected my eyesight. But let me emphasize that I have never claimed any special powers. Mutts don't believe in magic, Mutts can't afford to take the spiritual route in life. But one can always be tempted to think along these lines.

Because I am thinking if I can see them, maybe, just maybe, I do have some special powers. It's a tempting thought, but first we must consider other explanations. Maybe others see them in other colours. The earthy brown of canaries or boot-polish black of the crows. Maybe they actually see these red birds in red and don't think there is anything strange about their stillness, about their other-worldliness, as if they are flying through this place but don't need its polluted waters, don't want to feed on its charity-food grain.

Later, people would give explanations. Doctor, our man of science, will have the most logical and scientific expla-nation. Depleted uranium. Common canaries have been drinking water contaminated with low-strength uranium and have mutated into red birds, basically canaries dipped in colour and made dumber. I have this to say to Doctor. I have drunk from the same pond, I even relieve myself in the same pond, why isn't my ass red yet?

When my folks don't have a real explanation, they blame it on war. As if before the war we were all a brotherhood and didn't throw our trash into our neighbour's yard. As if war gave us bad breath and crude manners. It's like me saying that my Mutt ancestors ruled this land and then came the war and their glorious reign came to an end.

Doctor steals bad vegetables from the vegetable shop and calls himself a progressive. He believes that if we all started eating healthily the world would become a much better place. What can you do about him? We need a doctor even if he behaves as though he doesn't need us.

I know where the red birds come from. You will strain your imagination to believe me and point to a certain incident that fried my brains and turned me into a teller of tales, but Mutts can't afford to believe in myths. Or metaphors. A bone is not a metaphor. An electric pole doesn't symbolize phallic fantasies, it's a public convenience, and as I learnt to my cost, a brain-damaging hazard.

Red birds are real. The reason we don't see them is because we don't want to. Because if we see them, we'll remember. When someone dies in a raid or a shooting or when someone's throat is slit, their last drop of blood transforms into a tiny red bird and flies away. And then reappears when we are trying hard to forget them, when we think we have forgotten them, when we think we have learnt to live without them, when we utter those stupid words that we have 'moved on'. It's just a reminder that they may have gone but they haven't really left yet. They have not forgotten us. It reminds us that they might be gone but they miss us. We might go about our lives pretending they are not there anymore – we might give their clothes away, we might put away their notebooks in the bottom drawer, we might insist on remembering only the clever and funny things they said and plaster a permanently youthful smile on their faces, but all we need to do is look up and there they are.

I might be wrong. But Mutts are rarely wrong about birds. Mutts know a thing or two about love. Mutts don't breed in sewers all by themselves. They are the result of other Mutts making love. When you see a spotted brown Mutt with hazel eyes you can bet that it's senior Mutt's afternoon lust that also lives on in the form of a half-brother or a sister.

When I see the red bird I growl. Momo likes it when I growl. He usually says, *hey my tiger*. But this morning Momo remains under the jeep and says, *shut up Mutt*. I like it when he says my name. When he says shut up he only means, *go on my tiger, growl a bit more*.

I am hesitant to tell Momo about the red birds. Humans can be pedantic. They'll believe in someone sitting up there in the sky manufacturing bread and milk and strange sexual urges, they'll believe in souls, in djinns and fairy tales and sea monsters with breasts and fins, and political theories about the uses of inequality, but tell them where the red bird comes from and they'll shake their head as if you are trying to convert them to some Mutt religion.

Another reason I am reluctant to tell Momo about the red birds is that at heart he is a businessman. Even when he is watching television, even when his jeep breaks down, even when he is having murderous thoughts about his Father Dear, he is always working on a business plan which will make him fabulously rich. He has traded in nothing but junk but he is waiting for the 'markets to open up, for the situation to stabilize, for the reconstruction phase to begin' before he can embark on his financial adventures. *What comes after war?* he is fond of saying. *Reconstruction. And what do we need for reconstruction? Cement. Yes. But what else? You can't build cities just with cement. What is the other ingredient you need to build cities? You need sand. And we have got nothing but sand, zillions of tons of it. We can reconstruct the whole world with this sand. Hell, we can build an entire galaxy with our sand. And who owns all the sand?* That's the foundation of his new company called Sands Global.

I know what he would want to do if he saw the red birds. He would see marketing potential. He would want to trap them. He would do his cost-benefit ratio analysis. He would think of giant nets. He would think Americans would pay top dollars for them. Arab sheikhs will want them for breakfast for their mysterious magical qualities. Two hundred dollars a pop. He has been spending too much time watching late-night Nat Geo, where it's wall-to-wall animal cruelty. He thinks real life is the last ever sequel of *Fast and Furious*. Lady Flowerbody is doing strange thought experiments on him. You spend enough time with American-sponsored researchers and you start liking mustard, which smells of unrequited love. And you learn to say words like 'buck' and 'pop'. You begin to think you can make money out of sand and beautiful birds. Imagine selling the souls of your loved ones so that some horny sheikh can devour them to get a stiffy. You sell the memories of your dearest ones as part of the backdrop decor at some fancy wedding reception. Imagine the red birds fluttering in gilded cages. Imagine your most private grief as a party decoration.

Chapter 11

Ellie

Momo, the driver boy, has got two cushions on his driving seat so that he can be level with the steering wheel and he has to slip down and almost stand on the accelerator to keep the vehicle moving. I am not sure if this driver can even look out of the windscreen. But it doesn't really matter, because I can see outside and there is nothing but sand. I shouldn't have finished the whole flask of water in one go, my stomach is a wheat grinder churning out pure pain.

Momo turns towards the passenger seat after every few minutes and says, 'Who loves you, Mutt? Who loves you?' When the mutt doesn't respond the boy honks and screams: 'Mutttttt. We are going home, Mutt. Don't you want to go home, Mutt? Fast and furious, faster. We are gonna get you a doctor, we are gonna get you a bandage and you are gonna be fine. You are gonna roar like a tiger again.'

Mutt has got his nose stuck to the glass window, he whimpers in a non-dog-like voice and seems to be contemplating that eternal question: Can one ever really go back home?

'You shouldn't have been greedy,' says the boy-driver to me as I hold my stomach and moan. 'When you gonna be greedy, your stomach gonna hurt.'

'I was thirsty,' I mumble. 'I was very thirsty. I am in pain.'

'An American in pain, God help us. An American in pain is a fucking pain in the ass of this universe,' he says without looking towards me.

I can't believe the cruelty of this fifteen-year-old. Where is his humanity? Here I am dying after starving for eight days, and the boy is accusing me of excessive consumption.

I shut my eyes and hunker down in the seat and think of all the lessons I learnt in my Cultural Sensitivity course. 'There are many reasons they hate us and one of those reasons is our love for our pets,' our 'Cultural Sensitivity Towards Animals' module instructor had told us in our 'How To Defend American Values Without Offending Their Own' seminar. 'They think the money we spend on dog shampoos could feed the entire population of a Central African country. And they don't even know about the Americans who feed live rats to their pet pythons and hug them before going to sleep.' This kid driving me is a specimen of that very culture. I also hate that culture now; any culture that cares for whiney mutts more than it cares for starving humans lost in the middle of a desert needs a Cultural Sensitivity crash course. And we are not talking any stray humans, we are talking pilots, pilots on a mission, not the zoomies with rainbows on their chests, not the ones who go around spraying pesticides over forests, we are talking proper operational pilots on top-secret missions.

This mutt is going home. This mutt has a name, even if it's just Mutt. This mutt is getting love. I haven't even been asked my name. I know the boy's name because he keeps saying *Momo loves you* to his mutt.

I should be relieved, I should be happy that I am being driven out of the desert where I have been trapped for eight days and nights. But I am pissed off, because I am not getting the attention that someone who has survived eight days in a hellish desert should get. I feel that after all those near-death experiences, after all the sacrifices I have made for the country, I am being treated like an unwanted hitchhiker. One moment you are facing certain death in a desert, the next moment you are in a car sulking about your saviour's bad manners.

The last meal I had was an aspirin and a coffee. I wish I had saved it for now.

'You work for USAID?' Momo asks, taking an abrupt turn for no obvious reason as there is no difference between left and right, there are no tracks, no signposts to a destination – as far as I can see, it's all sand.

'Sort of,' I say and realize that I don't have a cover story. In all my misery I have forgotten to think up where I have come from, and why. I am supposed to have an elaborate story. What the fuck am I doing in the middle of a desert wearing a flying suit, starving myself to death? Am I the weakest link in some desert safari which has left me behind? I had thought about a cover story during the first few days, but my brain draws a blank now. Fleetingly I remember half the Strike Eagle but that is more than five days' walk away. Even if they found it they wouldn't make the connection.

Perhaps I don't need a cover story. If USAID is here and its staff comprises fifteen-year-old drivers, I can probably tell them any old crap, get some clean clothes, some medical attention, say thank you and then hop on to a homeward-bound US chopper which, I hope, would not be flown by a cocky teenager.

'Do you work for USAID?' I ask, trying to create a bond, or at least the possibility of sharing a joke or getting some information about the outbound flights. What I really want to ask him is *why the fuck aren't you at school? Have you got a driving licence? Why are you dressed in a football kit?* But I don't ask any of it. I only say: *Do you work for USAID?*

My own cover story should be simple; I could pass off as a pilot, on my way to delivering humanitarian aid, bringing in a plane load of rations, lots of footballs and candy, my plane crash-landed, and I was lost. Perfect. I am about to faint with hunger but my brain is still capable of coming up with believable scenarios. I'm a survivor, I am someone who can think on his feet even when he can't stand on them.

'I am too young to get a job,' says Momo with disdain, as if I have asked him about an embarrassing family secret. 'I am self-employed. You could call me an entrepreneur.'

I am relieved. I haven't been captured by some horny goatherds or bloodthirsty enemy combatants but by decent people who are self-employed and care about dogs. It's the kind of community where little boys pull themselves up by their bootstraps. The kind of place where they hopefully have flushable toilets and hot food. I shut my eyes and think of a medium-rare rib steak with a dollop of gravy on the side and a glass full of ice cubes.

The sand is whirling all around us and I have no idea how Momo is navigating his way. These are desert folk, they know it like the back of their hand, I tell myself. I trust this boy. A fifteen-year-old boy who has gone and rescued his injured dog is not likely to lose his way or abandon a fellow human being. He represents the best that the desert has to offer. This kid is our future. This kid is our hope. 'This is what I respect about Arab culture. You guys pull yourselves up by the bootstraps. Make something of yourself despite your circumstances. America used to have the same values but. . .'

'Who told you that I'm an Arab?' Momo roars with laughter. 'Look, Mutt, this man thinks we are Arabs. Don't give us ideas, we might become Arabs. Mutt, don't you wish you were an Arab?'

I faint with exhaustion and dream of vanilla shakes and pancakes that are stacked so tall they look like skyscrapers leaning into each other.

When I wake up we're approaching a massive structure that rises out of the sand like a concrete mirage. Miles and miles of barbed wire runs around it. Every few metres there is a very tall observation post laden with sandbags. The only colours in this grey-on-grey horror are the orange and white stripes of a windsock that hangs limp. A large sign says NOT A THOROUGHFARE. This gives me hope. A place with a white and orange windsock must have an airfield or at least a proper helipad. A place that's not a thoroughfare must be a safe passage meant for me. But our jeep takes an abrupt turn.

First we pass a series of abandoned checkpoints and sandbag bunkers and then arrive at a dirt track. We pass a donkey chewing on a plastic shopping bag, a few camels stand in the middle of the track; the boy almost falls over the jeep horn but the camels keep looking up towards the sky like a group of amateur cloud-spotters until, after a while, they slowly clear out as if disappointed by what they have seen.

'Stubborn like American,' Momo curses at the camels as the jeep starts to move again. What's with the fake American accent if he hates us so much? Why has he cursed the camels and called them American? He's obviously a wannabe Arab or from one of those countries that hate America because they aren't America. What does he know about my stubbornness? Me, I've always been easy-going – and given the circumstances there's not much choice.

There's a huge gate in the distance, like the entrance to a grand old city. The gate looks familiar. There is nothing around the gate – no walls, no fence – as if someone has erected the gate in the hope that walls will build themselves.

The top of the gate has something written on it, the letters are faded but carry an authority that still seems to hold, like a paean to a dead king. I bend forward, shooting pain in my stomach still shooting, and try to read the writing on the gate: USAID FUGEE CAMP. The RE seems to have dislodged itself out of embarrassment.

I guess it might have been a village once but now it's only a settlement of sorts. I have never seen a refugee camp for real, only in pictures and TV news. I expect neat rows of tents, gleaming ambulances, people standing in orderly queues waiting to get their rations from gap-year students with dreadlocks and nose rings. What I see is what I have already seen on my Strike Eagle's monitor, just before I hesitated to press the button: a series of junkyards, rows of burnt-out cars piled on each other, abandoned tanks and armoured vehicles, a small mountain of disused keyboards and mobile phone shells, piles of rubbish with smoke rising off them.

The camp is a sea of corrugated blue plastic roofs, stretching like a low, filthy sky, broken by piles of grey plastic poles and overflowing blue plastic rubbish bins. *This is the kind of place where evil festers*, Colonel Slatter had said. All I can see are failed attempts at starting kitchen gardens, neat squares marked with pebbles, half-grown stumps in little plastic pots. NO LITTERING signs over piles of litter. This seems like a failing effort to keep some distance between children and the impending plague.

This place needed no help from the skies.

What was I thinking? What was Colonel Slatter thinking? He came to bomb this place because he thought it was an existential threat to our great nation. He was doing his duty and I have done mine. Your zoomie goes down, you follow.

You'd think one-sided wars would have become boring by now. But they still keep at it. There are no dogfights now, none of that go after your enemy's tail and chew it up; mostly you are chasing your own tail as nobody seems to own fighter aircraft anymore. Down there they run around in vans or convoys of trucks like an army of ants scrambling towards a hole – or running away from it, it doesn't really matter. Or they stay in their compounds and watch TV. There are obvious ethical objections to calling the compounds houses, even though you can zoom in to see what's cooking in their pots. You can do the closest of close-ups but you still can't tell for sure if they are discussing a cut of lamb or planning to bring down western civilization. What you see on your screen is a traditional family, traditional because you see a group of men in a courtyard, reclining in their plastic chairs or on carpets watching TV, a brick house with a satellite dish on the roof, children playing catch in the courtyard. You circle, you pause. On your map the house is marked as a compound inhabited by enemy combatants. Now you're up there and you can't tell whether you are about to target enemies plotting an atrocity or innocent civilians waiting for dinner. You have two and a half seconds to make up your mind.

I hate those words: innocent civilians. Makes soldiers sound like child molesters.

As we pass the gate, there's an open-air school on the edge of an open sewer, with two buffaloes and about a dozen girls staring at an empty blackboard. Another open jeep overtakes us, it has half a dozen teenagers in the back, carrying rocket launchers, one of them waves at us. Momo ignores them. I half-raise a hand and then check myself. We pass a few rundown shops, a row of skinned chickens gathering dust on a wire, a couple of vehicles with a stack of bricks in place of tyres, a pair of teenagers taking their siesta under the vehicles, a man in a white coat tending to a drought-ridden vegetable garden, a few men and women sitting on the sand and occasionally looking up towards the sky.

'Thieves, all of them, like you,' the boy looks towards me and sneers. 'They are always looking for a plane. Can't drive a jeep, but always going into the desert, thinking, *ho ho ho, I'll find some fighter plane there.* No desert rabbits, now. Just looking for metal scrap. Some people are always gonna be losers.'

Should I be worried about these gun-toting plane-spotters? Have they found my Strike Eagle yet? Is this teenager driving me the shepherd from Colonel Slatter's legend, a bored, cold-blooded killer? Am I a welcome guest in the camp or about to become a prized prisoner, a bargaining chip to be traded for tinned food?

'Guess who loves you, Mutt,' the boy turns his head towards the mutt and shouts. 'Guess who is coming home, Mutt. Our war hero.'

In the Camp

CHAPTER 12

Mutt

Call me self-important, call me an attention-seeker, call me a miserable little self-important Mutt, but I do have a minor regret about the night the bomb fell on our house.

They were all settling in for the night, I was getting ready for my night patrol when Bro Ali came running, shouting *get out of the house, out of the house*. I was a little bit annoyed, because isn't it my job to sound the alarm, to issue warnings? But Bro Ali was running about like a crazed prophet and managed to create suitable panic, so of course I helped out by yapping at the sky, where I could already pick out the slow, familiar rumble of a plane approaching.

We were huddled in a makeshift trench in the courtyard, Mother Dear covering Ali and Momo under her arms like one of those mad hens who can gouge your eyes out if you mess with their chicks. Father Dear was waving at the sky, as if saying hullo to the approaching plane. Unlike everyone else I am not prejudiced against Father Dear. They are always accusing him of licking white men's boots – well maybe he likes the taste. I think with his hand gestures he was asking the plane to go back, like sometimes I wave my paw to shoo away a fly. But that thing in the sky was no fly. It said hullo back to Father Dear by dropping a smart bomb on our house. Father Dear had been given some money by them to build the house in the first place, but it was still our house, and now they had just spent a thousand times more money to obliterate it. I have never understood how money works. That's Momo's domain.

'What did they do that for?' Bro Ali shouted in a trembling voice, trying to escape Mother Dear's arms. The bomb had gone through the roof, windows were torn away, doors flew in the air, there was a shower of brick and wood and plaster and steel and it all settled into a heap of rubble where our house had stood. I was relieved that it wasn't one of those bombs which start a fire and burn everything down to a cinder. Even in times of mayhem – especially in times of mayhem – I can focus on small mercies.

'Maybe you gave them the wrong target?' Momo was angry at Bro Ali and was trying to squirm away from Mother Dear's protective custody. He thought he could run to the house and undo the destruction.

'I didn't give them any target today.' Bro Ali was angry at Momo.

Father Dear raised his hands in an attempt to keep them calm. Father Dear is the kind of head of the household who doesn't want work discussed in front of the family even when that work might have resulted in the complete and utter annihilation of the family's only abode.

'Sometimes there are mistakes,' said Father Dear. 'Even the best of us can make mistakes.' He was still on their side.

'This is not a mistake,' Bro Ali snapped at him. 'They never get it wrong. I know. They have done it deliberately.'

For Father Dear this discussion had already gone too far. 'Why would they do that, to their own colleagues? After all you have done for them.'

Bro Ali didn't seem very proud of what he had done for those people at the Hangar. I had accompanied him on his night missions when he used to jabber into his radio. He was trying to clean up the place by giving them targets. I didn't judge him; he sounded heartbroken enough. 'They have done it to show us that they can.'

'Who are they trying to show?' Momo was inconsolable. He had always looked at the blue plastic roofs with contempt.

'That they can bomb your house. They'll say they did it for our own good because people were beginning to be suspicious. They have restored our honour by making us homeless. Now we are like everybody else. This is their idea of being fair.' Bro Ali made a short speech as Mother Dear checked his hands and limbs for injuries. 'Thank God, we are all safe,' she said.

'They'll pay compensation. Maybe we can add a bedroom and get a new kitchen,' said Father Dear. He had already moved on to the post-war reconstruction phase.

'They better pay up,' said Momo. 'I'll draw up a damages list.'

'I have to go and work in the Hangar,' announced Bro Ali, still whimpering in anger and hugging Mother Dear. It was a startling claim, as if the bomb demolishing our house was not a senseless aerial attack but a job offer.

'They don't hire foreigners, not to work inside the Hangar,' said Father Dear, always the guy telling you things you don't want to hear.

'They have taken in many boys, everyone knows that. And what have they achieved? This.' Bro Ali pointed to the rubble surrounding us.

'You are not like those boys,' said Father Dear.

'I know that, I am the best they have ever worked with.'

Bro Ali's mind was made up. Did he want to turn them into peace-loving human beings by working with them? Did he want to work from within the system and change it? Did he want to blow it up from inside? Or did he want to learn? I could smell his rancid anger, milk at the boiling-point rage, but I had no idea how he wanted to achieve his objectives. If I want to go from point A to point B I dash, sometimes if a human is posted along the way to interrupt my journey, I'll lunge towards the left and as they stumble to stop me I'll abruptly turn right and reach my destination. That's the extent of my deception. Humans are different. If they want to make babies, instead of humping each other they'll invite the whole village, feed them, tell them about their noble intentions, then go hide in a room and try to make babies. When they want to fight evil they become evil.

I still don't know how but he has achieved one thing. Since Bro Ali went inside the Hangar there have been no more strikes. There have been no supplies. The gates have been shut. There's an occasional crack in the sky, occasionally an unexpected chill in the air, but they have retreated. Can a seventeen-year-old stop a long-running war? Or was our house the last target left on their list and now they have called the whole thing off?

Most people are indifferent to the basic question – why has he not come back?

Most people are indifferent; indifference smells like the bleached bones of your fellow dog.

I have my theory about why the bombing stopped when Bro Ali joined them. He said no more bombings, no night raids, no day runs. When you make profit from evil, you always tell yourself that if I don't do it someone else will. This is the biggest fib we tell ourselves. If I don't steal this bone, the other guy will steal it, if I don't hump this leg someone else will. When Bro Ali stopped, bombing stopped. Of course, there could be other explanations, we shouldn't always fall for that whole thing about how one man can change the world.

Maybe they got bored of bombing us? Maybe they needed those bombs elsewhere? It's a big, bad world out there. Maybe Bro Ali actually convinced them that they should stop bombing us, but those people in the Hangar, even if you convince them, don't just go away. Maybe this is the price that Bro Ali had to pay, he had to become one of them to convince them to stop bombing. That thought scares me. I can contemplate the mysteries of the universe and the perversions of the human heart, but I don't want to imagine Bro Ali becoming one of them.

Bro Ali had the power to be someone; he could fix tyres on a plane, he could cure homesickness, a total multi-tasker that Bro Ali. He could fight like a ninja and pray like a priest. And he never did it for any rewards.

That's the spirit, Bro Ali. I have lost many of my own comrades, some in the bombings, some while trying to rescue their human companions after those bombings, others have perished in horrible diseases that spread after the bombings. Do we ever ask for any medals? Do we have roads named after us? Do you really believe we all deserve to die a dog's death? Let me tell you, death is a bit more irksome than living with the memory of those who have already left.

Father Dear could have stopped Bro Ali but instead he went ahead and got him a job in the Hangar. Momo goes around saying Father Dear sold him. That boy can only see life as a series of transactions. We don't know what the deal was, but Father Dear got himself a deal. He never thought that his boy might also disappear like the other boys, because he was *his* boy. He was special. They needed him. He was almost as good as those people in the Hangar.

Momo doesn't realize how fathers hedge their bets. Having one son inside the Hangar and another one outside seemed like a sensible solution to him. One will be inside the heart of a machine and stay safe. The other one will stay home and keep us safe. Regret smells like burnt bread.

CHAPTER 13

Ellie

Here comes Momo's father. He arrives on a Honda 70 motorbike, sitting on the petrol tank as the seat is piled high with a stack of files. He beckons Momo, who comes jumping and skipping, unties the stack of files from the bike and takes them inside. He notices me as he parks his bike and rushes towards me as if he has been waiting for me.

'He is the man who tried to steal our Mutt,' shouts Momo. 'I caught him in the desert. He has stomach cramps.'

The light goes out of Momo's father's eyes; he comes and stands next to me. The man is wearing a striped shirt, faded brown corduroy slacks and carries a handkerchief in his right hand with which he dries his forehead periodically, although his forehead is perfectly dry.

'I should thank you probably but I wish you had taken that dog away, this Mutt's a curse on our house,' he whispers, as if he doesn't want Momo to hear our exchange.

I smile. A polite, culturally sensitive smile, which is supposed to mean I do understand but don't really give a fuck. What's a man to do? I didn't find the mutt. The mutt found me.

A woman's voice from the kitchen: 'I see you are back. First your son goes looking for one mutt and comes back with two and now you come back with your files. Am I going to cook these files? Did you manage to get some salt?'

This place is no fancy bistro but I am ravenous, and the water has settled down in my stomach. *How about some food?* I want to shout. *Where's your famous frigging desert folks' hospitality? Where's my chow?* I can smell onions being fried in the kitchen, hear the hiss of raw meat over hot iron. I've had some strange midnight snacks but this is the real hunger, for meat and bread and something that you can slurp down, something hot followed by something cold. *Oh bring me your spicy meats, give me your broccoli soup. Toss me some tofu. Feed me.*

I have seen these places, these compounds with their clay ovens, in our simulations, but there were no hunger pangs in the simulations. As part of our Cultural Sensitivity programme they sent us on a halal cookery course. As if I am going to find a fattened lamb here to practise my halal skills on.

'Have you come to reopen the Hangar?' Momo's father asks.

'What Hangar?' I say. 'I had an accident, I was lost in the desert.'

'But we have been waiting for you for seven months.'

'For me?'

'For someone to come. I have got all the files, all the paperwork.'

'That's not why I'm here. I told you, I had an accident.'

In the updated simulator exercise, 'Beyond Blitz', they introduced these old city centres where we could wing a building, almost scrape against a balcony and get a bonus red star. Then came compounds with families waiting for dinner. There were also lots of moving targets, dreamt up by some kid who'd never seen the inside of a cockpit but had watched plenty of video games; people, convoys, camels, occasionally trains. The basic rule was that if it moves, hit it. But then a technical problem: sometimes as you were about to hit it, it stopped moving.

We had workshops and brainstorming sessions and there was no consensus. Our capacity-building sessions turned into screaming matches. To bomb or not to bomb, or as Central Command started to put it, 'To B or not to B'.

I told Cath about this problem. We were told it helps to talk about such things if you are a long-term couple and love each other but have reached an emotional impasse. The stuff that confounds you in briefing rooms, or in front of simulators, should be discussed at the dining table and it will start to make sense. It was supposed to improve our relationship as well.

'And why do the targets move?' asked Cath, looking suspicious.

'How am I supposed to know, Cath?' It was the truth.

'Maybe they hear the planes approaching. And surely when they hear a plane approaching it's one of yours and they know that it's not there to take them somewhere nice for a holiday. Maybe they think you are there to kill them, or photograph them so that you can send another plane to kill them. And they don't want to get killed. You can't blame people for wanting to not get killed,' she said.

'In that case it's clear that they are the enemy combatants, otherwise why would they start moving when they hear a plane approaching?' I gave her a bit of my theory of modern warfare.

'What if they just need to go somewhere?' asked Cath. 'When I quit smoking I still used to get the urge to get up from my desk and go out every hour. That didn't mean that I was still a smoker, I just needed to get away from my workstation,' she continued. I was already regretting this. Even if I have an argument with a pizza delivery boy, she is always on the pizza delivery boy's side.

'But you were very depressed when you quit smoking,' I murmured.

I used to wonder what I would do if I was ever taken as a POW. What would I say? *My wife is depressed. I need to go home, please let me go.* Although she said that she was just trying to think things through in her head, things she was working through in her head were not easy to work out. I could see that. Some days she couldn't even change TV channels without letting out a sub-zero sigh. 'Why are you crying, baby?' I would make it a point to ask, and she always looked at me as if I had no right to ask that question. But sometimes she could work things out for me. I was stuck with the new scoring system on simulators, so I talked to Cath about it again. She wasn't interested.

Sometimes a discussion with Cath is like tossing a coin. It's not as if she ever tells me whether or not to do something, but after she asks why I would even think of doing a certain thing, the only way to find out is to go ahead and do it. So in the simulator I hit them, the moving and the stationary, and then felt lighter. Nothing better than shedding your load, that shoulder-sapping feeling, like the first few days of marriage.

'But those are only simulations,' she said when I told her. 'You can always change your mind when you have to go and do the real stuff.'

Cath always calls my work 'stuff'. I can't call her day-long shoots for Safe Cats commercials 'stuff'. I have seen desert simulations. Cath hasn't. With the air conditioner on full you can do as many sorties as you want and your butt doesn't burn. Yes sir, I have done many desert simulations but this is not a desert simulation. Because never did I get sand in my butt crack during desert simulations. And I have never felt so ravenous in my life.

'I was the local logistics officer for USAID,' Momo's father explains helpfully. 'I have to keep the records. You never know when the auditors might come.' Logistics Officer is a thin, wiry man with a neatly trimmed moustache, like a struggling jazz singer who hasn't landed a gig in years. He pulls up a camping chair emblazoned with UNITED NATIONS FOOD PROGRAMME and sits down, but he is so restless it seems he might get up at any moment and start running a marathon.

'Have you had any visitors?' I ask politely. I am the only visitor, I know. *And I'm not here to talk about your career prospects*, I want to scream. Where's dinner anyway? There's an entire fucking US of A government department to feed them, a five-star Hangar to protect them, all funded by my countrymen, by my taxes, to feed these guys, now where is my food? Why is that woman taking so long cooking whatever delicious thing she is cooking?

'They haven't visited in seven months but I have kept all the files updated. I have been writing to them regularly about the situation on the ground but I haven't been able to send my updates for obvious reasons,' he pats his files. 'It's all here because sometimes they like to catch us unaware.' I wonder what they could catch him doing? Being dull? He seems like the kind of man who is always getting caught without ever committing a crime. Waits for the police to knock on his door because he has been fantasizing about his neighbour's wife.

Things are a bit slow here. That woman in the kitchen is taking a century rustling up dinner, auditors don't visit for seven months. There is an annoying stillness in this place. Some people might call it peaceful, some might call it a sleepy town. But I'm hungry. You can't go to sleep on an empty stomach even if you're in the sleepiest fucking town in the world. No wonder nobody visits this shithole.

Momo comes in cradling Mutt. 'The doctor is coming,' he says, reassuring the mutt and his Father Dear.

'Doctor is busy killing dengue mosquitoes, he is busy growing vegetables without pesticides, he doesn't have time for naughty dogs,' Father Dear says. He doesn't seem sure of his authority in front of his son. A sissy father. A pussy-whipped, middle-aged man with a pretend job. I bet there's nothing in those files. I suspect he might be a closet poet, who doesn't share his poetry with anyone because he believes it's too precious and other closet poets will steal his metaphors.

Mother Dear's voice rings out from the kitchen, some-thing strikes a pot, making a call-to-attention noise.

'You have brought files?' asks Mother Dear, who as far as I am concerned is on a mission to make the slowest dinner in the history of dinners.

'Yes, I have all of them,' says Father Dear enthusiastically, as if he has just discovered a new source of fresh water in the desert.

'And have you brought salt?'

Father Dear gets up from his chair, clenching his fists as if trying to decide whether to divorce or kill this annoying woman who is insulting him in front of a foreigner.

'The plane didn't come today. But it should be here any day,' he shouts back.

'What am I going to put in the food if there is no salt? Your sense of duty?'

'Yes, yes, I know,' shouts the sissy logistics man. 'Your father owned salt mines, and you can't get a pinch for your stew. Heavens are not going to fall if there is no salt in your stew. No salt. No blood pressure. Half the diseases known to mankind are caused by salt. It's an addiction. They are not sending us salt because it's not good for us. If you don't like it here go live somewhere nice. You can go back to your salt mines.'

You fly around half the world, almost get killed, only to visit a couple who are arguing over dinner preps.

You get the feeling they have this exchange every evening. It's their version of 'Honey, I'm home'.

At least they're too busy fighting with each other to do anything about me. Momo is probably the designated assassin in the family but even he's fussing over his dog. He's laid out a small sleeping bag with US ARMY SURPLUS NOT FOR SALE inscribed on it and put the mutt on it.

'Doctor should be here any time now,' Momo reassures the mutt, picks up a football and goes out of the house.

'I think you must have guessed by now, the kid is a bit spoilt,' Father Dear whispers. 'We should never have taught him to drive that UN jeep. Now just because he can drive he thinks he is the commander of this Camp.' This man is quite a good storekeeper of his own regrets.

'Teenagers are the same everywhere,' I say, finally relieved that we are talking man to man. I wonder where the real commander of this Camp is. I should be sitting with him and not with this nice but lowly incompetent junior official who can't keep his son grounded or make his wife keep her mouth shut.

'If you are a father and if you are a fugee, what can you do?' Father Dear looks at me, waiting for a response.

'Nothing, I guess.'

'Right you are. We are fugees and we can't do a thing about it. We have been fugees for such a long time that it's difficult to tell today's kids that we were not always fugees. We were like normal people. We were nomads. We had goats and buffaloes and we followed the rains and stored our own grain in our own stores. We were becoming better, we built houses with flushing toilets, we bought tea sets and sofa sets and we bought electric fans because electricity was about to arrive, and it did come for a few seconds, and we all remember those few moments and are waiting for it to return. Now it's all gone – the house, the job. I think I still have my job but they have shut down my workplace without any warning – they were supposed to give six weeks' notice. It's not like them to ignore the SOPs. Thank God, we still have some goats and camels, but even they behave like fugees. They eat USAID grains, get USAID injections. These children think there was nothing before it and there will be nothing beyond this Camp. Well they know there is the desert but that's also like nothing. I mean when it rains, it livens up a bit, but it's not really Disneyland, is it?'

So here it is. Foreign. Fucking. Culture. All that Cultural Sensitivity racket. Parents moaning about their kids. Wives grumbling about their husbands. Why does anyone ever leave home?

But don't get too comfortable here. Go home.

'So have you been able to communicate with USAID? Any air drops? Surely they pick up their mail?' I'm charting my escape in my head. I don't want to ask directly about any existing connections to the outside world.

'No, but I have everything here on the files. There have been no air drops for seven months. Bombs stopped falling, auditors stopped coming.'

'Why?'

'I don't know. There must be other fugee camps. Probably worse off than we are. Actually, if you look at it we are doing OK. They must be very busy people. Probably busy in other parts of the world.' He bends towards me and lowers his voice. 'But there are some urgent matters, maybe you can suggest a way. . .'

Before I can answer him, Momo returns sans his football and starts giving Mutt a medical examination. The devious mongrel is whimpering, enjoying it.

I stay quiet and imagine a world that is so busy that it has forgotten me. No rescue parties, no airborne radar-carriers cruising the area, no woman hugging my picture on *Fox & Friends*, no flowers and candlelight, no vigils, no signs along the highways saying BRING HOME OUR BOY.

'You don't look well,' says Father Dear, pretending he wasn't about to start a conversation on an urgent matter.

Thanks for noticing, I'm about to faint with hunger.

Even if they are planning to slaughter me, I'd expect some food first. Is that too much to ask?

'I haven't eaten in so many days.' I try to keep my voice calm. Not complaining. It wasn't his fault I had not eaten in so many days. But he could do something about it now. And what is he doing? Sitting here, complaining about missing auditors and wayward teenagers.

'As you can probably tell, dinner is being cooked. There won't be any salt though,' he says apologetically.

I nod as if I understand the problem. I'll be happy to live on a salt-free diet for the rest of my life.

Fuck salt, fuck this politeness. Can't they just give me a piece of bread to begin with? Maybe some butter. What kind of hospitality is this? I survived eight days in the desert and now I am starving at the doorstep of a kitchen.

'I was lost in the desert,' I say to no one in particular.

'This happens quite often,' says Father Dear. 'Specially when people venture into it without enough preparation. Sometimes people get lost for weeks.'

'I was lost for weeks,' I say. 'Well, more than a week. Slightly more than a week.'

'Desert forgave you then, sometimes desert forgives and makes friends. The desert is immense but it's also lonely. It doesn't always kill, sometimes it just makes someone lose his way because it needs some company.'

'I am not sure if I needed that kind of company,' I say, and then remember my 'Basic Good Manners With Tribals' module which states that you must appreciate their local knowledge, their love for nature. 'You seem to know the desert like the back of your hand,' I say.

'What else is there to do? There is only one TV and Momo hogs it when we can get a signal. That's all the education he is getting. You know the interesting fact about the desert?'

'Go ahead, enlighten me,' I say, indulging my host, and then add, 'Although I'm never going that route again.'

'Women never get lost in the desert. In the history of this desert – and trust me it has a very long history – a woman has never lost her way in the desert. It ejects them, it doesn't let them spend even one night. The desert makes sure they are out by sunset.'

'Maybe women have superior navigation skills. Maybe they are not foolish enough to venture into it without first mapping their route.'

An empty stomach can make a man argumentative and forget his 'Good Manners With Tribals' in which it was emphasized that you must not mention women in any context.

Momo comes running, shouting. 'Mutt is dying, if the doctor doesn't come Mutt is gonna die. His blood will be on your hands.' He points towards me. And then towards Father Dear. 'And yours. And this will not be the first blood on your hands.'

Chapter 14

Mutt

I don't mind the pain but I do mind the fact that there are no painkillers. What is a better painkiller than unconditional love? You can say, what's better than Momo's arms around me? A bit of morphine, maybe. I know we are at war so maybe just a little aspirin. No, this is not delirium caused by exploding pain in my lower half, I have not gone sentimental after breaking a leg. No, I haven't fallen in love with my tormentor all over again. I realize how ugly life is out there. The world is not as big as they promised it was. You can call me whatever you call me. But I am not sentimental. Things they have tried to call me: Max, Charlie, Duke, Buddy. Buddy? As if by naming me after a white man, they can raise my status – or maybe their own? Things they say about me on the street: Mutt, kutta, son of a bitch. Now I am ready to be called a lame dog for the rest of my life. I don't care.

They can keep saying, *there goes the dog who has had a dog's life and will die a dog's death, oh such a miserable dog-eat-dog-eat-dog world.* Trust me I don't, I'd rather eat organic potatoes. Doggie style is not my style. This is what I do, this is all I can do. That's who I am. They are lowlifes but I don't bother with them because in the end they know that I am Momo's Mutt. Look who has got his head in Momo's lap? There is someone who cares about me. Look at the rest of them in this household. This white man doesn't even smell of anything. What kind of life is that? Lady Flowerbody is a bouquet of jungle smells that waft in and out of this house but she is out in the field. She is lonely at heart. Her heart was broken once by a boiled cabbage and she believes only a boiled cabbage can mend it. I don't blame her. Look at the role models in the older generation. Father Dear once loved Mother Dear when she wasn't Mother Dear, but that love has gone sour now, he wants to be appreciated for things he can't do. He wants to be worshipped for being who he is. Mother Dear could have led this pack but her heart is tangled in longing for her son, my son, my son. . .

It's only Momo who cares about me. And really, you are lucky if you have one person in your life who does. When in pain, ask yourself who cares about you. And if you can think of one person, that pain is worth living through.

And that still means something in this world infested with ghosts, in this purgatory where the living wait upon the dead, where when shadows lengthen hearts sink, and when a bird takes flight a precious part of your soul flies away with it. Maybe it's delirium. Maybe I am dying. But the place is increasingly full of things that I can't smell. Yes, they will say that old Mutt is finally losing his marbles. But I would like to be proved wrong.

One must suffer pain, one must feel joy, one must die, one must live. Sometimes I used to think they should just stay home and leave the outside world to me, I feel I can manage it better than them. I could take them for an occasional long walk, I wouldn't even put them on a leash, not even a collar. I'd let them run around the place and make sure they didn't get into fights that can be avoided with a few carefully delivered yelps. But their desires are complicated, always multiplying. They pick fights they can't win.

A few days after Bro Ali went into the Hangar and didn't come back, a three-vehicle convoy crawled through the main street. Children don't chase them anymore. Some parents stood in their way, waving, asking the soldiers in helmets to stop. Guns were waved, asking them to clear the way. Most people moved aside, still murmuring and cursing. A fourteen-year-old stood in front of the lead vehicle, his face inches away from the barrel of the gun.

'We don't want money, where is my brother? Bring him back.' He grabbed the barrel of the gun as if about to snatch it from the American. Idiot didn't realize that the gun was mounted, attached to the armoured vehicle with a lot of metal. Father Dear, who had watched the situation with increasing panic, shouted at the boy to let go. The boy ignored the shouting, trying to dismount the gun with the craziness of a fourteen-year-old boy.

As you can see, this was all bound to end in tragedy. Father Dear lunged towards the boy, a stray kite shrieked above in the air, a very short rattle from the gun and the boy had two large holes in his face. He stumbled before falling, a bit surprised at this sudden turn of events.

More crackling of the radios, and the convoy turned around and headed back to the Hangar, as if they had just realized that they didn't need water from our pond anymore.

There was nothing more to be done here, no alarms calling for survivors to be taken by ambulances. A father was standing over his dead boy, wailing. I went for a walk and when Mutt goes for a walk, Mutt goes for a walk. When Mutt chews a bone he is not acting out some suppressed violent fantasies. When Mutt humps he is not thinking of posterity. When a Mutt dies he stays dead.

I think I have come back to this house because I am a bit like them. Like all those who come here, to this house, the alive and the dead and those who are not sure whether they belong in this life or the other. The man with no smell keeps saying he wants to go home. *Home is in the Hangar buddy, yes Buddy, I can call you Buddy can't I?* Home should be in the Hangar. Why don't they take him there, blow up the gates, knock down the watchtowers, dig up the runways. Give them what's theirs, take back what's ours. Yes, I admit this is delirium speaking, it hurts, but you don't become a prophet just because you are suffering. There are all sorts of things they must do, go through life with an eye on sinners and salvation. I am just a Mutt, yes go ahead, say it, I'm a lame Mutt now.

Doctor is doing what he can, but can't he hurry up? He is one lazy messiah. I know he can't take the pain away, but can he take the edge off it. He doesn't want to. He believes in suffering. He is surely some sort of prophet. If you believe in suffering must you inflict pain on others? Why can't he score some drugs from Lady Flowerbody? Sometimes she smells like a sack of raw hashish but hides it well under a perfume called Opium. It doesn't smell anything like opium.

I can understand why she does it. Lady Flowerbody is fine, she is a working lady. They are different. They have a different rhythm. Their day starts and their day ends and sometimes the loneliness descends but she gets up the next day and gets on with it. Sometimes she says things which are not true but she believes them. I don't know anything about young Muslim minds but I know a thing or two about mutts. We don't go near drugs. Some of my comrades from good families have actually become expert at catching drugs. They give them two litres of milk every day and soft duvets to sleep on. I think Lady Flowerbody wants what everyone wants, I think if this was Nat Geo she would jump on Doctor's bike and they would speed away from this planet, a giant ball of fire. But there is something about her that tells me she'll be updating her CV. I don't think I'll figure in that.

This is how I see the world ending. Doctor will hang in here in the desert humping his Mother Earth, trying to impregnate it, but the rains won't come. The rains won't come, maybe more bombs will come. But, Doctor, can you hurry up and do what you are supposed to do. What are you saving those aspirins for?

CHAPTER 15

Ellie

I am dying of hunger but everyone here's busy with the mutt's medical emergency.

Doctor finally arrives on a very old model Triumph, a creased leather bag slung on his shoulder. Hunched over the handlebars, he comes very close to the plastic chair where I am sitting and listening to Father Dear's family woes. Doctor has the sunken eyes of a recovering fanatic, and the drooping cheeks of a malnourished child. He stops his bike but doesn't get off it and keeps looking at me as if he's lost his way and wants to ask me for directions. Bent over the handlebars he seems like an old woman kneading dough. A limp Red Crescent flag adorns the motorbike's rear. An array of blue and pink plastic shopping bags hangs in piles around his bike. It's probably his hospital on wheels.

'He thinks he is the Red Crescent rep here,' Father Dear whispers. 'That's why he insists on flying the flag. Although Red Crescent has not paid him for more than a year. I am not even sure if Red Crescent is called Red Crescent anymore. Or if it's red or gone some other colour. Thank God I work for USAID. Whatever they do I know they'll never change their name.'

Doctor is wearing a shabby white coat with ink stains on it and smells as if he has been sleeping in his medicine cabinet.

Getting off the bike he demands to know, 'Why did you send for me?' As if he could perform functions other than those related to medicine. He avoids looking at me. I am hoping for some medical attention for my blisters, for my parched throat, a little debrief about the impending Post Traumatic Stress Disorder but most of all something for my stomach, which seems to be on fire, hunger seems to have been replaced by a blaze which is devouring my innards. But Doctor ignores me and sits down on a chair with a loud sigh.

Momo arrives wearing a baseball cap, embossed with I HEART NY in bold letters.

'Your patient is here,' Momo says to Doctor who has an unlit cigarette between his lips and is rummaging for matches in his leather bag.

'And that is the thief who tried to steal him.' Momo points towards me. Doctor takes out a matchbox from his bag, lights his cigarette, two quick puffs, then produces a small pair of scissors from his pocket, clips the cigarette and puts it back in the pocket. 'Defeating cancer one puff at a time,' he says and smiles. 'I told you I stopped doing animals,' Doctor adds, mournfully. 'I am not trained for it. I have my oath to think of. And with my current job, there might be a clear conflict of interest.'

Momo listens to him impatiently, pulling his cap over his eyes, then adjusting it back. It seems the boy has seen this act before.

Momo takes Doctor by the hand and goes to the mutt. 'Mutt has broken a bone, he is injured. Bone is same, man or animal. Bone breaks, you set it, what's the difference?

Is Mutt bone not a bone? Is Mutt pain not like man pain? Can't you see he is suffering?' Momo talks to Doctor as if explaining the perils of playing with fire to a child. 'Do we have anyone else in the Camp we can call a doctor? Do you need orders in writing before you can save someone's life? Is Mutt's life not life?'

Momo has the making of a great preacher. He can accuse and plead in the same sentence.

Doctor looks towards me conspicuously, as if this is all my fault. Then he sighs and moves towards Mutt. He sits beside him in the dust and looks him over carefully without touching him. 'You'll have to hold him for me,' he looks up at Momo who's standing beside him, attentive; he has smoothly transformed from a bullying preacher to a doctor's caring assistant.

'Make him numb first,' says Momo. 'Rub some spirit on him. He doesn't like pain.'

'Who likes pain?' Doctor says without looking up. 'We haven't got any anaesthetic. I filled in a request form to replenish the stocks seven months ago, it's still pending action. This is how the world works. Remember the time when we had too much spirit and no gauze. Now we have so much gauze that we can wrap it around the earth and still have enough left over for all the injured mutts in the world.'

'He is not just any Mutt,' Momo protests. 'He is a golden retriever, just the wrong colour. When he grows up, he'll turn golden.'

'He is grey, he will stay grey. He is called Mutt because he is one,' Doctor mutters. I feel claustrophobic. Why are they bent over an injured dog debating his pedigree instead of providing him some pain relief?

'He'll cry but there is no other way. We need to inflict some more pain to make the original pain go away.'

'You sound just like the Americans and they don't even pay you anymore,' Momo says to Doctor. I bristle and keep quiet. You can curse your own country but when someone else curses it, you want to stand up and slap them. It's not patriotism, it's our damned human nature. But here everyone is accusing everyone else of being American. God save America.

Doctor takes out a piece of cardboard and cuts a strip from it with a US army knife, then produces a roll of gauze bandage as the mutt squirms and his yelps shoot up towards the sky. Momo squeezes his eyes shut as Doctor bandages Mutt's broken leg, covering it with surplus gauze. He pats Momo on the cheek, Momo squirms and tilts his cap. Momo has got Mutt's face in his lap, he takes off his cap and fans him.

Doctor comes and stands next to me, goes around my chair, and examines me without touching me and immediately reaches a diagnosis.

'Give the poor man something to eat,' says Doctor. 'It seems he hasn't eaten in many days. Give him some food before he starts eating your pots and pans.' I am first pleasantly surprised then scared by the accuracy of Doctor's diagnosis. My legs begin to shake and I am sweating despite a slight chill in the air. I resist the urge to faint because I don't want this quack putting his hands on me. Doctor has probably run out of disinfectants too. Father Dear goes inside and after a few moments emerges with a plate of boiled rice floating in milk with brown sugar sprinkled on top. He hands me the plate apologetically and whispers, 'She thinks the meat takes much longer to cook without salt.' I don't answer and start to eat with as much restraint as a man starving for eight days can muster.

Doctor watches me eat and makes satisfactory sounds as if his patient is responding well to treatment. He takes out his cigarette, two more puffs, clips it and puts it back in his pocket.

When I am halfway through my plate, trying hard to keep my food down as my palate rebels against this strange excuse for a meal, Father Dear disappears again and comes back with a big platter of what looks like large chunks of meat and a pile of bread. He starts to eat, sitting right in front of me, tearing off big juicy chunks of meat, dipping them in the oily gravy and stuffing them in his mouth. Doctor watches him but refuses to join him. 'That poison is going to kill you one day.' Doctor produces a dried piece of bread from his bag and a large green chilli and starts taking small, slow bites.

I was told they would slaughter their best horse if a hungry stranger arrived at their door. A hungry stranger has arrived at their doorstep, and they have slaughtered an animal and are happily eating it themselves. They have given me sick people's food, probably Mutt's leftovers, and are sitting right there in front of me feasting on the finest meat this desert has produced. Doctor has probably gone vegetarian. Even the lush green chilli in his hand seems appetizing. I have a feeling that I am being treated like a refugee. I feel insulted.

I feel homesick.

But I am here, I have not ended up like Colonel Slatter. I have food in front of me, my stomach is able to keep this food down despite the waves of nausea that engulf me. I feel I should be grateful but I can't bring myself to be grateful to this pair of crazies who live off UN handouts and are now smacking their lips right in front of me.

'What is it that you are wearing?' asks Momo, who has joined us, and is now picking out bits of fat from the meat on offer and feeding them to Mutt.

I look at myself. The inside-out flying suit surprises me. I feel as if I have come to this place inappropriately dressed. I must borrow the local civilian dress, if I want to blend in. I have to mingle before I can be rescued. But for now I have to tell the truth, earn their trust, even if they are being mean hosts.

'Flying suit,' I say. 'It's my flying suit.'

'You can wear that and fly? Go on, show us,' Momo says in jest. He is fully convinced that I am a con artist.

'This is what we wear when we fly an aeroplane, it takes care of the air pressure.' I am gobbling the rice, which is not doing anything for my hunger. It seems I am gobbling this mush into an endless void. I look at my cutlery which consists of just a spoon. It is made of stainless steel. Probably very hard to bite.

'If you were flying, where is your plane?' asks Momo, looking into my eyes.

I choke on my mush. 'I was bringing in aid, humanitarian aid. Food and football kits.'

'And then what happened?' Momo is an inquisitor from hell.

'My plane developed a technical fault and I had to eject.'

'You jumped out of your plane? Where is the plane?'

'Probably somewhere in the desert. When I ejected it was still flying.'

'And you were going to land at the Hangar, right?'

'Yeah, I guess.' There's a grinding pain in my lower stomach. I don't know if they have proper men's rooms here.

'They forgot to tell you that the Hangar is shut. There have been no flights for seven months.'

'I've got stomach cramps,' I mumble. 'When you eject sometimes you have short-term memory loss. It'll come back to me.'

Momo's eyes mock me as if he can see through my bullshit, as if saying *nothing will come back to you, nothing.*

'You are still hungry?' Doctor turns towards me.

'Yes. As you know I have been starving for eight days.' I wipe the last morsel of rice from my plate. 'A man can have an appetite. Especially in the middle of a war.'

'But this place is not America. You can't eat everything here,' says Doctor. 'The fugee food is poison. If it doesn't kill you, it'll make you impotent. You want to go home impotent?'

Who are these people to speculate about my intimate life? It's probably their culture. I need to be sensitive to it.

'Yes, I know all about halal. I myself prefer halal. Halal is healthier.' I am glad I took my 'Eat and Drink With the Enemy' module of my Cultural Sensitivity course seriously. A wave of nausea travels towards my throat and with it a sudden urge to get up and run, get away from this place as fast as I can.

I must find a way to contact Cath, I must find a way to send her a message. She wouldn't believe that I'm stuck here in the middle of nowhere, but I must convince her to come and get me out of here, take me with her. I must go to her. I get up in panic and start walking towards the door. My feet barely touch the ground, I feel I can walk through walls and locked gates. As I approach the gate, my head spins and an ancient fatigue takes over, I collapse.

A shout from the kitchen: 'Can you bring my plates back? This place is full of thieves.'

Chapter 16

Momo

When a boy wants to get with a girl, he tells her a joke. And if she laughs, it's a sign she is gonna be seduced. When a woman wants a man she tells him a story and if he pretends to be absorbed in the story, it means he is seduced. I know many jokes but I am not gonna waste any on Lady Flowerbody. She knows some stories and she is trying them on me. I am all ears.

'This modern family is not that old. It all started forty thousand years ago,' she says, catching her breath and picking out an invisible hair from her mouth. I can already tell this is gonna be a story with a moral. I like a good story. I am also very good at ignoring the moral. Also nobody has called my family modern before.

I can smell the faint maple syrup smell coming from her hair. I am not very good at smells. That's Mutt's speciality.

'You know how it came about?' she says, puffing on a rolled-up organic cigarette, her tobacco from the American Spirit pouch, her tongue licks the paper in a smooth prac- tised move. Smoking is bad for health so I'm never gonna smoke but I'm not gonna lie, she looks nice with that cigarette between her lips. It's a tough choice to make between looking good and lung cancer. 'It all started forty thousand years ago.'

I was thinking she was gonna tell me something about the origins of International Aid, and if they could outsource some of their work to me for the right price or if she could guide me to any venture capitalists who were interested in investing in my Young Muslim Mind rather than exploring it. But she obviously wants to tell me something more primitive, something that happened a long time ago before the young minds became Muslim and brought us together here, forty thousand years after it had all started. Her cigarette smells like stale incense that has burnt in the kitchen.

'When folks lived in caves, they didn't have partners. I mean they didn't think very hard about who they went to bed with and consequently when women gave birth to babies nobody knew who the father was. So maybe they did take care of them, like the community does, out of the goodness of its heart or for the larger common good, or maybe they just found the little babies cute like we do now, but the net result was that the world had lots of mums and no dads. And lots of kiddies died, lots of them. Sometimes they died because of all sorts of nasty diseases, or wild animals mauled them, or sometimes older kids killed them for fun, anyway they died in huge numbers and there were no dads to mourn them, only sad women digging holes in the frozen earth and later no partner to hold them, no one to promise them they would make another baby. Maybe they didn't even know how the babies were made. I am sure they had some idea but it was not as if they could google it and look at the illustrations or something.'

I know all about how babies are made. Father Dear forced sex education on us. He had even designed a module keeping in mind local culture and customs, he always reminded us, as if there were different ways of making babies in different cultures. I nod as if she isn't telling me the story of human evolution but narrating a tale of personal loss, something that has happened to her. When women are telling you stories about history, they are telling you about the present, something that started a long time ago but is not likely to end any time soon.

'So the kiddies kept dying, and men kept denying that they had any role in their birth or death and women kept digging holes and starving themselves to feed their children. Then there was this smart girl who one day gave a man her baby to hold. As the men prepared to go out to work – I mean go out to hunt or forage for food or whatever it was that they called work back then – this woman comes up to the man who she had slept off and on with, they haven't really done anything, not the things that she has done with other men, it was sort of like *sure we live in the same cave, sure we know each other, you were on top of me last week, or last month* – don't know how and if they measured time – *weren't you?* So she just asks him to hold the baby for a minute while she goes out to relieve herself. And she said it at the exact moment as she was plonking the baby in his lap, so the man didn't have the time to grunt or hit her or throw the baby away, or say *wait a minute I am a man*, or make whatever gesture was in vogue to say a clear *NO, I am not holding this baby*. Before he could get up, swing the baby at her or yell at her, she was out of the cave and gone and this guy was left holding the baby. And she didn't come back all day. A number of times the man left the baby on the ground and walked up to the cave's entrance determined to join the others in their daily toils, but as soon as he reached the cave's entrance the baby gurgled and laughed. Not cried, mind you, because that would have been normal, that's what children did, they cried.

'So the man spent practically the entire day walking up and down the cave, picking up the baby, plonking him down, holding him upside down and swinging him; he did everything he could remember having seen women do with a baby, he just did it in a more manly way. There was not much you could do with a baby back then, I mean there was no baby gym, or prams or soft toys, so he ran out of things to do with the baby very soon. They both sucked a yam, he sucked it and put it in the baby's mouth and the baby threw up and he felt obliged to clean it up with a banana leaf or whatever it was that they used for wipes in those days. They probably took a nap together because that's how the men and women returning after their day's toil found them, the man reclined against the wall of the cave, the baby with his arms tightly around his neck, smiling in his sleep.'

'You're making this stuff up,' I say, propping myself up on an elbow and trying not to look below her neck. She digs into American Spirit, another lick on the paper and she holds an unlit cigarette between her fingers.

'So he became the first man to not leave the cave, to stay with the baby. And when the people came back they were divided in their response. Women were scared, they didn't know what had happened. They wondered if the man had given birth and that was considered a monstrous thing even back then. Men were in awe, they had been out all day chasing dangerous animals and weeding out poisonous roots for food and here was a man, one of them, fast asleep with a smiling baby hanging around his neck.'

'How do you know all this?' I ask, getting up.

It is getting late. Mutt is yelping in the distance. Mutt has the impatience of a juvenile who thinks his lazy owner is standing between him and his destiny. A potted history of the nuclear family is standing between me and the door.

She holds my hand tightly as if she has read my thoughts and my escape plan and is determined to foil it.

She is gonna make one determined storyteller.

'They started to emulate him after that. Some of them at least. Others were repulsed. How can a man, a hunter-gatherer, a lurker in the jungle, stay all day in the cave hugging a slobbering little baby? But there were many who took to it enthusiastically and let the women wander the jungle, go out and hunt and find food. And these women who otherwise might have gone to bed with whosoever might be lying next to them always went back to the man with their baby. And that's how the word "baby-man" came about.

'They didn't all live happily ever after, men got bored, sometimes in their anger they smashed the baby against the cave walls and moved on to the next cave and the next woman and sometimes the next child. But many of them stayed, many of them kept the baby alive and then many of them left the baby with the woman and ventured out and came back to the same woman and picked up the baby. And when they were out hunting wild animals sometimes they thought of that baby and smiled. Now that's parenthood for you, that's family for you. You might want to call it love or evolution or survival or the desire to sleep with the same woman every night of your life.'

'And then what happened?' I ask, now half standing, ready to bolt but oddly fixated with this history of love in the caves.

'Boom,' she says, exploding an imaginary bomb with the palms of her hands. 'Fewer and fewer kids died. But the more people lived together, the further they drifted apart. You have six billion people now and we all still feel lonely.'

Then she looks at me with those sad eyes of hers. 'Your Mother Dear, she refuses to leave that cave.'

'What has she got to do with it?'

'She needs to be strong. I think in the end she'll find a solution to this problem of yours. She also needs to lower her expectations. She needs to get out more often.'

'She has no expectations. She used to be strong. She could carry three pitchers of water on her head, but with age of course. . .'

Lady Flowerbody has no idea how Mother Dear is raring to go out. She has no idea how I have managed to keep Mother Dear in.

'She needs to let you go. She still lives in the caves and you are her baby-man. But you are too young to carry the whole family's burden. And history's burden.'

'I am old enough.'

Look at the do-gooder's trickery. One moment she is teaching me how babies are made, the next moment she is trying to snatch that same baby from his mother.

She is definitely gonna be on my team. Now if only Mutt would shut up. I am right here, I am not gonna leave you and go somewhere, you should know that by now, Mr Fried Brains.

Chapter 17

Mutt

Today is the third worst day of my life. How do I know? Because one is wise enough to know that the worst day is already in the past. Maybe other bad things will happen, in fact today came close to being like the day my brains got fried, but I have lived an eventful life and I can safely say that the worst is in the distant past.

I keep running after the Jeep Cherokee; Momo can see me in the rear-view mirror but he keeps pushing the pedal down. He pushes that pedal hard when he is on a mission. Today I need to be on this mission with him but he doesn't want me to see him cry. I can smell his unhappiness at having to leave me behind. It is stronger than ever before, the smell of withering jasmine flowers. It's a smell very common amongst your masters when they are abandoning you for your own good.

I do not wish to write a treatise about the terms of abandonment between humans and their canine comrades, but may I just venture to ask what he knows about my own good? What's worse than somebody unilaterally defining your own good for you? Yes, there is something worse than that; when they actually, sincerely, from the bottom of their lovelorn heart, believe they know what's good for you. The stench of certainty, the rot of unshakable faith. It always reminds me of the smell of dead members of the domestic canine fraternity, freed from the daily humiliations that I have to suffer. I have smelled it too often. It's not pretty, that's why one suffers. If the ultimate freedom comes with that stench one will choose to stay an abject slave for a few more years.

This morning I could smell it already. Momo was feeling bad for himself because he had to do that thing that he thinks, nay he knows, is treacherous but he is certain it's for my own good. He was scheming and plotting and walking about as if he was just distracted by the new arrivals in the house. He doesn't realize that the white man has no smell and she is a bouquet of wild flowers.

I was lying under the jeep and Momo knew it. Our relationship is such that he doesn't need to see me to know where I am. He is aware of my presence. And I am not only aware of his presence but what's going through his genius head as well. I can chase his anxieties and hunt them down for him even before he has been able to give them a name. I can tell his enemies from his friends. I can't divine a future for him but I can tell you that his future is my future.

I was waiting for him to open the door so that I could walk through it and guide him to the point where our mission would begin. To show him that there were voices coming out of the Hangar. I could smell frying butter and other food smells. We have to mount surveillance and find a way to get into the Hangar. If we don't go to the Hangar how can we find out where Bro Ali went? I had the information, I had a plan, not a set-in-stone plan, but a pretty rational plan, but was Momo listening?

He was listening, alright; to his own raging hormones.

He was more interested in the Lady. He is consumed by Lady Flowerbody. He thinks he can seduce her; even worse, he believes he'll allow her to seduce him. He also believes he can get her to invest in his new business venture and help him find information about Bro Ali. The eternal human folly, looking for sex and salvation in the same person. That's what boys do. He pretends that he doesn't care, but is consumed by thoughts of her all day long. Showing that you care means admitting that you have a weakness. We are not afraid of showing that we care. And nobody has ever called me weak. I want to tell Momo that God promised an interesting world. He never promised a fair world. He definitely never promised a two-for-the-price-of-one world.

Hovering around the jeep Momo suddenly remembered something and went back inside the house. I followed him, reluctantly because it could be a trick. I could smell a faint whiff of trick. Tricks smell like onions. This house always smells of tricks. Everybody doing something for the other person because it's for their own good. The air in this house is like a thick onion soup.

And as he stepped inside it grew stronger and I didn't follow him in as I normally would. He was expecting me to come in. I know Momo's deceits. Like most things in life I can smell them but I can't stop them. I turned back to the jeep and waited on the passenger's seat side from where I usually get in. Momo came back, took the steering. The jeep coughed, Momo didn't even look towards me. The jeep lurched. I knew this was the end. But I know I can't give up.

So I run. And since I run with a limp I don't expect to catch up with the jeep. Even if I didn't have the limp you can't really keep pace with that Cherokee monster. My hind leg is almost healed but it still hurts. I have found a way to put my paws on the ground so it hurts less. This is what life is all about; you live and learn to manage your pain. I know he has abandoned me for the day. But I have to appear optimistic. I cannot be seen to abandon him.

I don't blame him. It's not about loyalty, it's about his out-of-control urges. He thinks he is headed for an amorous rendezvous. Lady Flowerbody thinks she is meeting her lab rat. He believes she has designs on him, that old myth about older woman hankering after young boys that middle-aged men have cultivated for centuries. She needs to study him for her report. He thinks he can score some dollars and lose his virginity in her experienced hands. Of course, the boy pretends that his life is all about business and Bro Ali, but go on, have a sniff, he smells of lust on the verge of self-combustion.

Delusions smell of synthetic vinegar.

He thinks all it takes is a trip to the bush to realize all one's teenage fantasies. You go into that bush as a free man – or as a free dog in my case – but you come out a slave, a slave to your own recurring desire. And in these teen years the desire recurs a lot. I can't go into details about my own exploits but just remember that when they call me Mutt the Rutt they are not praising my intellectual capabilities. People who boast of their sexual exploits usually have bad teeth and shrivelled testicles.

You would think Momo was in the middle of planning an expedition to bring his brother back. He is also in deep mourning. Can you have tears in your eyes and fire in your loins simultaneously?

These are some of the questions that the Lady should be working on. Instead she is interested in studying the effects of bombing, mild drugs and extreme flirtation on young

Muslim minds. I am glad she has no interest in the minds of middle-aged reformed Mutts with fried brains. It's not my job to criticize well-fed do-gooders but I can tell you a thing or two about what goes on in the bush. It should stay in the bush but there are lessons that young Muslim minds can learn. And the first one is that depression and sexual depravity are indeed first cousins.

Momo is the victim of his own hormonal imbalance; I am mere collateral damage. He has left me here with the smell of sadness so overwhelming that I could be in a salt mine. It's Mother Dear's time for morning tea and tears. And her rosary.

What a way to spend the third worst day of your life, watching a sad woman making her afternoon tea and working the rosary with the passion of a teenage boy self-pleasuring. Ellie has sneaked into the kitchen. I suspect he is trying to make tea. That man is trying to go native.

Why do they drink tea? Maybe for the same reason I sometimes eat grass and then throw up? At least I am cleansing my own digestive system. What is their excuse? Why do they put that black dust in milk and boil it? You might as well slurp the milk. Not that I would know what it tastes like. OK, I did take a sip or two when Mother Dear left her mug on the floor. I was exiled for a whole week. 'This is not a family dog and I won't have him gulping tea that is meant for my sons.' She repeated that for one whole week. She is such a family person. Look where her family has got her. One son gone, the other one out of control, running around the bush in the hope of humping a lady twice his age and stealing her money, and a husband who has brought that very lady friend home. But in her grief our Mother Dear is as stubborn as those lizards on their ceilings. Those are poison, those lizards, I had one as a little afternoon snack a while ago, its tail kept dancing even after I had gulped down the rest of it. I was sick for two days.

Sometimes Momo is not afraid of showing his soft side but ends up betraying his hard edges. During my exile after my first drink of tea Momo kept bringing me food, usually a slice of dried bread. Not even a whiff of butter. Momo thinks putting a bone in his pocket is not hygienic. That boy really has a free-floating concept of hygiene.

Like most people he is ready to pay lip service to his duty to his family by which he usually means Mother Dear. And this woman has got nothing but sadness as her family value system and, be fair for a moment, can there be a more useful family member than this humble Mutt? How many times have I saved this house from the plague of cats? How many smelly rats have been dispatched to rat hell with these teeth? But a few sips of that disgusting tea and I am not family. And who is family? The boy who is not even here. But that boy is family and will remain family.

I am Mutt and I can excrete gold and spout Rumi but I will remain Mutt.

I am having these melancholic thoughts sitting on the street, trying to shoo away the flies. These are the real nemesis. I have taken on a pack of deranged cats, avoided the butcher's bad moods, I even hope to outlive Mother Dear's misery, but you can't win against these pesky flies. They are like a manifestation of God's irritation with His own creation. So I have no doubt that when I am dead and gone my cadaver will be covered with these flies, and if I get a burial, as I hope to after all that I have done for the family, they will manage to sneak into my grave as well.

I doze off fighting these little pests, and when I wake up evening is approaching. A walk around the compound for evening inspection and what do I see: Lady Flowerbody is sneaking into that deserter Ellie's shack. When they decided to put him up in this plastic cubicle next to the main gate, I had a pang of nostalgia, the place was my own personal love in a past life. I thought this boiled cabbage would use it for some higher calling. But he is using it for the same purpose I used it for. Momo has deserted me for a rendezvous with her. And now it seems she has deserted Momo for a world-class deserter. It's not just cheating in the traditional sense but a grand circle of treason.

I don't intend to present myself as some kind of infallible character but increasingly I am coming to the conclusion that I might have more moral fibre than this whole family put together.

That's why Momo runs away from me, he doesn't want to confront the sad truth about Bro Ali. You are embarking on a mission to save your brother, you ditch your second in command for a few moments of humping. And when he returns, he doesn't smell of any humping, only the frivolous rot of small talk. I should know. What a shame. Now I feel bad for him. The boy deserves a hug, if not shameless humping.

And this is only the third worst day of my life. There was another day. Oh that really was the worst day of my life.

CHAPTER 18

Ellie

At night the stars are ridiculously low, as if trying to come closer to see if they can hear anything in this silence. I dream of a giant simulator, its sole purpose simulating herb gardens. As if there are not enough gardeners in the world. And this simulated garden is a geeky little patch, with herbs and inverted cactuses. Was I supposed to learn something, turn this desert into a vast herb garden? Did I fly 637 sorties, drop a few thousand tons of the smartest bombs, so that in the end I could shovel shit or whatever it is that you have to shovel to keep those herbs alive and cactuses inverted? I try to remember if I've ever taken a gardening course. They planned one once, but too many officers volunteered. Central Command don't like it when too many people want to do the same thing. Apparently this kind of thing was called mutiny once, a bad bit of history that Central Command don't like to remember. In my dream Colonel Slatter is standing on my head and shouting, *dig Ellie dig*. I am ignoring him and digging calmly as if I am digging of my own accord and Colonel Slatter is providing a drumbeat for my voluntary actions. I dig and dig into this garden and my shovel hits something hard. I put aside my shovel and dig out the earth with my hands, my fingers touch a smooth surface, I clear up the surface and it's a baby's head; the little bugger is giggling away.

I wake up in horror.

One thing they never teach you in Desert Survival: in the desert the morning comes too early. First there is a distant call for prayer, a bit more hurried and stilted than I had heard in movies and in my 'Sensitivity Towards Religious Rituals' module. I had heard it so many times in our training that I had actually started liking it. It seems the person calling out to the people has been dragged out of bed and wants to get back to sleep. I pull the duvet around my head tightly as if trying to steel myself against the allure of Allah. There is a special sub-module on the potential side effects of hearing Azan while in captivity. We were told about the magical qualities of this call for prayer, we were told real-life tales about how staunch disbelievers, militant atheists and at least one Jehovah's Witness had found themselves mesmerized and forced into the embrace of their captors' faith. Neil Armstrong, the first man on the moon, heard it and converted to Islam. It was never made clear whether the conversion took place right there on the moon or after he returned to earth. Just imagine, you are the first ever human being to step on the moon and what's the first thing you hear? You don't hear a song about the moon, or stars or star-spangled banner, but you hear what I am hearing now: *Prayer is better than sleep, oh yeah, prayer is better than sleep.*

But I am sleepy and no desert god is going to convince me otherwise. We were told in our module that you can take local brews and local lovers but don't try the poison of native religious practices. *Don't shove your Jesus in other people's faces either*, we were told, *we've already got that covered*. The more ridiculous a religious practice, the more respect you must show towards it.

Now that time has come to put my training into practice I realize how ridiculous our fear of conversion to another faith was. I have survived heat and hunger and a bully little saviour boy, I am not really in danger of being taken in by a plea to pray to a desert god when the stars are still shining. I slip the duvet from my head and take in the view.

I am surprised that it is still night, proper night with stars hung low, as if straining towards me to say hi. I look out and see that the call for morning prayer has stirred the refugee community, but not everyone is rushing to pray. Some have started collecting their goats and herding them towards the main gate, others are probably hugging their wives or their concubines tightly in their sleep. Some are off to collect firewood for their morning tea, others are fiddling with and cursing their malfunctioning gas cylinders. One of the women is abusing her husband loudly because he is still busy drinking from a bottle. He in turn is protesting meekly, 'Let me finish this, then I'll go, there is still half an hour before morning prayer.' It is a cacophony of voices and smudges of bright colours and smoke rising from a thousand clay ovens. It's pitch dark and they are already busy making breakfast.

Some people, it seems, are going for their morning prayers, shadows rushing to answer the call of their creator. Others are making their way towards the edge of the desert and disappearing behind the shrub that defies the elements.

I observe all this activity and wonder about the sanity of a culture where people start doing stuff at a time of day when stars are still burning bright, when you can't even see the next person's face properly.

I was having an argument with myself the night before and the argument had gone on for such a long time that I had drifted into sleep.

I had been trying to argue with Momo in my head and trying to answer that silly, existential question: What am I doing here? Why don't we first establish what I am *not* doing here. I have not bombed this place; that is plain and simple for anyone to see. The Hangar is intact. So is this refugee camp, more or less. Maybe Colonel Slatter had tried to bomb it and ended up with the same fate as me. Maybe Major Stratford had bombed it; definitely Major Stratford, not in the current campaign, but definitely in the last campaign. Maybe there were others who had bombed this place. Other Americans. Maybe the odd French pilot.

I just followed my orders. I flew my mission.

I might have done some bad things but I didn't do anything to these people. I'm doing my job for fuck's sake. Since when did doing your job become a crime against humanity? Don't fuck with my head. Fuck the makers of zero-zero ejection seats that don't eject. Fuck Martin-Baker. Don't fuck with my head. Let me get some sleep.

Someone tugs at my duvet and without thinking I cling to it. I am an over-sleeper. My St Moritz childhood has taught me that the real sleep, the deepest and the sweetest sleep, only comes when it's already morning and someone is trying to wake you up or the alarm is about to go off. I was often told by Cath that I was the kind of man who would fly eight thousand miles to take out a target any time of the day but couldn't be expected to get out of his bed to meet the FedEx guy at the door.

Here and now I am aware that the world around me has an advantage over me. Not only have they lived for generations in the same place, they have managed to become refugees in their own land, they have woken up before the sun has shown its hopeful face and they're already busy scheming about what to do with the rest of their day. They're cracking their breakfast eggs and bowing before their god and I am drifting back to sweet oblivion.

The tugging on my duvet is accompanied by birdsong.

Suddenly I am wide awake, I am ready to leave this bed, ready to follow this song, this voice into a new day, to a new destination, even if it leads me to morning prayers and to an angry Arab god.

I pull the duvet from my face. 'Yes.'

Lady Flowerbody stands close to my feet, a yellow plastic bucket in one hand, the other trying to pull the duvet off me.

'I am off to milk the goats,' she says, as if sharing some intimate routine with me. 'But first I need to count my duvets and put them away. Sometimes they disappear after sunrise. This place is full of thieves.'

I sit up, startled. I am an officer waking up at the crack of dawn in a new place and my duvet is needed elsewhere.

And suddenly the light changes and I see a smudge of orange in the sky, the sun struggling to pull off its own duvet, and I realize why they call her Flowerbody. Even at dawn, her eyes shine, the curls around her face are as dark as the night, and beyond that I can't see her face. But it is her accent that shocks; she speaks as if she is speaking to someone she has been expecting. She stands above me, pulls the duvet off and starts to roll it, and speaks with a European accent, softened Ds, and abrupt Rs.

'I don't think they know who you really are,' she says.

If I wasn't sitting in a bed, under low stars, I might have thought I was still lost in the desert, here's another mirage to consider. But I feel she'll take me out of here. She'll take me on a journey. She'll take me home. Here's somebody who knows who I am. She can see beyond, she can see that I'm more than just a lost American soldier.

'I think they are keeping you here for a purpose,' she says. 'Don't forget that.'

CHAPTER 19

Momo

One good thing about field scholars like Lady Flowerbody is that after they have asked you about your innermost feelings they give you a Cadbury Mini. They also thank you for your cooperation, for your time. Time my ass, I want to tell them, time is all I got. They used to say time is money. They were right. My time is gonna make you money. One day that's gonna change.

Another good thing about field scholars is that when they give you that Cadbury with fake milk, fake sugar and fake chocolate (yes, the wrapper is real) they themselves retreat into their offices and eat real chocolate that is at least seventy per cent pure. It's supposed to be good for your heart, it lowers your blood pressure and tastes like life, bitter and sweet, crunchy and soft at the same time.

Pure chocolate is not what I am looking for in Lady Flowerbody's shack, I am looking for information on her real mission. She goes around the Camp all day, her clipboard in her hand, asking everyone, *how do you feel?* What kind of researcher wants to know so much about feelings? Why does she think anybody is gonna tell her about their real feelings? And what exactly are her own feelings about all these fake feelings that she keeps collecting?

In the top drawer of her desk is a stack of filled-out forms, her comments in the margins, scribbled in a hurry, as if she is listening to people and scribbling her own thoughts rather than theirs. I shuffle the forms, looking for something familiar. At the bottom there is a form with my name on it and it's completely blank. It's strangely reassuring that she is still so curious about me that she has left my form blank. And there under the stack of papers I find her little pack of dark chocolates. One is open, half eaten, leftover bits wrapped in silver foil. I take it out of the foil, roll it in my fingers, a bit too moist, probably melting in the desert heat. I put it in my mouth and wait for that bitter and sweet darkness to spread. It's dark and bitter alright, it's so bitter that I feel I have swallowed a whole neem tree. It gets stuck on my palate, I try to spit it out and in the process somehow manage to swallow the whole thing in one go. I pick up another file and flick through it, trying to ignore the bitter taste in my mouth.

Words float up from the paper, my head first feels heavy then light. Mutt is outside the door whining, probably thinking I am having a snack without sharing it with him. I pull the chair from under the table and try to sit, I keep sinking and sinking. The stack of paper slips from my hands and covers the floor under me. *My land, my people*, I mutter and look up. My heart is a soaring eagle. The roof on the shack dissolves and I can see a pink-hued sky with a large black moon, the size of Mother Dear's bread-maker, dangling in the sky. Mother Dear and Father Dear are framed in the moon, rubbing their cheeks, even smiling. In the distance an old plane with twin propellers floats towards the moon. As I look closely I feel airsick. Bro Ali is flying the plane, wearing a leather helmet and massive aviators. I am not sure if he can see me or not. I try to raise my hand and wave towards him, he wiggles the wings of his plane like a clumsy dancer. Behind his plane comes Mutt, floating in the air like a champion swimmer.

There is something wrong with this. Mutt is supposed to be here, outside the door, on lookout, he is supposed to warn me if anyone approaches the shack. What is he doing up there in the sky? For that matter what am I doing here on this chair? What a mess I have made in this neat little makeshift office.

Why do I care about this office? My heart suddenly sinks, it's somewhere between my knees. I look up again and Father Dear and Mother Dear are still framed in a full moon, now wagging their fingers at each other. My heart swoons, I feel I am flying, I want to go up there and give Mother Dear a hug and tell Father Dear to calm down, I have got everything under control. Centuries pass, our Camp turns into a lush valley, this very shack becomes a tourist attraction, Mutt is driving my brand-new Range Rover Vogue and I am running after the vehicle, my heart is a frantic criminal trying to get away from the crime scene.

That thing that I gulped down probably wasn't a piece of dark chocolate. I have polluted my young pure body with some unheard-of intoxicant. How am I ever going to come back to earth?

Breathe.

Read. Bro Ali used to say, *read, what are you afraid of? That you might learn something?*

I pick up another file and try to concentrate. Breathe. Newspaper clippings. 'Colonel Slatter: desert sucks in our hero'. Planes have been disappearing and the government is wasting taxpayers' money and getting the people killed for what? Camp gets a mention: 'evil has been wiped out'.

It's a bit sickening to be described as evil. We are entre-preneurs, not evil.

Why is she investigating this? Is she interested in our feel-ings or their feelings? I throw the file away and rummage in her drawer. A silver box with a picture of a woman clutch-ing her skirt. Inside a variety of painkillers. I wonder if any of these pills will help me with my nausea gathering in the pit of my stomach. There is no warning, no yelping Mutt, no sound of a door creaking, she is just standing there, loom-ing over me like a giant with lipstick. My nausea disappears, I try to wave my hand to say hi. My hand is heavy.

She says something and her voice is coming from a distance. *Are you OK? What are you doing in my office? You look ill.*

I am OK, I say. *I just needed some pen and paper. I was making notes for your research. I can only describe my feel-ings by writing.*

She takes the silver foil from the table and puts her hand on my shoulder.

You didn't take this, did you? Are you OK? Should I call the doctor?

No, no, I am fine. I just feel hot and cold at the same time.

She picks up a file and fans me. *Calm down*, she says, *breathe, I'll make you some tea.*

Another century passes as she puts on her kettle and keeps looking back at me with grave eyes.

Young minds, my ass, I take a sip. Well, let's say it is sweet and I don't puke. She takes my hand in her hand, which is unexpected and probably a violation of her researcher's contract but nice. But I am not gonna fall through the chair and I am not gonna fall for a honey trap. History is full of tragic stories about people who try to mix up their business targets with matters of the heart.

Do you need a list? Do you really believe that Alexander the Great fell to a poisoned arrow? No sir, he fell to a Hindu temple girl who said if you are such a conqueror, here's my heart, have a go. Do you think Warren Buffett goes around with a broken heart? No sir, for me business is always gonna be my first pleasure. Matters of the flesh should wait in the queue. And it's a long queue.

That tea was a good idea.

We sit quietly and look at each other furtively as if to see who is gonna lose their brains first. My jaw relaxes, I notice a mole on the left side of her neck which I hadn't noticed before, I look up and the sky is clear and a single white bird streaks through it and I look at it with satisfaction as if the bird has taken off on my orders and is headed to a destination predetermined by me. For the first time since she arrived in the Camp, I feel relaxed; better than relaxed, I feel still, for the first time I am in no rush to get into my Cherokee and rush to a business meeting, I can just sit here forever staring at the sky or looking at that mole on her neck. I mean what exactly is the point, the sky is the same everywhere; all you need is a piece of bread and a cup of tea and a companion. Mutt doesn't like tea so I am sure he doesn't mind.

She seems to have some answers in those files.

I feel I have everything a man needs. Somewhere in the distance, Mutt yelps thrice. I think he approves. In fact if she has something to tell me I'll listen, but I am not nervous in this silent moment, I am not thinking about what she is thinking or what she might tell me. I would like it if this could last forever.

But even forever doesn't last forever.

'Feeling better? Nice,' she says, 'isn't it?'

I nod my head and realize my eyelids are heavy. 'What?' I ask.

'The thing that you just had that you thought was chocolate. Opium.'

I should panic but my heart is tired of panicking. I am averse to herbs of all kind, Class A drugs are for movie stars or people with poor upbringing. I don't pollute my body with chemicals.

Drugs kill your ambition, unless your ambition is to do drugs.

'I don't feel anything,' I say defensively. I realize that my voice is low, almost a whisper. 'Why do you take it?'

'I take it for my migraines.'

'What are migraines?'

'It's a headache with many heads. But otherwise it's the preferred drug of the kings,' she says, as if trying to make me feel better; distressed drug-dealer talk.

'What kings?' I say. 'We don't have kings anymore.'

I have seen people on Nat Geo Late Night who make so much money through drugs that they are called narco-barons. I prefer to call them businessmen who make money off junk. I am always gonna support the free market but I am gonna stay away from the drug trade because let's not forget that there is way more money in weapons and oil and do-goodery and it's all legal. Apparently there is money to be made by going around asking people how they are feeling about their missing siblings.

She shakes her head slightly, disagreeing with me but not with too much enthusiasm. If she ran the world there would never be any wars, only post-war reconstructions. 'There are things about substances that you need to know. It's part of my research to discuss things they would never talk about in school. It's good to avoid drugs for reasons of faith or because your parents disapprove, but you must know what you choose not to do. You drink alcohol and you are a depraved man, you talk nonsense, you don't notice the traffic lights, every girl or boy it seems is willing to go to bed with you, you cry because your mom loved your sister more than she loved you, and then in the morning you wake up with a dry throat and pulsating shame. It doesn't matter whether you drink fancy, fruity cocktails or cheap whisky straight from the bottle, you end up behaving like an ass.'

For a moment or two it feels she is warning me, telling me stuff that Father Dear should have told me instead of the stuff he told me about sticking my penis into rubber balloons. There is no chance I'm ever gonna turn into a drunkard.

I am in a place far far away, her voice comes from underwater, she is trying to prepare me for the facts of life, she is trying to prepare me for a fight. But what side of the battle is she gonna be on?

'Take a sliver of this and what happens? Nothing. It makes you normal. It makes you rational. You put one foot after the other as you are supposed to, you pour tea into a cup without your hands shaking or the cup running over; when the doorbell rings you think it's the courier bringing you the goodies you ordered, not an unknown assassin who has been sent to finish your meaningless, miserable life. You become the man that you should be.'

One of her eyes is slightly red. Her lips quiver. The beginning of madness must look like this. She needs help. How am I gonna help her? I wanna tell her that it almost made me puke. But she is not finished with me yet.

'You know why the Mughals ruled for so long?'

I have no clue who the Mughals were or for how long they ruled, or the reasons for their long rule. Taj Mahal,

I remember, they built that white palace for a dead princess. Seventh or sixth wonder of the world or some such nonsense. They were probably good at ruling and killing their princesses and building palaces for them.

'Because they discovered this. Before making life or death decisions they swallowed a bit of this and it gave them the clarity to send their armies to slaughter their brother's armies. You need a steady heart to send one hundred thousand men to do a job when you are certain that most of them will not return. I am always surprised that our government can do it without using this. They sit around a table in a conference without taking any opium and still manage to start wars that kill millions.'

'All I see is unopened bottles of Perrier. It's like sitting in a boardroom. Restructuring their business. War is business, no? Or is there more business after war? The business you are in?'

She looks at me as if the invisible thread connecting us has snapped.

And then I know what needs to be done. With the clarity of a king who sends an army to slay his brother, I realize I don't need an army to bring Bro Ali back.

'Why are you going around collecting the records of missing boys?'

'Because that's central to my research. I have told you that their people are missing. Your boys are missing.'

'What have we got to do with their people?'

'See,' she says, as if I have already proved her point. 'They say the same thing. It's a deadlock.'

'What deadlock? They had planes in the sky, tanks in the Hangar, guard dogs on chains, what did we have? How can you even compare?'

'So tell me, what did you guys have?'

'What you see is all we have. Not even our own roof over our head. But tell me, whose side are you on?' I say, finally feeling the clarity that her drug is supposed to induce.

'I am just researching trends, really, and hoping to bring about some kind of closure.'

'Closure? They already closed the Hangar, what else they gonna close now?'

'No, closure as in putting things in the past. Moving on with our lives.'

'You are moving on with your life?' I point at the paper-work and files surrounding us.

'Look, closure means that after something bad has happened you accept that that bad thing has happened and you get on with your life.'

'I am gonna get on with my life as soon as Bro Ali comes back. I have plans, he can have his jeep back. I was gonna get a new one anyway.'

'And how are you going to find him?'

'We need to find a way to get into the Hangar,' I say.

'Why haven't you tried so far? Definitely not because you are not authorized to go in? You do a lot of things you are not allowed to do.'

'They used to have tanks and planes and guns that mow down entire cities. I don't know what they have there now. You don't go into a battle without knowing your enemy. The gates are shut. There are probably booby traps.'

'So you are afraid to go in?'

'I was,' I say. 'Now I have got one of their own. I am going to put him in my jeep and find a way to get in.'

'Have you asked him? It doesn't seem like he wants to go anywhere.'

'What are his choices? I am gonna put him in my jeep and drive right in. What's he gonna say? And if you really wanna see my young mind, then you need to see this young mind at work. You are gonna come with us. I am gonna give you some real meat for your book.'

And that's an offer even a pretend researcher scholar is never gonna refuse. The alarm from the Hangar starts to ring. And it rings forever. That's where we are gonna have to go.

Chapter 20

Mutt

Last summer it rained, some dancing peacocks descended from nowhere and Bro Ali got chickenpox. This was a time when Momo had to have whatever Ali had. Slashed jeans, bad breath, double entendres, Vin Diesel accent. He did it without much effort, he pretended as if he had thought of it first but was a bit slow in implementing it. If Bro Ali started making a figure of eight while peeing, Momo would pretend to write the first letter of his name. I pretended to applaud their juvenile actions. I don't believe in piss artistry, I just relieve myself at any suitable place when I need to. This was a particularly auspicious time, new electric poles had gone up, high-strung wires shimmered when lightning struck. You could go from pole to pole and celebrate the impending end of darkness from our lives. Electricity is coming, we were told again and again by Father Dear, who single-handedly tried to take credit for the compulsive philanthropy of the Norwegians who had donated poles and wire.

In retrospect anyone could see that these poles were a series of tragedies waiting to happen. There was a freak monsoon, peacocks flashed their amber wings and did their ridiculous dance, big, fat, grey electric transformers sat on pylons like big, fat omens. And everyone was happy.

Mother Dear finally managed to lay her hands on Bro Ali. She brought out an old cotton dupatta of hers, it was so soft and so white that I didn't even go near it, worried that even my breath would soil it. She went to work, making a paste of turmeric and fennel and goat's milk. From a distance it smelled like the promises of a compulsive, cheating lover. Bro Ali lay face down as she scooped up her cure and applied it to his back, covering the hundreds of little red dots that had bloomed on his torso. Momo joined in applying the paste, alternately pinching him when Mother Dear was not looking. Bro Ali giggled and then sighed as the paste burned the dots on his body. Bro Ali's torso was covered in the white dupatta that he had wrapped around himself.

Momo took off his shirt and showed some red bruises on his chest. He was certain that these were early symptoms of a superior variety of chickenpox. The bruises were from my paws, my daily struggle to wake him up. But when Momo insisted that he must get his share of chicken pox cure, who was going to say no? A black cotton dupatta was produced, Momo wrapped it around himself and lay down. Now Mother Dear and Bro Ali took turns looking for non-existing red spots on his torso and kept dabbing the paste on his body randomly. Momo giggled and sighed and pretended he was really sicker than Bro Ali.

'Don't wear any clothes, your body needs fresh air but don't go too far from the house,' Mother Dear warned, but there were dark clouds in the sky, there was a gentle drizzle, the desert sand was sending out all kinds of dizzying smells, bright red velvety insects were on the march everywhere, it would have been a sin to stay indoors. So we all ran out ignoring Mother Dear's warnings, as she shouted, 'Don't get my dupattas wet.' Ali in white, Momo in black, yours truly clad in monsoon carelessness, we ran around, frightening peacocks, disrupting the long march of the armies of velvety red insects. Momo jumped into the Cherokee, Bro Ali in the passenger seat, both bare-chested, with their bodies daubed in their mother's home cure for chickenpox, we drove around aimlessly from pole to pole. We counted eleven, stopped at the twelfth, got down. Momo and Bro Ali started their piss artistry, I decided to baptize the twelfth electric pole.

The moment of my misfortune. The worst moment in the worst day of my life.

As I lifted my leg, unknown to me, about eight hundred miles away the gates of a dam, the largest earth-filled dam in the world, opened. According to conservative estimates about six million cusecs of river water, monsoon muddy, wild and foamy, dropped like a native Niagara onto the eight waiting turbines, each weighing more than thirty tons of metal and blades. As the turbines span the generators converted it into the electricity that the Camp had been waiting on for years; the electricity travelled through eight-gauge, substandard copper wires and, travelling at the speed of 1,860,000 miles per second, arrived in the pole exactly at the moment when my clear, healthy urine made contact with it. Of course the bastards had forgotten to earth the pole, as they were sure from their past experiences that this whole pole-wires-transformers business was just a showpiece to steal more money. But someone had a bout of seasonal goodwill and released the electricity. It travelled through my piss stream through my blood veins and straight to my brains. This is how my brains got fried.

The electric shock sent me flipping into air, it was more like I shot up, and the scream that poured out of my mouth was strange, as if I had learnt to speak like my human companions and was just like them, screaming gibberish. I could hear Momo and Bro Ali giggling behind me. I was screaming and yelping like a Mutt prophet who has just received his first prophecy and who is terrified and who wants to return it to the sender. More giggles behind my back. It took me a while to realize that there might have been comic potential in my situation. It occurred to me later that my brothers with their black and white wraps around their waists and their young torsos glistening in the drizzle had no malice towards me. But in that moment I felt like a Mutt. My brain turned them into these neon devilish figures, who were breathing fire and cackling like mad djinns and were about to tear me apart and throw me to other hungry dogs.

Yet in that moment I became me. Before that I was just another above-average Mutt with common desires, beastly urges and an appetite for home-cooked food, but in that moment I rose above the ranks of common strays who had adopted troubled families and were trying their best.

Momo says my brain got fried in that accident. I think I became a philosopher that day.

It was the worst day of my life.

But, who knows, maybe it was the best day of my life.

CHAPTER 21

Ellie

I have had enough of that stupid cockpit–womb analogy. Don't tell me the cockpit is like a slick womb, paid for by taxpayers, where you can go and hide and feel safe from this world because you refuse to engage with it. Don't tell me I take things too literally when I remind you that no womb comes fitted with Sidewinder missiles.

When I'm on a mission Cath usually acts as if wars have been started in twenty-three countries so that her husband can stay away from her. I am not personally involved in all twenty-three wars, nor is my unit, and even if it was I wouldn't be allowed to tell her. But it is quite a stretch to think that your husband finds your evenings together on the sofa so terrifying that he'd rather fly halfway around the world to bomb some place that is already a ruin because of all the previous bombings. That's not how war works, that's not how nations operate.

The cockpit isn't a womb I retreat into; it's my work-place. I go there to perform a certain task. And, like every task, it's divided into subsets of tasks. And, after a success-ful mission, like a home run, one is allowed, how should I put it, a little celebration. And that's an essential part of the task, it gives meaning to your work, even if your work involves flying two thousand miles up and down very low over enemy territory just to draw fire, so that your buddies can pinpoint hostile pockets. Flying low over potentially hostile settlements and breaking the sound barrier is part of the job. But how do you explain this to your loved ones without freaking them out? So I keep quiet and just say stuff like: *That's work, babe, it's noisy work but someone's got to do it.* But even when I'm saying it I sound like some kind of ageing geek who tinkers with old transistors in his garage and wants to be respected for having a passion. A passion.

I can't really tell her that I've sometimes volunteered for missions when I could have taken time off and stayed home, building that fence, mowing that lawn, making that curry for which I stuck a recipe to the fridge three months ago.

I can't really tell her that I find it much easier to drop a load from forty thousand feet than to have a quiet weekend afternoon under her watchful eyes and answer questions like: *Is something the matter, you seem quite distant today?*

How do I tell her that there actually is something on my mind. I have been contemplating the lemon-scented dishwashing liquid she's started using. I don't really hate lemons, I mean who does; everyone likes them in one form or the other. But do you really want your morning coffee cup smelling of industrial lemon? I mean you have just woken up, you're having your first cup of the day, is it an unreasonable expectation to smell some real coffee? But what you get is a nauseating waft of lemon first thing in the morning. And you can wash your cup before you use it, but what do you wash it with? The same lemon-scented Vim. And even if you rinse it seven times after that, your day has begun with a bad smell.

If you want to smell lemons first thing in the morning that's your choice, it's a gender-neutral choice, I am sure there are men out there who start their day by drinking warm lemonade and call it lemon tea. Or there are people who start their day by drinking a litre of warm water and then throw up, yes deliberately throw up, and that is supposed to improve their digestion and keep them virile in their later years. Who am I to judge them? To each their own. It's a free country, if people want to start their day by smelling and drinking disgusting and smelly things, they can. We're fighting this war and the previous war and the ones budgeted for next year in order to bring some of these freedoms to the other parts of the world. But if she prefers Vim lemon, if she likes its smell, does it give her the right to shove lemon up my nose first thing in the morning? I mean I am all for equality of the sexes and the distribution of labour between a couple, she chooses to do the dishes and she chooses it because it soothes her, calms her down, and then she goes and does this.

So there I was, sitting on the sofa while she asked me why I have that distant look on my face; she was trying to talk about my condition and I was thinking here's someone who has no qualms about shoving lemons down my throat every morning and then pretending to care about my mental condition.

In our 'Suppression of Inexplicable Urges' module I learnt to let your emotion stay with you, let it grow, and then only let it come out when you can create an ambience that is pleasant.

I can exercise extreme patience in such cases, I have learnt. Because when you are living with someone, that other person is in your domain, and you are in their domain, and it doesn't matter who is paying the major part of the mortgage or who picked up the bill when the hot water tank broke down last, you are both in each other's domain.

You must preserve yourself. Don't let the other person un-self you.

So I didn't say a thing, I didn't mention lemons, in fact I didn't mention any fruits, any washing liquid. Instead I said, 'Cath, when was the last time we went to Traviata?'

She gave me a puzzled look as if I was asking her a trick question, and I swear upon my unborn baby's head that I have never in my life asked her a trick question.

'I don't know, it's been a while,' she said in a non-committal way, as if she believed there was a right and wrong answer to this question. 'Yes, it's been a while. Why don't we book a table?'

La Traviata is the kind of pretentious place that tries very hard not to be pretentious. Mismatched chairs, fake old newspapers instead of tablecloths, crockery that looks like it has been made at a hobby club. Salt and pepper shakers adorned with tribal art. In fact, exactly the kind of place that Cath's mother would have started if she had been interested in home-cooked Italian food as a small business opportunity and not thrown herself under the train that was carrying Cath to college.

We got a good table, the kind of table that Cath considers good anyway, we were sitting side by side and could see everybody. I guess everybody could see us too. We didn't have to look at each other while talking, we could look at other people or at our food while talking. Before we had ordered our mains, in fact even before our starters arrived, the waiter brought a small bread basket and a large ceramic dish with a dollop of pink butter and a tiny dish of olive oil. No problems there, one is a citizen of the world and if that means getting a dollop of pink garlic-infused butter with your complimentary bread, that's fine. But along with the dollop of pink butter sat two lemons wrapped and tied in white cotton gauze. I had come to this establishment to discuss the lemons which are causing me early-morning stress and here I am being served a pair of cut lemons cleverly tied up in white gauze as if in an attempt to disguise them for my personal benefit. There is an interrogation technique that we were taught in the 'After You Are Captured' module. Your captors will try and provoke you by doing small things that irritate you in order to get under your skin. The only sensible response is to resist this provocation and focus on something else. I didn't mention the lemons and looked around to distract myself. Next to our table an old couple were completely absorbed in each other's company. It was kind of sweet, him whispering things in her ear and her giggling loudly as if she had heard her first dirty joke at this late age.

'That's a nice touch,' said Cath.

'It's very pretentious, why camouflage a lemon in white gauze? Why are there lemons in the first place? They are probably Indians pretending to be Italians,' I added.

'It's just practical,' she said. 'How many times have you been annoyed by crunching on a lemon pip in your salad?' I was left speechless. Of course Cath was on the lemon's side. It's like a torture victim being told that he is being hung upside down to build his character.

'Hmmmph,' I said, and mauled a piece of bread with a knife slathered in pink butter. The old man had thrust his tongue into his old lady's mouth. I jumped in my seat, then put my hands under my thighs and sat still, trying very hard not to look at the old couple. I have nothing against people expressing their affections for each other, I am not a puritan by any stretch of the imagination, but can't they do these things in the privacy of their own homes? I know the romantic dinner is practically an institution of western civilization, but how is civilization being advanced by sucking on your partner's tongue while eating a perfectly good beef lasagne in the middle of a restaurant? Why couldn't they just order takeaway, get naked if they want to and then smother each other with their couscous salad and feed each other dough balls dipped in each other's body fluids?

'That's sweet,' Cath caught me trying very hard not to stare at them. She was good at that, my Cath. At catching me staring. And I guess I must have been good at it too. Getting caught, staring.

'I know people of that age fuck but do we have to watch them doing it while we wait for our dinner?'

'They're only holding hands,' Cath said, staring into my eyes. I dug into my salad and caressed the fork with my tongue with every bite. Sometimes all a man can do and should do is to make his point and then move on and keep eating his food. I could feel her eyes boring into my forehead.

'Sometimes I lose you,' she said in a calm, sad voice, the scariest of her many voices. 'I don't know where so much anger comes from.'

She looked more puzzled than angry, as if she had suddenly discovered an aspect of my personality that she was unaware of. I can report that I made the same joke, maybe in a different tone of voice, a few days after we first met and she laughed out loud and gave me this look which said *oh you make me laugh so much, how could I ever live without you.* And now the same Cath, lovely Cath, is sitting there wondering if I should be institutionalized for cracking a joke in the middle of our romantic dinner in our favourite restaurant.

'Sorry,' I said, taking a sip of water. 'Bad joke. Too much time with the boys in the squadron.' My apologies were sincere.

I told her I'd spend more time at home, and I did. I made her pancakes, bought her a yoga mat, made love on the right days. And for a while it worked. And then it didn't. I tried to make myself feel better, hoping it would lead to us feeling better. I started telling her again that the world is overpopulated, we should adopt a baby. *Are you afraid to commit?* she would ask. We are married, we make love, we don't use protection, we share everything, why would she think I was afraid to commit? *Maybe you are an unhappily married woman*, I told her. *Is there any other kind?* she shot back. I should have kept my cynicism out of bed. And she said, *here's the place you come to produce another human being to fill the void that lies between us.*

'You know I have been working very hard on our marriage, you just don't. . .'

She looked at me with unbounded pity.

No, the problem wasn't too much time in the briefing rooms, the problem was too much time with Cath. I was clocking up as many hours with my therapist as I was in the cockpit. Bombing runs in the morning then going home to get a scolding for not caring about her feelings. Fuck this, I told myself. I need more missions. I am going to sign up for that extension. She doesn't need to know that it's optional. I am going to volunteer for more missions just to get away from another romantic fucking dinner. Bring on the war.

Sometimes a distant war is the only way to resolve domestic disputes.

Yes, that's how I ended up in this mole hole. That's how I ended up being told what to do with my life by a gung-ho teenager.

CHAPTER 22

Momo

After I put my Falcons for Ethical Hunting programme on hold, I had reached a plateau. And that is when divine intervention took place and someone fell from the sky. Yes, a stranger fell from the sky. Now he says he wants to get out of here. How do you return a gift from the skies? I have to pretend that I don't know that he fell from the sky but look at his flying suit, look at those sunglasses, look at that pulled-down, depressed crocodile face that he has acquired after pulling a million negative Gs, his skin as pale as my Mutt's jaundiced eyes. He is dreaming of a lost plane. He is gonna keep dreaming about that plane. I am in the middle of recruitment for my rescue mission and although I have asked him many things there's one thing I need to ask before I can put him to use.

'I am gonna ask you a question and I want a straight answer.' It's time to be straight with Ellie. I am not gonna have someone on my team who I can't trust. You can't go to a boardroom meeting without knowing whether your team has divided loyalties. You don't go into a battle without knowing what is in your top general's past.

'Are you a spy?'

My tone is neutral, almost friendly. I am not interrogating him, just asking him about his day job. He is sitting there with his back to the wall holding his head like a war widow. I think sometimes he pretends that he is a prisoner of war. Although we have been treating him like a guest. Give them a roof, feed them and this is the gratitude you get. He needs a dose of reality and I am gonna give it to him.

'That's a trick question,' he says, still holding his head. 'What kind of spy would admit to being a spy?' There you go. He has laid himself open. And he has shut up at the same time. I can tell you that if he is a spy he is not very good at it. He is the kind of spy who wishes that they owned a café and ran a book club.

'If you were being true to yourself, you would tell me. I promise I am never gonna betray your secret. One shouldn't be ashamed of one's day job. I have been thinking of starting a small surveillance unit myself. Information is the new oil. Maybe I can even help you with your spying.'

He looks at me as if I have asked him for a million-dollar loan.

'I want to be able to trust you fully. Help me help you.' Sometimes white people only understand things when their self-interest is gonna be involved.

'I'm homesick. I'm worried about Cath,' he says, looking into the distance. 'I have never been away from home for such a long time. Mine was mostly a stay-at-home kind of war. I could be over Mosul at lunchtime but I'd be home to take out the trash, cook dinner or at least help clean up after. She must be worried sick. If a person dies you bury them and you manage your grief. But what do you do when you don't know if your person is alive or dead?'

There you have it. All lies. Who calls their wife their 'person'? She is a pretend wife.

This pretend pilot needs to sort his ways. He is always going *Cath this* and *Cath that*. I am gonna tell you what I think about Cath. There is probably no Cath. He is probably a cupboard gay and has been in that cupboard for such a long time that he has an imaginary Cath in the cupboard of his mind. Don't get me wrong, it can happen. For about six months Bro Ali and I used to have an imaginary pet tiger, we took him for walks and fed him imaginary goats. Even Mutt would have imaginary wrestling matches with our pet tiger.

I know this can happen, it's a much more common condition than people ever admit. Even now when Mutt feels lonely he plays with his imaginary friends. He has been yelping at birds that come and go all the time but he thinks only he can see them.

When you are dropped in a desert and wander around claiming half your plane is gone it's obvious you are not on a straight bombing mission. Probably his brain is fried too. He keeps talking about Cath and pancakes and a baby which was never born. What can you do? I mean not with the unborn babies but with pretend pilots who dream up unborn babies. And a wife. Sometimes I want to shout at him: Stop imagining a wife who is not there. Stop imagining sons who are not born, never conceived. If you are gonna make love to a ghost wife, you are gonna have to take care of a ghost baby.

I don't believe in ghosts though. I believe in dollarized profit margins and better mental health management. If he was supposed to bomb Mosul and has ended up here then God help him and his country.

I don't tell him that though. Because he is my ticket to Bro Ali and I am his get-out-of-here pass. I want him here, I want him on my side. This is what one has to do: you listen to them. You let them talk. You let them think you are the only person who understands their pain. This is how friendships work. This is how global alliances are formed. This is called team building. This is called Management 3.0.

Sometimes Ellie tests my patience: listening to him is like listening to Mutt whining about the ghosts who don't let him sleep. All his dead doggie friends turn up every night in his sleep and want to party. And when he wakes up from one of these dreams he climbs onto my bed. And wakes me from my own dreams.

Sometimes I think I have got two people with fried brains. One is a native Mutt, victim of a technological advance. Not only his brain got fried in that accident, he has also lost control over his bladder. The slightest sign of trouble, a little change in weather, the appearance of anyone wearing the colour red, he's gonna go bat shit and do things he never did before his brains got fried; he jumps and tries to reach for the jugular but he usually ends up sniffing someone's crotch which, for a person with my reputation, is quite embarrassing. In his attempt at posing as a militant, crack dog, he relieves himself in all the wrong places.

And the other one is a victim of the failure of war technology, a man separated from his machine.

Ellie is essential but a potential risk. But he has what it takes. He is the right colour. He is the key. If we have him, we have a chance at negotiating with Bro Ali's kidnappers. My bro for your man. My Ali for your Ellie.

'So they sent you to bomb us? And they didn't tell you that your planes have been falling in this area? Then nobody comes looking for you? They must not love you very much.' Sometimes you need to make them see the truth.

'I can't talk about operational details. I lost my plane, now I want to go home,' he doesn't look me in the eye. He never looks me in the eye.

'Take a walk. There's the desert. But if you decide to come back, our doors are always gonna be open for you.'

He is not gonna go anywhere. What are his choices?

After I sort out this mess I am gonna move into real estate. That Hangar is prime property, if we take it over, imagine the potential. How many housing units, how many shops could we put in there. I'll reserve a floor for my company's headquarters. I am not God's mercenary. I am God's entrepreneur. Mutt is circling us at a distance, wagging his tail, wanting attention. I have asked him to keep an eye on Ellie and this is his idea of surveillance, running around in circles making question marks with his sad tail. My Mutt is God's joker. Whenever I look at him I think the creator must be that man who tells a lame joke then laughs the loudest and the longest.

Chapter 23

Mutt

'Have you got any bad potatoes, small ones?' Doctor believes if a vegetable is small or deformed it has to be good for your health. He is on a mission to score organic veggies. He arrives on a motorbike, a Triumph 175, old with shiny double silencers, it seems he is carrying his whole household on this Triumph. There was a time when chasing his motorbike, yapping after him was the high point of my life. But my limp has restricted the speed of my movement, even though it's added a certain elegance to my gait. I see his motorbike roll in, I lift my head and give a customary yap, which turns into a yawn. Momo is having yet another session with Lady Flowerbody, having his young mind studied, and I am taking a break from my daily inspection tour of the Camp.

The main square is deserted. Royal Hardware scrap dealers have shuttered their shop and are taking a siesta under the carcass of a Bedford truck.

I wonder if Momo will need Doctor's help to get over what his young Muslim mind is being subjected to.

Doctor himself seems ready to set off on a world tour. A rolled-up blanket tied to one side of the bike, balanced on the other side with two pairs of leather boots; an array of plastic shopping bags hangs from the handlebars of the motorbike. He wears the blue overalls of a US Army infantry sergeant complete with stripes and standard-issue Ray-Bans, held together with Scotch tape and a USAF helmet with WE DARE emblazoned on it. A long thin antenna shoots up towards the sky and quivers like an angry man wagging his finger at a tentative god in the sky.

The store owner of Allah's Servant's Fresh Chicken and Veggies waves him away. 'No bad potatoes today. It's not the season.' I sniff some chicken feathers. Doctor pretends as if he hasn't heard. Doctor has heard the call of the apocalypse. *We survived the bombs but we are not going to survive our own greed*, he is always saying, always warning us about the perils of plastic bags and processed proteins. He has seen doomsday and he is not going to pay attention to a lowly trader who uses God's name to sell vegetables and chicken.

He goes and stands next to the large blue drum used as a garbage can for rotting vegetables, it is overflowing with partially damaged greens, slightly bruised cauliflowers and moth-eaten spinach. Doctor believes that dignity lies in scavenging and not in a queue outside a ration depot. The vegetable-shop owner jumps from his till and comes and stands next to the blue garbage bin as if protecting it from some raiding army. Doctor takes off his helmet and turns around as if about to leave, even takes a step, then in a flash bends down, retrieves a partially rotten onion that has fallen out of the garbage can and rushes and mounts his bike. He kickstarts his Triumph after depositing the onion in one of his plastic bags. The owner takes a step towards him and then changes his mind.

'I have got money,' shouts Doctor, taking a bunch of crumpled notes from his pocket and waving them in the air. 'Sell this to me. You can't take rotting vegetables to your grave.'

Doctor is champion forager in a community which lives on handouts, but insists on preaching about honest living, daily toil and daily bread. Doctor just turns up and takes what nobody wants. I watch him from behind the fruit baskets where the only fruit are small bomb-sized watermelons. Doctor is considered the biggest thief because he steals the smallest things.

'You must have small, damaged potatoes, here, I am buying. I am not begging,' Doctor waves his fist in the air again to demonstrate his buying power.

Look at that motorbike again. It seems he has prepared it for a journey through treacherous terrains, its mudguards raised high, a camping gas stove hangs on its carrier. On his fuel tank is strapped a large Nestlé bottle, with an amber liquid sloshing in it. Doctor takes it out of the strap and waves it in the air. 'I have got petrol. Low lead, super. I can get out of here when I want. If you keep hoarding those rotten potatoes, I'll report you. I'll report you to the World Food Programme. There are laws against hoarding potatoes. Even rotten potatoes.'

The shop owner stands his ground next to the blue garbage can as if guarding a precious treasure. 'Read what it says,' he shouts at Doctor. 'USAID doesn't give us potatoes, Allah does.'

Doctor straps his Nestlé bottle to his fuel tank, revs up his engine as if whispering a threat. 'Those potatoes don't belong to you. They were sent for us, the people. There will be a price to pay. There are red birds flying this way, little birds, the Hangar is filling up with hungry visitors. They don't want your potatoes, they want their lives back. They are not bringing you cheap vegetables, they are bringing fire to roast you and your greedy brothers. I have got petrol, I'll be out of here while you burn.'

He disappears in a cloud of dust and the growl of his engine. I think thank God there is someone besides me who sees these red beauties.

Poor man. He thinks he'll escape the apocalypse because he has got a conscience and a bottle of low-lead petrol.

'Bloody theatre nuts,' says the owner of Allah's Servant's Chicken and Veggies. 'They think every place is a stage where they can just start delivering their stupid monologues.'

'He is an actor?' asks Ellie, who has been watching this from behind a mountain of Persian watermelons. I followed him here to see what this white deserter is up to. It's always wise to keep an eye on deserters. If they can betray their mother country, imagine what they are going to do to hostile nation states. White Ellie has a scientific mind. He sees fresh vegetables, he thinks transportation, he thinks here's a way out. He is ready to desert again.

'An impostor, more like,' says the shopkeeper. 'A born liar. He has probably got more cash than half the Camp but insists on stealing from garbage cans. A born thief. He thinks he cares about the environment. He wants to save the earth by eating bad potatoes. He keeps going on about ghosts. I'll welcome those ghosts. Better than the thieves we have here.'

I don't know why they all keep saying this place is full of thieves, why they can't see the exceptions all around them. I have been under the chicken slaughter table for half an hour and I haven't stolen a feather. There is no community pride left even when they see decency personified, limping around them with such élan and grace.

'No, I don't believe in ghosts, but I can understand why people believe in them. It helps them deal with their loss,'

Ellie puts the watermelon back on the pile and picks up a smaller one. 'Nice melons, really fresh. Where do you source these from?' he says. He is obviously not here for fruit shopping. I am sure they have good enough watermelons wherever he comes from. He is picking up information, trying to cultivate moles.

Allah's vegetable seller is in no mood to share his supply routes.

'You must have people like Doctor in your country? People who stuff their mattresses with currency? Who bury their gold under their bed and then go around panhandling, *gimme a coin, I am a coin short of making my life worth living.* And if you don't give them a coin they tell you that the world is coming to an end.'

'Oh yes,' Ellie says. 'We had one on our street. He had a dog and a sleeping bag and about a thousand plastic bags stuffed into a shopping trolley. He froze to death and then they found that every single plastic bag in his trolley had a chequebook in it and the sleeping bag was full of jewellery – many imitation pieces but some gold too. So how often does your supply truck come?'

'And who took it?' asks the shopkeeper, looking at Ellie suspiciously, as if he had killed the homeless man, taken his money and gold and was now hiding a world away, in this Camp.

'The government of course. Our government is the biggest thief. It steals from the living, it steals from the dead.'

'Thank God we don't have that problem,' says the chicken and vegetable man. 'We just steal from each other.'

Everything in the shop has a smell. Chickens smell of death by boredom. Bitter gourd smells of eternal struggle against that boredom. When Ellie walks out there's no change in the olfactory map. The man doesn't have a smell and he is going around cultivating an information network checking out our supply routes.

He huddles with the vegetable man, two conspirators caught in the act. I can hear words like US visa, witness protection. Our man sells Allah's vegetables and chicken and wants a US visa: traitors are us. There is no way out of here, not while I am responsible for the security here.

Constant vigilance is what I have to do. Momo has plans for white Ellie, he thinks he can trade him for Bro Ali. He also thinks he can take over the Hangar and turn it into a shopping mall with a fountain in the centre. But why would Americans give us anything for free? They might have shut their military operation from the Hangar but I think they have other plans for it. The temperature has been dropping around the Hangar, it can be sizzling hot in the Camp but as you approach the Hangar perimeter the weather shifts as if you are walking into an air-conditioned room. Sometimes I can smell stoves being lit. Right now I can pick out a whiff of butter, real proper butter hitting a hot pan.

I make a dash to check out the Hangar. And as I approach I can see that it's back in business. I am just lurking around trying to track down the source of the butter smell when I see my first ghost. Of course, when I see it I have no idea that it's a ghost.

Chapter 24

Ellie

A few days loitering around in the Camp and I am thinking maybe I was better off in the desert. At least I had some hope of being rescued. This place is an open prison. Mutt follows me even when I go for a walk. I sneak in the Jeep Cherokee hoping to drive away and he starts barking as if a thief is trying to break in. Even Father Dear, that mouse of a man, stands in the door blocking my path when I try to sneak out in the middle of the night. 'How can you leave us like this? There are people here with unpaid salaries. They keep asking me when should they expect their salaries now that you have returned. And now you want to leave? There are boys missing, what do I tell their families?'

He is almost in tears and hasn't even mentioned his own boy yet. 'I was just going for a walk,' I tell him. 'Where do you think I can run away to?'

This place reeks of neglect. An outpost in a war that the war itself is not interested in. Nobody is going to come and invade this place. Nobody cares for a bunch of goatherds, veggie smugglers and junk dealers and an abandoned Hangar. There is nothing to destroy here, nothing to be saved. Who wants to save angry teenagers and pampered mutts? No decent country takes these people into consideration when drawing up next year's war plans. If they are searching for me, they are likely to search for me in the desert. Or invade a country far far away. Here, even the next plane carrying tinned food doesn't arrive.

They also keep telling me that they are a proud people. What does that even mean? Having a blue plastic sheet over your head, a little gas cylinder tethered to a small stove by a chain and lock, some songs they occasionally sing together and sweet memories of the time when there used to be a USAID plane every week, soldiers pouring out of the Hangar, patrols on the streets; that's the sum total of their culture and their economy and they call themselves proud people. I have seen homeless folks back home who were better fed than this lot. And they only asked for loose change, they didn't wave their pride in your face.

'You can't judge a whole community by making a list of things they don't have', Lady Flowerbody tells me. I can't decide whose side she is on. One moment she is sweet on me, the next moment she wants to be Mother Teresa. A bunch of young men loiter around her makeshift office, probably waiting to get their young minds examined or desperate for some career counselling or fantasizing about losing their virginity. 'Surely there is some skill you know that you can teach these people?'

'Like what? I should teach them skydiving. Oh wait, we are in a no-fly zone. Should I teach them how to weave baskets from date palms, teach their goats how to jump through fire hoops? Sorry, I am not good at any of those things. Look, all I can do is fly and that's niche work, I mean not just here, anywhere. You can't just get together a bunch of people and start a flying club.'

She is not the type to take a no after no for an answer. I was warned about her. Momo's visceral hatred for outsiders disguised as news: Lady Flowerbody is a crazy lady. She is a spy but there is nothing to spy on. So she has become a welfare organization worker, a surveyor of Young Muslim Minds. She keeps hoping for more raids so that she can study more Young Muslim Minds, but nobody takes her seriously. If you believe Momo, she is the resident evil since he got rid of the last resident evil researcher who came down to study his mind, his people's way of life and share their observations with the world. He is quite proud that he made the writer of *The Way of the Nomad* bet on his first scorpion racing circuit. The author of *And the Sands Wept. . .* was offered mining rights on equity share basis.

'You could teach in the school? We can reopen it, lots of boys have gone but there still some around who should be in school. Think of the children. Think of all these children who should be in school.'

Think of the children. That is the basic premise of extreme weather survival. Any kind of survival, desert, snow, cannibals' dinner party. I saw it first in a preliminary brief for Advanced Desert Survival. Think of the children: a picture went up on the wall, a child without arms, a child without legs. I thought, as fucked-up ideas go this was pretty fucked up, especially for my childless self. Why would I think of children? Why would I think of children without hands and feet, like the ones they showed us in that slide, half human, half gauze bandages. Sick fucks. What has this got to do with survival? What has this got to do with the desert?

I raised my hand. 'Why the children?' *Let's talk about it after the coffee break*, I was told.

Faced with extreme cold or heat or someone beating steadily on the soles of your feet, always think of the children, we were told. Now, it may not be normal for someone my age not to have any children to think of. They don't give you and your wife a fertility test before they hire you, but when it comes to desert survival they want you to think of children after the fifth day. But it's probably not normal for someone my age – someone of any age, children or no children – to be stranded in a desert after wrecking a Strike Eagle and with no children to think of. You are still supposed to. Something to live for, they say. How the hell am I going to think of children? I can think of all the things about to go bad in my fridge. I can worry about an avocado turning pulpy grey because Cath refuses to use it. How am I going to think about children? The last time I thought of children was when I was a child myself. The only time I think of children is when I am on a commercial flight and even then I only think *there'd better be no children on board*. If there are some on the plane then their parents better be carrying some sedatives to administer to them, they better not scream because they scream louder than a five-thousand-pound bomb and by the time they leave home and go away to start their own shitty lives they have probably cost you as much as a five-thousand-pound bomb. But Strike Eagle's cockpit doesn't accommodate any children, not the weak black ones with bloated tummies and not the gurgling white ones with their pink bottoms.

Now she is telling me think of the children.

'That school by the sewer? It's not even safe for grown-ups and you have got five-year-olds running around on the edge of a twenty-foot-deep gorge. It's a buffalo shed.'

'That's not a sewer, it's a dried-up stream. And we have never had a problem.' Her positivity would be bothersome if it wasn't so fragrant. She has the certainty of a war survivor, the ones we were warned against, whose only possessions are a crutch and a Quran and the memory of a missing limb, the most dangerous people in this most dangerous place.

'You could help out with my research, this is going to be a very serious study, local yes, but it'll shed light on the global plight of young Muslim—'

'I have no interest in the young Muslim mind. It's probably full of football and filth like young anybody's mind anywhere in the world.'

She has probably got her heart in the right place but this callousness, this arrogance, is appalling. Trying to fix all the world's problems with a blackboard and a box of chalk.

'Why can't we all just stay home,' I mumble and she hears me.

'Yeah right, why can't we? Tell me. I volunteered to come here after you forced these people out of their homes. You should have stayed home.'

'I can probably teach some basic arithmetic,' I mumble. 'But let's first try and put up a fence. I don't want little kids falling into the ditch while I teach them prime numbers.'

She looks at me with kind eyes. 'So maybe we can get the Hangar open, shift the school there?'

'You can't just walk into a military installation. You don't have the clearance. Children definitely don't have the clearance.'

'But you do, you lead the way. Think of the children.'

'I don't interfere in administrative matters. If a place is shut, it's shut. Why ask why?'

Lady Flowerbody is definitely not here just to study Young Muslim Minds. It seems she has been sent to play around with my mind.

A Jeep Cherokee drives towards us and stops perilously close to where we are standing. 'Now there is somebody who should be in school,' I change the topic.

Momo kicks the door of the jeep open and jumps out.

'You still here, dog thief?' he addresses me, his eyes full of mischief. 'Still having stomach cramps? It seems you don't wanna go home. Why are you running away from the wife? Or are you planning to settle down with the Lady? Spy falls for thief, who she gonna spy on?' Momo is trying to be friendly. I wonder what he wants.

'Can't wait to get out of this hellhole. But you are going to get arrested for driving that thing. Even here it's illegal.'

'If the police can find this place on their map, they are welcome to come and arrest me. If your new friend can find me a better vehicle, you can have this and drive back home. Look, she wants a peep into our minds, she doesn't care about our transport needs.'

There is nothing more irritating than cocky fifteen-year-olds. What happened to respect for the elders? In our 'Significance of Elders in Tribal Cultures' module they emphasized that it's bigger than class, it doesn't matter if you have fifty camels or drive a Land Rover, when you see an elder you stand up in respect. Even if you are in your fucking uniform, even if you are driving an illegal vehicle. And here is a kid terrorizing the Camp with his rash driving. He represents everything that's wrong with this Camp, with its dependent refugee status, its eternal wait for some plane to appear in the sky and relieve everyone of their misery. I haven't raised children myself but if I had a boy that age I'd make sure that he walked to and from school every day. To toughen him up. But he is not my respon-sibility. Every badly behaved fifteen-year-old in the world is not my responsibility. That's not what I signed up for. I signed up to fight in a war, not to foster a family of juvenile delinquents.

He stands there and stares at me. She walks away as if this boy and his illegal jeep has got nothing to do with her, with us. She has the air of a permanent do-gooder who will just leave when they stop feeling good about doing good.

'Do you want a lift?' Momo says, fiddling with his I Heart NY cap.

'Where you going to drive me to?'

'Wherever you wanna go. Back to the desert?'

His *wannas, gonnas* irritate the hell out of me. He sounds like he was born in New Jersey.

'I don't *wanna* go anywhere. Not with you. I can walk.'

'Come with me,' he says. 'I wanna show you something.'

I can't imagine what there is to see unless he has got a secret tunnel out of here.

'Yeah, sure,' I say, and start walking away from him. He comes after me, cap in hand, and starts to walk in step with me, as if we are two old friends out for an evening stroll, friends so familiar that we don't even need small talk.

'I wanna tell you something,' he says, looking straight ahead.

'Everybody wants to tell me something. The only thing I want to hear is a set of directions out of this place,' I say, making it clear that I have no intention of involving myself in local gossip, petty disputes or family squabbles.

'You've seen the Hangar, do you know what is inside?' he says.

'What's in there? A departure lounge for passengers stuck in these boondocks?'

He looks at me with the confused eyes of someone who is genuinely trying to help but has been rebuffed.

'It doesn't seem you wanna go anywhere in a hurry,' he says. 'I understand, sometimes I don't wanna go home either. In the desert we have an ancient saying about families. They fuck you up.'

The boy has been acting grown up for such a long time that he sounds like a middle-aged bar-stool philosopher.

'No, seriously, if I don't get back home very soon, or at least if I don't get in touch immediately and explain my situation, I'll be in trouble. Missing in action isn't what it used to be.'

Momo raises his hands in the air and looks at me as if reminding me: *Look at yourself now. You're seven thousand miles away from your home base, you have lost your plane, you are at the mercy of the very people you came to kill and you are still worried about trouble at home. You must really love your wife who doesn't even exist. Or you must really love that fucked-up country of yours that sent you here in the first place and then forgot all about you.*

But for the moment he is not interested in me or my country. He has got family on his mind, which is definitely the most fucked-up country in the world. 'If Pakistan screwed Afghanistan and USA was the midwife you'd get a country called FAMILY,' I say.

'Yes, I know about these things.' He says Mother Dear is very angry with Father Dear. Very very angry. And he comes home every day, before sunset. But she is still very angry.

'I know,' I say. 'You can't blame her. Nobody should have to cook every day without salt. It's a strange kind of punishment. And your father doesn't know how to show love. A man must show love. Even when he is not feeling it.

Especially when he is not feeling it. That's how relationships survive. That's how the world survives. And you don't keep count of the number of times you have to show love. When monkeys pick lice off each other they don't keep a count of how many lice they have picked.'

'Interesting you talk about monkeys,' he says. 'I tried to train a monkey once. More stubborn than Americans. Always jumping up and down, but completely empty upstairs,' he puts his forefinger to his temple.

'Families are the same everywhere. Cath's mother was popping painkillers all her life but Cath turned out OK. She even runs a book club.'

He looks at me as if I am trying to give him a life lesson he doesn't need.

'She cries,' he says, looking down examining his sneakers. 'She cries every night after we go to sleep.'

'How do you know if you are asleep? You are probably having nightmares.'

'I can't go to sleep until she stops crying. Some days she is still crying when Mutt comes to wake me. That's why I used to be late for school. That's why I got expelled.'

I don't know what I am doing here but I am definitely not here to cure depression amongst middle-aged married women. There are more chances of world peace breaking out.

I used to think that if I am ever taken a POW I am going to plead that my wife is depressed, I need to go home, please let me go.

Cath had called during the last Desert Survival Course, and for some reason they put her call through. To think, they have been more kind to Cath than they have ever been to me. There are still some old-fashioned controllers untouched by emergency rules who believe that any call from your spouse is as urgent as any order of the day. I thought she was calling to tell me something significant like she was pregnant or she had lost weight or our kitten was throwing up again. She had only called to say that she was feeling hungry and lonely. She didn't say she was lonely because I wasn't with her, she didn't say she missed me or that she would have liked to be with me – not that they would let her be with me, there was no way they would allow a spouse to be on a survival course with anyone. But if you are feeling bored and lonely and your husband is away learning to survive in a desert, the least you can do is tell them that you miss them or you would like to be with them. There is no law that says you can't say that. But all she said is that there was nothing in the fridge.

'This meat is raw, how am I supposed to eat it?' she said, and then added abruptly, 'I am bleeding again.' I never knew what to say to that. She made her monthly cycle sound like my personal failure. I ignored the accusation.

'Depends if you are making breakfast or dinner,' I said. 'There is a time difference, you know, our watches are set to different time zones. I don't know where I am—'

'And even if you knew you are not allowed to tell me. . .' She cut me off sharply. I could tell she was hungry.

I could have given her a tutorial on how to cook a snake on a hot stone but I just grunted and told her to order a takeaway and hung up.

I wish she would call now so that I could tell her some-thing about the desert, the real one, not the shimmering fantasy in our simulator. So that I could tell her family is trouble anywhere in the world.

She doesn't call anymore. She only appears and disappears.

*

Momo takes my hand and pulls me down with a jerk, bringing his mouth to my ear. For a moment I panic, thinking he
is about to plant a kiss on my cheek. But he whispers in my
ear. 'Father Dear sold Ali to your people. That's why Mother
cries all night.'

'Who is Ali?' I say, snatching my hand away from him.
I should probably ask him where his father sold him and
why.

'Don't speak so loudly. Everybody in the Camp knows, they
think he has gone with the Americans and sends us money.'

I can't believe that mild-mannered logistics officer is a
seller of children, of a human being called Ali. He sees my
perplexed face and says, 'Bro Ali, my older brother. Two
years older. He worked in the Hangar when there was a
workshop. He could fix anything. They let him change tyres
on planes, when they used to have planes.'

A pickup truck hurtles towards us. A teenager sits in the
back, cradling a gun. A very pregnant goat stands behind
him and it looks very scared. Momo greets the boy, the boy
ignores us and hugs the goat.

'Why would your father do a thing like that? And why
would the folks at the Hangar buy him? We don't trade in
humans. It's not even legal anymore,' I say.

Momo takes my hand and we start walking away from
the Camp. 'Are you gonna keep playing stupid or are you
stupid? He says he didn't do it. He says he got him a job in
the Hangar and then he never came back. But it's obvious
that he is lying. He never looks you in the eye when he says
that. And he never cries.'

'Some people don't cry. Your brother probably got lost in
the desert,' I say.

'Nobody gets lost in the desert unless they are a complete
stupid,' Momo says, angry now, then looks at me. 'He knew

the desert very well. I do too. And he taught me everything I know.'

Then he starts talking like an irritated lawyer trying to explain a fine legal point to his dumb client.

'This is what happened. Before, he used to go to the Hangar sometimes, worked for them and came home in the evening. Sometimes he did things for them which were top secret. Even I wasn't supposed to know. Mother Dear used to give him breakfast before everybody else. Then one day Father Dear says pack his lunch and he says iron his Boss T-shirt, he says it's a special day. Bro Ali has got a full-time job. And he goes with Father Dear and Father Dear comes back alone and pretends he knows nothing about why Ali hasn't come back.'

'Surely he gave some explanation?'

'Yes. He said he must be on his way, fixing radars on the plane. Official business, even Father Dear is not allowed to go in the operations area. Double pay. Special job. When he finishes the job he gets a green card and the same job in San Jose.'

'And then?'

'He never comes back. Do you think they might have sent him to San Jose? Why wouldn't anybody tell us anything? Hangar also shuts down, no planes, no bombs, nothing. Only an alarm that rings sometimes. Mother Dear screams at Father Dear, Mother Dear threatens to go there to find him. He was Mother Dear's favourite.' He says this in a state of despair, as if he has lost in a rigged contest.

'Firstborns have that kind of advantage. I'm sure she loves you too.'

'I am her only son,' says Momo, then adds, 'until we find him of course.'

Until *we* find him?

And I suddenly realize that behind all the swagger and sharp tongue and fancy boots he is still a child struggling to understand what his parents want from him, what else is in store for him.

Come on, man, don't get involved. It's probably treason to help the enemy against your own country. What if High Command finds out? Even if it's not technically treason, it's stupid.

'Maybe he just left. Maybe he ran away. Kids are always running away from home. I always used to dream of running away. One day you'll run away from home too.'

'Mother Dear has told me she is not going to forgive me her milk if I don't find him. What does forgiving the milk mean? I can't ask her because what if it means something really bad. It sounds bad enough.'

I try and remember some piece of wisdom from my Cultural Sensitivity course. Nothing. We were told they respect their mothers. The more sons a mother has the more respect she gets, but it also means she has to do more housework.

Nothing about milk. Nothing about forgiveness.

'She probably wants you to focus on your school work, not drive around aimlessly. All mothers want that.'

'Did your mother want that?' he says thoughtfully. 'And how about you? Do you have children? What would you do if one of them went missing?' This is not the first time the little brat has messed with my head. I say nothing.

'I know what my mother wants me to do. She doesn't realize I can't do it alone. But now I have got an idea. I have got a team. I have got a plan; but for that you are gonna have to go inside the Hangar.'

I am pretty sure I am not going to like his idea. I am dead sure that it's a bad idea. I can't break into a locked-up military facility along with enemy combatants. I am sure a whole universe once existed there; planes being refuelled, war plans being implemented, pilots sitting in their waiting rooms with their extra hot cups of coffee and their aspirin for breakfast, where master sergeants stood waving orange batons at taxying aircrafts, where you could breathe in aviation-grade gasoline and get high for a few moments.

'What we gonna find in the Hangar?' Momo asks.

'As you are saying it's not operational anymore, I wouldn't know. Probably only an R&R facility?'

'What's R&R?'

'Rest and Recreation. When soldiers are tired, when they need a break but there is not enough time to fly them home.'

'Did they send you here for rest and recreation? When are you gonna go and check it out? There is not much rest or recreation in this Camp.' It sounds like a mission brief. The sun is glinting in the green shards on Momo's house's boundary walls. Maybe I need to do exactly what Momo wants me to do. Find a way to get into the Hangar, there has to be some comms equipment, I could get in touch with the Roaming Angels and get the hell out of here. But Momo wants to hitch a ride.

'I think the way to start is that you need to talk to Father Dear,' says Momo. 'In confidence. That should be the first step. He considers every white man his boss. I think you can convince him that we should go into the Hangar.'

I am not here to solve your family problems, I have enough of my own, I want to say. I don't say anything, but Momo already seems to have a strategy in place. I am supposed to talk to the logistics officer. In confidence? About what?

'I don't think your father trusts me,' I say sheepishly. And I think it's this moment when I sign on to the project that will seal my fate. I could have said *I have no desire to talk to your father.* I could have said *I don't want to have anything to do with a man who allegedly sold his firstborn to an invading army.* I could have said *I am the invading army.* I could have said *I don't understand your culture and hence am the wrong person to take part in any local adventures.* I could have just walked away. Anyone in my place should have said *this is not my culture, I am going to run from this place.* But I didn't. Why? Because my mission isn't complete yet.

Say hi to Major Ellie.

CHAPTER 25

Mutt

Whenever I hear the alarm from the Hangar, I know we are gonna go into action soon. It is a shrill sound that stuns the morning birds, pierces through every mud wall, stirs everyone in their dreams. It is the sound of a thousand dead American soldiers screaming their last scream, it rises and falls like their fathers whispering to their dead sons' pictures and then it rises in cacophony, like all the dead from their bombing, pulling themselves out of their graves and trying to tell the stories of their abruptly ended lives.

First there is one sound, as if an ambulance is moving in slow motion, carrying someone who was distressed but not dying, then the voice grows louder, and more shrill, and stray dogs lie down on the ground with their bellies pressed against the earth, as if the earth will absorb their fears, migratory cranes lift off in their vast formations and leave the Camp in panic, promising themselves to avoid this route in next season's migration. The noisy children in their courtyards shut up, and thrust their fingers in their ears and pull faces at each other, goats go around their business, occasionally raising their heads, then, getting bored with this whining world, go back to the essential business of avoiding poisonous berries and chewing the leaves. The alarm sustains itself at its highest pitch for about a minute and just when I think it will ring till eternity, it begins to die down and then, like a choking dragon, it takes a few loud hiccups and comes to an abrupt halt. Its presence vibrates in the air for a few moments, goats pick up their heads and note the silence with approval and then go back to their day-long lunch.

CHAPTER 26

Momo

I look around for Mutt. Trust him to disappear when the alarm went off. I am suddenly aware although the alarm is heard all over the Camp it carries a personal intimate message to me. It tells me that there is an American base, that's where Bro Ali went, and never came back.

There are rumours and rumours surrounding the Hangar since Bro Ali went and the planes stopped coming and the bombs stopped falling. Many spread by Mutt. When there is nothing to do he runs around it howling on moonlit nights. And sometimes, just to confuse the rumour-mongers, on pitch-dark nights as well.

The alarm goes off at random hours, a three-minute shrill symphony that reminds everyone that this place, abandoned for the last seven months, is still protected, there is an electrical mechanism, which monitors the potential intruders, petty thieves looking for scrap metal, ambitious thieves hoping to find hidden treasures. They make sure that the alarm is tested at an unpredictable hour, sometimes when people are in the middle of their lunch, sometimes when they are about to put their heads on their pillows, giving people the impression that there is a clever bit of planning that goes into the security of the Hangar. Here's a place where there has to be a clue about where Bro Ali is, otherwise why all this security after it has been abandoned?

Sometimes you need to ask Father Dear things even when you are sure you are not getting any answers.

He is sniffing his files like Mutt sniffs his female friends.

'Is it just an abandoned base, or are they hiding something in there? Why don't we just move in?' I am not expecting a straight answer from him and I don't get one.

'People here are suspicious by nature,' he says, putting his file aside. 'They think if something is locked and has an element of security there has to be something worth stealing in there.'

You have to be tactical with Father Dear. And, as Lady Flowerbody says, you always have to manage your expectations.

'And are they wrong to be suspicious? Why still miles and miles of razor wire, why these signs saying IT'S NOT A THOROUGHFARE, INTRUDERS WILL BE SHOT, THIS PROPERTY IS PROTECTED BY GUARD DOGS, why don't they want anybody near it, why this drama with the alarm going off, if they are not gonna protect anything inside it? Do you think they might come back?'

The only way to keep him talking is to not mention Bro Ali.

'My job description included ensuring that nobody goes in, not even me. It doesn't say anywhere that if there is nothing inside it you can forget your duties. When there is nobody watching at a traffic signal, are you still supposed to stop or do you just say oh look no traffic, no cops I can just keep going.'

'Why don't we just move in so that you won't have to worry about security? It's our land after all.'

Father Dear shakes his head as if I am suggesting an act of treason. 'Who says I am worried about security? I am doing my job.'

I respect his achievements. You don't just become USAID Logistics Officer and keep the job seven months after they have left unless you know something about what's in the Hangar. Or more likely in Father Dear's case you are afraid of finding out what's in the Hangar. Or what isn't in the Hangar anymore.

'There were people from fifteen countries in there,' Father Dear says, clutching his files. 'Daily review meetings. We had twelve thousand gallons in reserve fuel. There were eight types of bread on the buffet. We used to open a new box of brass polish every Friday.' Father Dear is finally showing some emotion, he realizes it and retreats into his own head.

'And then?' I ask.

'They took away my security badge,' he says with such misery, as if they took away his manhood along with his badge. 'They said they were restructuring.'

I don't want to remind him that they took away something more precious than his security badge: his firstborn.

'Can we go in and have a look?' I say and I don't forget to look in his eyes. He is reluctant to give a straight answer. 'It's dangerous,' he says, lowering his voice. He knows something about the place and doesn't want to share. He is also afraid of losing his other son.

'Father Dear, I know it's not your fault, but do you have any idea why the bombings stopped after Bro Ali went in?'

He looks down at his feet. I am never gonna be good at reading depressed people's feelings but I think he sheds a tear.

'You know that he wanted to go. And the people in the Hangar wanted him also. Who can say no to a son?' he says. 'Who can say no to Americans?'

I don't tell him my own plan: we have got a white man in the Camp. So he goes in and we follow him. It's that simple.

I think we are gonna have to drag Father Dear there too. With respect of course.

Chapter 27

Ellie

'They know who you are,' she says. 'There are no secrets in the desert.'

We are sitting at the edge of the pond. A couple of goats are eyeing us suspiciously as they take turns grazing and sneezing over the thorny bushes. She has asked me to follow her here. I am happy to follow her, hoping for a moment of privacy where she could give me a road map that will take me from here to a room in Diego Garcia, a couple of days to check if all my bones are intact, to give some of those taxpayer dollars to the folks discovering a new strain of PTSD, to make sure I had not surrendered any state secrets to the desert folks, as if the desert folks were interested in anything other than their next shipment of tinned beef.

And now she tells me they know about me.

What is there to know anyway? My whole CV could fit onto two lines: one man, 637 missions, a few thousand tons of the finest explosives deposited in some of the world's most evil places. Some hits. Some misses. Current status: lost.

How do they know? I thought I had been doing a good job of looking like a mid-level USAID executive, it basically involves listening to everyone patiently and then saying let's continue the meeting after the lunch break. It is the kind of job for people who say they are interested in people because they are really not interested in anything. And although I couldn't give a rat's ass about people before ending up in this shithole, I was beginning to like this, people talking earnestly about sewage and cheating spouses, about the need for winter shelters and better ways of teaching maths. I had started to sense the possibility of a post-retirement career in the parallel universe called International Relief. Cath would approve. We could get posted to Darfur and maybe adopt a baby. It'd shake up the neighbourhood, the colour of the baby that is. Make them orphans, then adopt them, that's how the world goes.

'How do they know?' I ask in an accusing voice. 'I am sure they are used to people like me coming and going. I haven't got my job description engraved on my forehead. Or have I?'

She picks up a pebble and throws it in the pond. A small cloud of mosquitoes rises, hovers over the surface, then settles down.

There are voices in the distance, vehicles stuck in sand, revving their engines, hushed voices, twigs breaking. Probably a bunch of kids trying to start a wildfire. It is probably against the Camp rules but then kids everywhere start fires because starting fires is forbidden.

'You talk weird,' she says. 'Sometimes people are only guessing what you are saying.'

I feel hurt. Why can't I speak my own language? Half the damn world speaks bad English. Do I ever mind? She is talking to me in English. She is objecting to my presence, my speaking in English, in English. I can speak a few words of Arabic. Five, to be precise, if you count the word 'Arabic' itself. Now is it my fault that they don't speak Arabic around here?

'They call themselves Muslims and still don't speak any Arabic. Why don't they speak Arabic?'

She looks at me like I'm a moron.

'You are Christian, why don't you speak Aramaic?'

What the fuck is Aramaic? I want to say. But I need to steer the conversation away from religion and languages; no one ever wins. 'I am only a cultural Catholic.' And then she goes into a righteous rage, typical of do-gooders far far away from home. 'What the hell is a cultural Catholic? Someone who only half believes that His mother is a virgin? Someone who nails himself to a wooden beam over the weekend?'

The twigs are crackling now, but I still can't see any fire. In a very low voice which occasionally rises above the audible level, someone is singing. They might be sending a coded message, but it definitely sounds like someone singing. A gang of amateur singers trying to form a band in the wilderness, a promising subject for anthropology graduates but a bloody nuisance when you are trying to have a conversation about how to escape the barbarians and get home. But what is left of home? A three-bedroom condo, and a car gathering dust in the garage, and memories of Cath everywhere.

'And why do you have to wear this flying suit all the time?' she says. 'Just borrow a local dress. And please stop calling this place a camp. This is home for the folks out here.'

'People here wear all kinds of uniforms; that proves nothing. And everybody calls it a camp, it says so out there on the gate. Does it have another name?' I decide to shut up. It is the kind of argument that got me in trouble with Cath, when she would hear me out quietly for fifteen minutes and then would only answer after four days. And now when I see her she doesn't speak to me at all.

But what I just said is kind of true. Half the refugee kids wear discarded uniforms from European police forces and paramilitaries. Anyone venturing in here for the first time could easily mistake it for a grand reunion of forgotten armies. There are teenagers who strut around in NATO generals' uniforms, grandfathers puff on huqqas wearing overalls from the British infantry, a bunch of teenage girls have taken a shine to the French Foreign Legion's berets.

Why is an air force pilot with a simple flying suit considered a total alien in this freak show?

'And my suit's considered proof here in this humanitarian world of yours? If they were to start judging people by what they wear, half your camp's population would end up in war crime tribunals in Amsterdam.' I am positively furious now. I had taken for granted that she was an ally. That in this lost world she was my traffic controller, my direction finder, my navigation map. I thought we were natural allies, indispensable for each other. If two well-educated people stranded at the edge of a desert can't stick together we have already lost half the battle.

Yesterday we were natural, even spiritual, allies; today I am told that I don't speak good enough English.

'The war tribunals are held in The Hague,' she says dismissively. 'And nobody ends up there. That's just for show. Unless you are some poor unlucky Serb and can't afford a good lawyer.'

I can't decide if she is acting dumb, doing some essential part of her job or if she is just refusing to acknowledge how indispensable we are to each other. The only two like-minded people in the Camp, refusing to help each other.

'Aren't brown people back home always whispering to each other, in their own language? I'm not saying they are always scheming or plotting against us but isn't that the truth? Don't they do it in the subway, standing in Gap checkouts? Forget colour, forget nationality, aren't we mutually dependent on each other? How are we going to defeat the forces of darkness if we can't even help a good soldier get into a rescue helicopter and go home? Aren't we together in this? Don't we complete each other?'

I want to continue but I stop. There are some simple facts of life that she is not ready to face, sometimes a man must hold back.

If I didn't bomb some place, how would she save that place? If I didn't rain fire from the skies, who would need her to douse that fire on the ground? Why would you need somebody to throw blankets on burning babies if there were no burning babies? If I didn't take out homes, who would provide shelter? If I didn't take out homes who would need shelter? If I didn't obliterate cities, how would you get to set up refugee camps? Where would all the world's empathy go? Who would host exhibitions in the picture galleries of Berlin, who would have fundraising balls in London? Where would all the students on their gap years go? If I stop wearing this uniform and quit my job, the world's sympathy machine will grind to a halt. You don't hold candlelight vigils for those dying of old age and neglect. You need fireworks to ignite human imagination.

I can see now that she belongs to that civilian world of eternal deceit, of well-earned loneliness, people wanting to arrive somewhere without risking the journey. She is as devious as anyone who has never stared death in the face, someone who has never looked at an eight-inch LCD screen and had to decide whether place X should exist or not; she has never had to guess if a convoy of vehicles was a wedding party or an advancing army. The only choices that she has had to make are how much powdered milk to order, how many boxes of mosquito repellent; she only has to count people or look at old registers to get the approximate population, then guess the number of surviving children and make sure that there is enough Play-Doh for everyone. And then study their young, hopeless minds.

Goats are jumping up at the only tree around the pond and flailing around the poisonous-looking yellow berries. A vague homesickness settles over me. In the first flush of love, sometimes you hug someone and linger a second longer, you know that it's going to be over now, but you linger. That's what I need now, a hug that'll last a moment longer than is customary. A hug that'll say *keep me here, keep me safe from sinister-looking goats and their poisonous yellow berries*. I need a hug.

'There was a tip-off that the Camp was going to be bombed again,' she looks into my eyes, still not sure if she should be sharing this information or not. 'There was a very reliable tip-off. International Relief is kind – well at least reliable – when it comes to these tip-offs. Their supply chain is touch and go, poor things are always sending us beach volleyball gear, but they are good with tip-offs. They let us know that a plane was headed this way and it was not theirs. Also, that Doctor predicted it. You might think it's mumbo jumbo, but people here, they believe him. He has a track record. He is not some kind of stargazer or spiritual healer, he has foretold stuff that has happened. And I am not talking about predicting rains, which even kids here can do quite well. He has been going on about ghosts in the Hangar. It's not haunted in any conventional sense. But perhaps there is something more there, not just your people's ghosts trapped in there.'

I try hard to concentrate. The sun is suddenly above our heads and no more a gentle source of muddy light, but a determined torturer wielding a blowtorch. Sometimes all you need is a hug and all you get is political analysis.

'So we were all in our shelters, all the cattle pushed into the desert, and yes, there was a plane, it circled and circled as if looking for us from up there and then nothing. After midnight we heard a little snap in the sky and then again, nothing. We waited and waited in our shelters listening out for that whistle your missiles whistle before they visit us, but it was all quiet. We came out in the morning and everything was the same. The goats and camels were back. And we were receiving congratulation from Helping Hands who we haven't heard from since the last USAID drop and they are saying, your people in the Camp shot the Eagle down. We're like yes the fuck we did. Should give us some cred with them. The bigger the guns behind you, the bigger the aid package you attract. What have you got? And we are pretending, yeah hell we did, we haven't got anything to show for it though. But we go on pretending we have got something that can shoot down planes. But no, we haven't got any such thing except our prayers.

'Those clowns in the Camp, they are always looking for visual material. Optics they call them. So these boys are in the desert and they film this wreckage, a crashed plane, half a plane apparently stuck in the sand. Also pictures of a dead guy. Now I have to say this, he is strapped to his seat, charred mostly so not recognizable but has a nametag with your name. Now they want to produce their own video. Everyone wants to make a grainy little video. But they have footage and you look quite dead in it. But here you are and they want more footage. They are quite determined.'

The world is full of struggling film-makers. So what if they have filmed some dead zoomie in the desert. When they are dead they all look the same. They wouldn't kidnap me. What'll they demand in ransom: happiness? They don't want to lose their refugee status. Who wants to stop getting free packaged food and almost-new Nike attire?

'And on the eighth day you are found roaming the desert,' she continues. 'They bring you in and you start pretending you were doing milk runs in the desert and took a wrong turn. And now you are here and you don't even want to go home? Don't you want your medal, get your picture in the paper, collect your bonus, play golf? You'll have to get out of here, sooner or later, but first there is work to be done.'

'What work?' I am through with work.

'Colonel Slatter's crash was all over the news back home,' she says. '"American hero's last mission" or whatever nonsense. They found his plane's wreck but not Colonel Slatter. And then you walk in talking about some stupid army ritual.'

'It's a matter of squadron's honour. Your officer crashes, you fly the same mission. So I did.'

'I am all for traditions and respecting the military culture but something new is happening here. Your people took in their boys and they didn't come back, and then you took in Momo's brother and your planes started crashing. The boy was a nerd but could he be bringing the world's largest air force to its knees? Anything I am missing here? You followed Slatter, right? So who is following you here?'

I know it is time to be square and firm. 'I have taken an oath and I am not going to discuss our war plans with anyone. Not even you. And who are you anyway, my rescue party? We might be on the same team, same ball, same park but our shit is different. I fly missions. I do my work and I go home. I don't live in some godforsaken commune and poke into other people's minds.'

She looks at me as if she knows I need a hug. 'You see those boys in the van, you hear that singing? They are getting impatient. They saw one of their own shot in the middle of the Camp. They have found your plane. They have found you. There's no way you could have survived that wreck. You lost your men here, didn't you? Many more than you are willing to acknowledge? Were they ever taken back? I don't buy it but this is what they believe: their ghosts are roaming the desert trying to find their way back home. They believe you have been sent to take them back. So you were sent on a mission, weren't you?'

'Nobody told me anything. I had my coffee. I had my aspirin. I took off. I thought I was doing my last mission.'

'Well there is one more to go. You got to do what you got to do,' she has suddenly assumed the authority of a veteran commander.

'And I am on your side. They think I am keeping you for myself. That's all men can think of even in the middle of a war.'

Chapter 28

Mutt

Momo thinks he found me, he adopted me, he trained me, he kept me and when I ran away into the desert after his brutal assault he brought me back. I let him think that. It's good for his fragile ego. I think I am the one who adopted him, has kept him out of trouble, seen him at his weakest and still kept faith in him. I was there when Bro Ali caught him stealing petrol and thrashed him. There is the petrol tank outside the Hangar and Momo got a rubber pipe, dipped it into the tank, sucked and sucked and then filled six empty Nestlé bottles and started a home delivery service. Fuel for Almost Free. Bro Ali caught him and gave him a thrashing so severe that I flinched and I yelped and finally managed to rescue him.

Some nights I ran after Bro Ali as he sneaked out and set up his radio thing and started talking to people in the sky. Momo followed us; I pretended we hadn't noticed. Even Bro Ali pretended we didn't know he was following us.

But I let Momo think he is God's gift to humanity and me. Some people might call it a servile attitude on my part; I call it love.

And it's this love and not greed that makes me go to the Hangar now.

There is the smell of cooking, of butter and sugar. How many times have I tried to nudge Momo to look in here so he might find some answers. But he is stubborn. If it's abandoned, if all the troops have been withdrawn then who is cooking up a feast? Preparation. Preparation. Preparation. He wants to strike at the right time, he wants the right team, he is obsessed with the right gear. He wants a takeover. He wants to turn the place into a shopping mall with a fountain in the centre. He wants to keep the top floor for his own offices. In his head he has choreographed homecoming celebrations. I agree it's not like one of his business plans where even if you botch it up you can move on. Here the stakes are higher, much higher; a mother's heart, a brother's love and the family lineage and something about my land, my freedom which I don't understand. All I know is that you have no chance of earning any respect in this desert if you let them take your brother.

Sometimes Momo deludes himself by assuming that they have taken Bro Ali to some place called San Jose. He is having too much fun there, that's why he hasn't contacted his family. I want to scream at him: *Don't just make plans, do something. They took away your brother, now you strut around in the jeep that they gave him, so that he could roam around with his transmitter.* He always said he was helping root out evil. I thought he was talking about smelly cats before I knew better.

I am circling the Hangar, hoping to catch another whiff of something that will give me a clue to what's going on inside. Barbed wires are rusting, booby traps have dozed off, ghosts of sniffer dogs still sniff the winds for any approaching enemies. I can smell cinnamon, which is the smell of summer holidays in childhood, and whipped cream, memories of nice things that never happened, I am lost in these smells when I hear steps. I don't smell anything but I hear footsteps. And she comes at me, almost floats towards me, sits down in front of me, like pretentious dog-lovers do because they want us to believe they are not larger than us, *no you idiot you are much bigger, you are sitting down that's why our eyes are level.* She ruffles the hair on my neck and gives me a hug. I am looking at her like *who the hell are you? Where is your smell?* What kind of person doesn't have a smell? I think I know someone else who doesn't have a smell. *Where's your shadow? Why are your hands and cheeks so cold? Whatever the hell happened to you? What are you doing so far away from home?* Because she is blonde and has translucent pale skin and blue eyes that seem to look through me. *Why aren't you scared? Don't you see these teeth? Do you even know who I am?*

Then I realize that it's my turn to be scared. For the first time in my life I am afraid of the human touch. Before I can yelp or put my paws on her, she gets up and starts walking towards the Hangar. And she is not the only one. There are others like her, some dressed in uniform like those soldiers who used to come out in convoys to get their water supply, now a bunch of tired soldiers returning to their base. They are floating over the sand heading towards the Hangar. The temperature suddenly drops. My brain is exceptionally slow. There is a person who doesn't have a smell. I thought maybe they use some special perfume to disguise their smell. Because if you can't smell them you can't scare them.

I can see them now. A ghost army is coming together for a reunion. Momo is never going to believe it. He is a man of science. Even if ghosts come brandishing chequebooks, Momo is not going to believe it. The only way he would believe this is to come and see this for himself. It's just like the old days but much colder. The gates of the Hangar are open, the floodlights have been turned on, there are no aeroplanes but the windsock is fluttering, the giant machines in the Hangar are squeaking and whirling. Why have they come back? Have they brought our bro back? Suddenly I remember. My fried brains might be slow but they can do the job. I know the person who doesn't have a smell. I need to go tell Momo that there is a ghost under our own roof.

Chapter 29

Momo

When Mutt wags his tail or curls it into a question mark I can usually ignore him. But when he comes with his tail in a tight coil and runs circles around me, he is bringing some important news and we need to tend to urgent business. We get into the jeep and drive and what do I see? The gates of the Hangar are open, the barriers are up, the floodlights are on. We drive around it in our Cherokee, I honk the horn, *anybody there?* I don't see anyone on the checkpoints, or the silhouette of a woman, but I am ready to bet that Mutt is right about her too.

You must have heard that God created couples so that his creation could multiply and overpopulate the world. But God also created couples so that they could hound each other in life, betray each other and then haunt each other after one of them dies. I have no idea if there really is a ghost in the Hangar. Who cares? There's a white woman, and we already have a white man amongst us. He has been going on about his wife. Wanting to go back to her but never really making a move. Now she has come to him. I can tell when Mutt is barking the truth. So Ellie runs away from his wife and his wife tracks him down. A good wife is always gonna do that. Even when your country forgets you, your wife is gonna remember you. What's not to believe?

I find him in Lady Flowerbody's makeshift office, studying a file. My tone is celebratory, as if I have brought the good news he has been waiting for all these days. 'They have come for you. I think there is also someone special to meet you.' My tone is full of mystery, full of promise. I am gonna entice him gently. When you are outnumbered by a powerful enemy, you can't rely on brute force. It's my negotiation skills that are gonna win the day. I can't really put a gun to Ellie's head and take him to the Hangar. That only happens in the movies. In real life everybody is gonna talk and talk and only pull out our guns when we have run out of words.

'You gonna go to the Hangar. Your woman's come to get you.'

'Where? How do you know it's her? Why didn't you bring her here?'

White man is gonna keep thinking he is smart until that smartness is snuffed out of him.

'She's gone inside the Hangar. You know that I can't go in. And why would she believe me, why would she listen to me? I am only a little boy.'

What is he gonna do? He can't say that there is no wife, that I am imagining her. That Hangar is open and letting in white people. What kind of man is afraid of his own people? Someone who thinks he is not one of them. Someone who doesn't want to be one of them. But what is he gonna do? He is our ticket into that place.

'Your father said that place is haunted, that there is nothing in there except ghosts.'

Father Dear said that, really?

So Father Dear has been hiding behind the occult, he is trading in ghosts now. I am the one who is not superstitious but Ellie is a step ahead of me. I am gonna beat him with logic. White man is gonna believe in whatever is convenient for him.

'Use your brains. It's a warehouse. Full of redundant tanks and aircrafts and artillery. There is a rescue team that she has brought with her. To take you back. She travels halfway around the world to look for you and you are afraid of a short ride? You must really love her.'

I can see that he still doesn't wanna go but there is a strange glow in his eyes. Suddenly he looks like a crumpled paper bag.

'I was going to go anyway. I don't know what I have been waiting for.'

'Not just you. We are all gonna go.'

As we move towards the Jeep Cherokee, I see Mother Dear rushing out of the house. I can't remember the last time she stepped out of the house. On her heels, Mutt, proud, a bounce in his steps, even his limp looks like an act of grace. It seems as if his brains suddenly got unfried.

CHAPTER 30

Mutt

When I emerge with Mother Dear's long-lost white dupatta that covered Bro Ali's chickenpoxed torso, I am expecting a thrashing. Mother Dear is sitting there putting green gooey stuff in her hair. It's henna. I can't stand the smell because it's the smell of wedding nights and trembling virgins. She hasn't gone out in a while and this is her way of getting ready for the big, bad world. It's my turn to tremble though, and nobody has ever accused me of being a virgin. I didn't really steal the dupatta, I just put it under the sofa because it so strongly smelt of Bro Ali. It brought back unbearable memories. But I know she needs it now. The time has come to stop being fearful of these memories.

I put it at a safe, respectful distance from her and sit still. It's against my restless nature to stay still but I don't want to send the wrong message. I don't want her to think that I have soiled her lost son's memory or that I have been messing with her personal piece of clothing. Sitting still is not that difficult if you haven't done anything wrong. I haven't. Not with this dupatta. She comes and picks up the dupatta, she smells it and in her smelling it I can smell all the love in the world.

I keep my tongue in my mouth. I keep my tail still. When she lunges at me I don't move. I am not sure what I am in for. A kick or a slap? With Momo I can always tell if I am going to receive a kick in the butt or a kiss on my snout. She slaps me. Gently. It's not really a slap, it's the kind of gentle shove in the face that you give someone when you want to say, *you beauty*.

Then she bends down and nuzzles her nose against my snout. She has never done that to me. 'My son, I think it's time to go.' Nobody has ever called me my son.

There is a clamour outside, and suddenly everyone – and I mean everyone – is talking.

It's definitely time to go.

To the Hangar

CHAPTER 31

Mother Dear

I am not going to sit here with smoke in my eyes, my chipped nails and a bad conscience and wait for a miracle. I have already waited enough. In the end I have to do everything with my own hands. Miracles don't happen when your existence is tied to your stove and when you spend your days thinking: Am I a bad mother? When did I become such a bad mother?

Then there is no salt in the house. I might be a bad mother but I am not a stupid mother. I know when it's time to do something.

I can see the preparations all around me. I can see a journey in Mutt's eyes. Momo has been stealing oil from the kitchen for his rifle. That deserter Ellie wakes up in the middle of the night and thinks of running away and then realizes that he has no place to run to.

Even Lady Flowerbody has been trying to get me to join the sisterhood. She tells me that I am not a bad mother, that I shouldn't blame myself. She says that it's common amongst mothers to think that they are not good enough to be mothers. I tell her to shut up and work on her report and make sure nothing is stolen from my home. How can people make a living telling others not to blame themselves for anything? That good-for-nothing slut tells me that I should wait a bit, let things take their own course, turn my grief into my strength, put my loss into a global perspective. She wants me to be a strong woman who makes her own decisions.

Who does she think makes decisions around here? I made one bad decision; it didn't seem like a bad decision at the time. Boys need to go out in the world, so I let him. A proper job in the middle of the war, a job that didn't involve fighting. I swear I thought he'd be safer in the Hangar. They had the guns and the alarms and could decide where to throw bombs. He would be better off, I thought, after a bomb came through our own roof. Maybe I was a stupid, selfish mother but now I don't need any more strength, I need my son.

I have waited enough. I waited nine months. You know what that wait was like? Every other minute I thought what if he was dead inside me? And then he would kick, I would say, *thank God he is not dead*. I'd be relieved for a moment and then I would think what if he has no eyes? And I would pray *O merciful, O giver of eyes please give him good eyes*. What if he is six-fingered? Well that would be OK because I had a six-fingered friend when I was little and everyone thought it was cute. We envied her because everyone wanted to count the fingers on her hand just to make sure.

I didn't want him to come into this world. I wanted to hold him inside a few days longer. I wasn't afraid of the pain. I wasn't sure if he had something missing, a limb, a toe. I couldn't imagine a face. And when he came out he pulled my whole being out into the world with him. It hurt but it felt good. It was awful and it was beautiful. There was burning in my stomach but stars bursting in my eyes. My nipples hurt but my nipples hurt even more when he didn't suckle.

Now to sit and wait and not be able to hear him come into the house, banging the door and shouting *Mother Dear, I am hungry, I am so hungry I could eat a whole cow. Where is my food, Mother Dear, why is there never any food in the house, why do you feed it all to Father Dear, he doesn't even do any work at his office? You feed Mutt before you feed me. Come on, Mother Dear, where is my food, I am so hungry.*

I was not always a bad mother. There was always food for him; you just could never tell when he would be hungry. By the time you had lit the stove to warm the food he was jumping up and down the house showing you how hungry he was. I did alright there, fed him and clothed him as his limbs stretched and his hunger kept growing.

They should have taken me. Why did I agree to send him on his own? Why didn't I insist on going with him?

CHAPTER 32

Mutt

Our jeep travels at a steady speed, it makes no sound. Father Dear is sitting beside me, slumped in his seat as if he is being taken to attend his own trial. White Ellie the deserter is sitting beside him, fidgeting. Momo has got one hand on the steering of his Jeep Cherokee and the other one on his M16. The safety catch is off. *Momo, can you please put the safety catch on? Let's not show off. You could kill someone or maim someone without meaning to.* Guns smell of idle lust.

I have got my nose in the air. And I see the first red bird and then another and another. I yelp. Momo looks up and nods his head in approval. I don't know if he can actually see them or is just indulging me. Mother Dear is sharpening a crystal dagger on a little black stone as if she'll bring the whole army down with it. She raises the dagger above her head to check its sharpness, it glints in my eye. Momo stops the jeep. We are being followed.

He is only a speck in the distance, a man on a motorbike, but he's catching up. Here comes the traitor, I think. First we'll have to deal with the traitor. Momo waits for Doctor to catch up.

Doctor stops his bike at a safe distance from us. As the dust settles, we realize that he has got a pillion rider: Lady

Flowerbody. She has got a hand on his shoulder. They'll make a good pair, two reluctant saviours, if they can save themselves from each other.

Doctor has no interest in our mission, he is non-partisan, he eats objectivity for breakfast; objectivity smells of stale piss. He is not going to take any sides. He is not interested in saving Bro Ali, he is not even interested in saving humanity. He wants to save the desert. He thinks the desert is the source of life and continually reminds us that there are more than thirteen thousand species in the desert. He should try and sample some of this biodiversity for breakfast. Most of these species are poison disguised as life.

'Why are you following us?' shouts Momo. You can never expect a straight answer from Doctor.

'I am most certainly not. You are going your way and I am going my way.'

'But why are you going to the Hangar?'

'I am not telling you my travel plans. Is there any place that I am not allowed to go to? You might need me. Your enemies might need me. I prefer it when nobody needs me but I have to be ready when someone does.'

Momo is looking at Lady Flowerbody, he was expecting her to come but not with Doctor. 'Where do you think you are going?'

Lady Flowerbody shrugs, she is looking for another chapter in her book. 'I just got a ride. I thought you wanted me to come. I heard the siren too. Basically just doing my job.'

Mother Dear puts her hand on the steering. 'Go on, Momo, we are not wasting time on people who don't give us straight answers. We have work to do and we'll take any help that comes our way but we won't wait for any time wasters. Enough men have wasted my time, I don't need one more.'

Chapter 33

Mother Dear

You know why I am a really bad mother? I am a bad mother because most nights I lie awake and ask myself why we didn't send Momo. He is the clever one, the devious one, a wily little man at fifteen. He should have gone but the older one said *I am the older one. And I have unfinished business with them.* I wonder what would have happened if Momo had gone instead. Then I have to stop myself. I am not just a bad mother, I am a monster. I have lost one son and now I am wishing I had lost the little one because he would have had a better chance of coming back. As if he deserved it more. As if this was experience. As if this was a game of chance that one could play better than the other.

This can't be left to chance anymore. Flowerbody tried to teach me to manage my grief. Managing your grief soon becomes a full-time, dead-end job. It's like managing a small business that never makes any profit. Everyone has got their weapon. I had to choose. I am no good with knives, or daggers, guns are too loud. I used to chop wood when I was young, I was very good at it. There was a machete somewhere. It was rusting in the shed, I did clean it up, I sharpened it and kept it ready after Ali went. Just in case they tried something with Momo. Raising a son is like sharpening a weapon day after day and then waiting. Even when you have no appetite for weapons, you need one because you don't know who might come after your child.

A mother is mortally wounded when she gives birth. After that it's only a matter of time before her sons drive her to her death.

My father carved little objects out of salt slabs, first as a hobby, then as a small business. *My salt craft,* he used to call it; add a dash of pink into any material and it becomes a craft. And the salt from his mine already came with a splash of pink in it. He mostly made table lamps, sometimes shaped like a turtle, sometimes like a camel, and once a flock of doves holding each other up from their beaks, a circle-kiss of doves.

For Ali and Momo sometimes he crafted little replicas of weapons, pistols, toy machine guns. They would go around the house shooting each other.

Why have you given them guns? I said.

There is a war coming, these kids have to learn to handle a weapon.

But these are toy guns.

We can sell these toy guns to tourists and with that money buy a little pistol and with that pistol rob a caravan and with that money buy bigger guns, and you will get to a stage where people will come and buy guns from you because they are scared of you.

My father was like that. Momo gets his business brains from his grandpa.

I am not starting an arms business, I said, *but Father, can you actually make something that works?* And he made me a dagger.

This dagger.

Does my dagger look decorative? It's sharp. And the nice thing is blood doesn't stick to it. It's like the frying pan I have, with that shiny coat, not sticky, that my man got for me when he still used to get things for me. I have been saving my non-stick dagger for this day. There have been days I have been tempted. After all it's made of salt, why not use it to make food? But I have always resisted the urge. I always told myself I was being a sentimental fool, saving a little slab of salt. But every irrational fool finds out, one day, that their irrational belief was a good investment for the future. What you have saved for sentimental reasons becomes your weapon on the day you need it.

CHAPTER 34

Doctor

They think they are going to have a quiet chat, present their charter of demands and return home with their boy. I expect some casualties but not a whole lot. For me personally it's a difficult choice to make; both sides are a bunch of criminals, they have all been robbing the earth blind. I'll be happy if they all perish, but I have to think of the doctor's oath I was told about. Not many people realize the dilemmas that medical professionals caught in such situations face. When the fatalities begin, as I know from experience will happen, whose side am I on? As far as I can tell I am the only medical professional on site. Lady Flowerbody flagged down my bike when I was leaving Camp. I thought she might want to assist me but she said she had her own work to do. I don't blame her. Who wants to be a paramedic in a battle with ghosts?

If one from this side falls and within minutes one from their side falls, who do I save first? I am supposed to save lives without looking at the colour of the flag or even the colour of their skin. There is a personal risk here as well. Tending to one side or the other will immediately make me a target. I am woefully ill-equipped to deal with the kind of damage that's about to happen here. People are scared of big battles, involving tanks and bombs falling from the sky, but it's the small battles fought at close range that cause the most vicious damage to the human anatomy. A bomb will shatter you into a hundred little pieces and although it looks ugly the exit is relatively peaceful. Take a bullet in your gut and then lie there as other combatants trample on you and you'll wish for that bomb that never fell. The battles are ancient, and the way they intend to fight is also not very evolved. The so-called enemy has bigger guns and even bigger food supplies. They also tend to hover above the earth instead of walking, a condition that I have observed but not treated. I don't believe in the paranormal and I am not going to start believing now. I am a doctor not a sorcerer. And I am definitely not a negotiator.

My personal beliefs shall not interfere with my duties. I personally believe that the human race is completely expendable. It has turned raging oceans into deserts and deserts into wastelands. My personal feelings can't come into it. I have a job to do and later I'll prepare a report. *Get on with killing each other, you morons. The earth will be a happier place without you.* Look at their idiocy now. Mother Dear has suddenly appointed herself the leader. The power struggle that is destroying this planet. She is standing in front of Momo blocking his gun. Momo is trying to take aim and avoid his mother's head at the same time. My work is about to begin. I am wearing a white coat, for additional clarity I have tied a white bandana around my head. *Hey you all, who fight this morning, know that I am here not to fight but to manage your wounds. The fewer bodies, fewer limbs lost, less work for me. Get on with it, talk if you want to talk, fight if you want to, finish each other off. Be quick about it, doctors need their lunch break.*

CHAPTER 35

Mother Dear

He is scared. Maybe my man uses his own fear to control me, to keep me chained to the stove. I have got nothing against the stove, it feeds me, it feeds my family. He tells me they have gunship helicopters that can see in the dark, and they have big scary dogs on very heavy iron chains that will devour you when unchained. He wants us to be grateful because we are alive and we have food. Sometimes he hints that even Ali might be better off without us. He says things like: *They have air conditioning, you know. And real beef. And biscuits with lemon cream.*

My Ali loved those lemon-cream biscuits.

Can you trade your son for his own happiness? Will you give him away for his own security?

First he used to say our Ali is on active duty. I say what about working hours? Weekends? Independence Day holiday? What kind of job? Why can't he write a letter? When my husband lies, he looks me in the eye.

'It's a secret job. When armies work in strange lands, they need help, local knowledge, interpreters, it's all official. All confidential. All paid up. Sometimes there are delays in payments but they do pay up.'

But why doesn't he come home?

Last year my Ali would wake up from a nightmare and sneak into my bed and hug me. Now he is a fully paid-up, official secret.

'Have you met with him? Have you seen him? Can you bring him back for a little while?' I found it hard to believe and still do that my man has become a child-trader. Did he know when he was sending him away or was he just careless?

I try to hold Momo back sometimes. He is always looking at the door, always pretending that he has got to go somewhere more important, do something urgent. Learn to sit still, Momo, listen to my story. You have to listen. Remember when you punctured Ali's football and he hit you and I hit him? I shouted at both of you.

Father Dear wouldn't come home for days, after the Hangar shut down. He was scared. He was scared of you. He is still scared that you'll kill him one day. When men run out of words they want to kill. Or at least start thinking about killing each other. I see blood in your eyes. You say these are dollar signs. You blame everything on your Father Dear. But sometimes I suspect you might have inherited your father's love for white people. It's a disease. I know you can say that love is a disease anyway but I can tell you love of white people is a special kind of disease.

But listen, Momo, your father wasn't always like this. He was the son of a chief. People would come around asking for bootleg sugar and petrol. He was quite the smuggler. One day he said, 'People are always coming to do business with me, sometimes to pay their respect, you better start covering your head.'

I said OK, I started covering my head. It became a joke between us. I would see him and I would cover my head, and I would giggle and he would come and give me a squeeze and then go away to do his business. I was covering my head and becoming respectable, but I still had to bring water from the pond. And then one day I forgot my dupatta at the pond, it can happen, it's a piece of cloth not your body part. I approached the house and there was a group of men loitering around waiting for your father, the smuggler in chief, to show up. I reached for my dupatta and it wasn't there. What could I do? I didn't want him barking at me in front of these strangers so I took off my shirt and covered my head and marched right on. What had I got to hide? Everyone has arms, right? And he told me to cover my head, which I was covering with my shirt.

Everybody looked down as I approached the house and there was a sudden hush and prayers being murmured as if they had seen the devil himself, then he emerged and yanked me inside hissing and puffing, and tried to beat me with clumsy hands. I kicked him in the shins.

'What's wrong with you, you idiot?'

'Look, I am covering my head.'

'But look at yourself.'

'There is nothing to look at, I am wearing an undershirt, OK, my arms are exposed but you never told me to cover my arms. And what's wrong if my arms are showing? My head is covered. Isn't that where all your honour lies? Or is it in my arms, tell me for once.'

I realized that day that I am stuck with a confused little husband. Here's my man who will go around licking the boots of every white man he can find, who will grovel in front of an office file, yearn for an insulting cable from his Headquarters, but my exposed arms bring him shame.

Now he is coming with us, sitting here in the same jeep. I didn't ask him to. Momo went and told him the only thing that'll make him get off his lazy ass: that white soldiers have returned, that the gates of the Hangar are open again. He doesn't ask why everyone else is coming along. He can see it in our faces. He knows when to shut up.

I don't object to him coming with us. He can watch.

CHAPTER 36

Mutt

All myths. All lies. Folk wisdom is nothing more than the accumulation of centuries of prejudices and fear. Global security is nothing but social engineering through job creation. First build a facility, then man that facility, then hire more people to protect that facility, then hire some dogs to protect those guards, then hire more men to destroy it, then start dreaming up reconstruction contracts.

I am ahead of the pack, on a little reconnaissance mission. Or maybe Momo is using me as a bait to lure them out. But I get to have the first look. Barbed wire is cleared from the main gate. They are expecting us, they are facilitating us. I also expect a welcoming party. From the inside, the Hangar looks like an abandoned shopping mall. Big shuttered gates. Boarded-up offices. Half an aeroplane hanging from the ceiling. Murmurs, echoes of murmurs, people in shadows, shadows within shadows. People inside are no better than file-pushers of yore. Look at them now; their feet are not inverted. Sniff, they don't smell like the insides of the coffins. I should know, I have smelled all sorts from inside and outside. They smell like nothing. They have been left behind. They were serving their God and country and then they were suddenly forgotten. They are dead but they don't know it. Because nobody has bothered to put them in flag-draped coffins, fly them home, march them through the streets, nobody has given them state funerals, celebrated their sacrifices, named little country roads after them. They have just been forgotten.

If they were not heathens, they would be called martyrs. They need to keep the war going even when it has ended.

They have good taste in food though. Can you remember when was the last time you tasted a good, authentic pancake? Me neither. They have got mountains of pancakes and pools of maple syrup. I am not complaining. They are setting up positions around a buffet for the dead and I set up a position under a table with the maple syrup. I am not a combatant. I signed on to the mission after I was promised a strictly non-combatant role. I have always been a logistics guy anyway. I'll stay here near this mountain of pancakes and try to figure out who needs what. In this fog of war sometimes people don't know what they want.

The first one to walk in is Ellie. Clever of Momo to send in one of their own first but perhaps way too clever. He's probably got nothing to offer us.

That man is not only a thief and an absconder, he lacks any kind of self-confidence or conviction. Lady Flowerbody thinks he needs therapy and a pep talk. No. He needs a life but he can't get one now. I can see through him. His nametag has turned neon. One used to wonder what happens to people when they die. So this is what happens, they eat pancakes. I wouldn't be complaining.

They have all got their nametags in neon. They are worse than ghosts. They are fashionable ghosts.

These are lost souls looking for a way back into life, looking for that golden sunshine back home. They want their military ranks back, they want to collect their gratuity cheques, they want to go home and start stalking their girl-friends who they hope are already unhappy with their new lovers and are ready to take them back. They had trained themselves to be brave, they were ready to lay down their lives for their God and country but they didn't know that bravery comes with high noise levels and then an abrupt silence that lasts forever. You can't be brave when you are dead. And then promptly forgotten.

It's the eternal human folly, hankering after things that are lost. Mutts don't want their youth back, we don't go through life thinking about that bone that we misplaced somewhere.

Let's not underestimate them though. Lest we forget, they don't know they are dead.

Chapter 37

Mother Dear

I am still not sure about him, my man, the man sitting behind me in the jeep, the man pretending to be not here. He wasn't like this, not this devious, not so slippery, not like the last sliver of soap in your hand. He begged for my hand on a moonlit night; he was on his knees after waking me up by throwing pebbles at my window. I thought he wanted to sleep with me. I let him in. I didn't think there was anything wrong with a boy wanting to sleep with me. I could always say no, but it was good to hear.

'Do you want to sleep with me?' I asked him, but he stood and stared.

'I want to have babies with you,' he said, 'I want to marry you and then I want us to live in our own house.'

'But you are the son of the Chief, you can marry anyone you want.' Everybody knew that the Chief used to beat up his children with a whip if they played with other children and sometimes he beat up other children if they were foolish enough to accept his children's offer to play with them.

He said that he had run away from the house because he was whipped after refusing to join a hunt. Why wouldn't a man join a hunt? I should have seen the beginning of that slippery slope right then. He had father issues. Who doesn't? But if your father is a cruel idiot must you become one too? These are the conversations he was having with his father: 'If you don't hunt, what are we going to eat? That deer is not going to slaughter itself and turn into kebabs.'

'I told him we'll eat grass,' he told me as he tried to hold my hand. I let him, but I should have guessed right there that he took pride in his idiocy, his passive stubbornness.

'What'll the deer eat then? There is never enough grass for them. You might be the runaway son of a chief, but you are not a real prince who can refuse to eat anything he doesn't want to.'

'We'll go and live in the desert, away from my father's house so that we can enjoy our freedoms.'

'I would very much like to enjoy my freedoms but who is going to pay for these freedoms? Who will feed us?'

'I'll join USAID,' he said. 'My English is very good.'

'What is USAID? What is English?'

He didn't bother answering but I knew that my own father was right; the war was coming. And what comes after war is USAID. So we lived on rations of tinned beef and complaints about logistical delays. The man who could have been a small-time prince became a petty bureaucrat. My family gave me their blessing but now they wouldn't even send me salt. They have probably run out of it too.

CHAPTER 38

Momo

My land. My people. And here they are refusing to go away. What's their excuse to be here? Why can't they just give us our man and take theirs? What do they need that sky-high roof for? Look at those massive beams. They built this place as if it's going to last forever. They think they are going to last forever. I want to tell them *you got killed, now you are gonna stay killed. It doesn't matter whether you died bravely or left this world shitting in your pants. White or brown, dead is dead.* I take a peek inside the Hangar to assess the situation.

They are hanging out in the Hangar as if they were invited for a Sunday barbeque. Slogans like NO FEAR are scrawled in electric bolts all over the walls. It doesn't seem like they intend to put up a fight. They are not afraid of dying. They are not looking for cover. They are not interested in giving each other cover. They seek death. They are already dead but they want to be released. They want to be obliterated. I am gonna give them their heart's desire. For now they are acting as if they are in a circus and are perched over tanks, hanging from the barrel of a rusting artillery piece, one of them brandishing not one but two M16s and a much later model than the one I have. Some of them are huddled around a buffet table contemplating their food. Ellie's there, all back-slaps and high fives: 'You are welcome but who allowed these other people in? It's authorized personnel only.'

Ellie is the authorized personnel. I am gonna show them who is the authority around here.

When you are fighting ghosts, wouldn't it help to have one on your side? But this is not how life works. You protect an asset, you cultivate an ally and when the time comes to put them to use they cross over to the other side. How do I know if my own Bro Ali is with me or with them? We have heard about birds who refuse to fly away even when the cage door is left open.

No ghost is gonna care about their blood relations.

It doesn't bother me that the deserter has turned out to be a ghost. What really matters is that he is not on my side. I'm not gonna lie to you, this is a setback.

My land, my people and now they are telling me I am not an authorized personnel on my own land. I am here though, so let's see what they are gonna do about it. I am gonna take Bro Ali home but before that they are all gonna fry.

Chapter 39

Ellie

Colonel Slatter has thrown himself a farewell party. We must look like an all-you-can-eat buffet to them. I can see them now. Friends turned enemies. Comrades-in-arms who want to turn their guns on you. Ex-commanding officers wanting to show you who's the boss. I never had much appetite for these fist fights but here nobody's asking for my permission. We are in it so we are in it. Do or die, why ask why when the only answer you are going to get is a punch in the gut or teeth in your jugular? How do I know? We'll have to wait and see.

They are all waiting for some news, waiting to be told it's over. Wait some more. See some more. Then die.

You wouldn't have that problem if you were already dead. Calm down, learn to talk. You can't threaten them. You can't motivate them. Maybe you can plead with them? Maybe they are worried about posterity. They are probably thinking we were good guys fighting good wars and now we are dead guys. There has to be something beyond this.

Maybe I can plead with Colonel Slatter? He still looks the same, precise movements, no syntax. *Sir, I am so glad we found you. We have been looking for you for five months*, I want to say something reassuring, something suitably banal.

I hear ghosts take language seriously. No cuss words. There was a time when if Slatter said fuck your fucking mother, your mother stayed fucked. But Slatter has cleaned up his act. He hasn't grown wings but Slatter is polite as an angel. Angels are polite because they have nothing to lose.

'Ellie,' he shouts. He looks more normal than I had ever seen him when he was alive, his head shiny and freshly shaved. Maybe people become themselves after they die. Maybe that's what we mean when we tell people to 'be yourself'. 'Ellie boy, did you think war was a picnic?' Then he tears off a pancake and starts to chew slowly. 'But this is.' He grunts. I move towards him. To shake hands. They used to say drink like Slatter and one day you may fly like Slatter. Nobody said anything about living like Slatter or dying like Slatter.

When you were in trouble nobody ever said go talk to Slatter. Now I have got no choice but to go talk to Slatter. *There is the small matter of this boy that you hired, his family is here to see him, maybe you should just let him go, eh Slatter?*

He looks at me and waves a gun towards me: 'You too, Ellie, you too.'

CHAPTER 40

Momo

In the end it comes down to this: a man and his sweet 16. All ready to go. There is chaos in here, as if we have gate-crashed a bachelor party. It looks like the kind of place where runaway car thieves stop to buy Coke and burgers and then, seeing the place is run by an old woman, decide to rob it. And then get stoned at the scene of the crime.

Something odd though, some of them are stuck to the roof, others are leaning against the walls. A bald man with a shiny head runs around the Hangar wielding a machete. He seems to be the main troublemaker, others are minding their own business. A crazy white man is better than a crazy white man who says *I used to be crazy but now I am fine*. I am gonna start the fight with him. I am gonna blow some neat holes through his bald head. He seems like the head of this rogue unit; I am gonna chop the head off this monster. My sweet 16 has a gun-sight with a cross hair that reduces the risk of error, but even a blind man could take out a target at this distance – specially when the target is a head so big, so shiny and so repulsive. And Ellie is with him, whispering into his ear, exchanging high fives, seems like a proper reunion, good old-fashioned white-on-white action.

We are here for a purpose. The enemy is pretending as if we are not here to collect our debts, as if we are here for leftover rations.

I believe in battle as a soccer game. It's not always the sharpest shooter who wins, it's the one who sees a gap and can find the right angle. The game is won by people who know how to use their elbows.

Their leader is in my cross hair now. If only Mother Dear would move out of the way. She is blocking my sight and all I can see is a swirl of red hair.

I am not even thinking about where Father Dear is. He is probably lurking at the back. That'll be his real legacy. Lurker at the back. Waiting for the battle to be decided before choosing a side. This time he might be too late.

CHAPTER 41

Mother Dear

I know my Ali is here. I can smell him. He still smells of my milk. And my son is not a ghost. I am looking at these ghosts and my heart melts, because they all look like lost sons. They are probably homesick too; knowing that you are never going to go back doesn't really help you get over your homesickness. My Ali could cure homesickness, a disease worse than love. They are still reluctant to meet their maker. Life barely began, how can life be over so soon in a place so far away? But they can't go home, even when their mother has left the door open for them. No son, you are dead. You are in her dream. They look like the kind of people who are not sure they are done with this world yet. But the world is done with them. There is no point in lingering.

I think I can cure them of their homesickness. I have got a dagger carved out of a pink slab of salt. The blood doesn't stick to it.

I think they are hiding him. I think they need our help. I think we can get out of here with my boy without shedding some poor mother's son's blood. I wonder if these ghosts have blood. I realize that Momo is raring for a fight, I fear he's going to mess it up. We are not here for revenge. We are not here to save our national honour, we are not here to save our national anything. They are soldiers. OK, they are ghosts but they are still wearing their tattered uniforms and medals, their families are still getting pensions. I'll hold on to my dagger but I'll talk first. There can be no victory if I don't take my firstborn home. My son's safety is my victory. That's my entire war plan. That's my ideology. That's my tactics. That's my strategy.

You have to cover all bases so I have brought my rosary with me. My left hand praising God, my right wielding a dagger, just in case.

I decide to stand between Momo and them. This is the only way to ensure order and avoid unwanted casualties. No, I am not saying shoot me first, I am not saying kill me before you harm my son. God knows there are enough of these man-martyrs, always ready to embrace death with open arms. I am bringing some home economics and common truths to this arena.

They seem to have a lot of food here. I hope they have been feeding my boy properly.

Chapter 42

Mutt

People looking for human qualities in me and my clan are actually giving themselves a backhanded compliment. Look at this mongrel, so intelligent, so compassionate, so human; can jump through fire hoops, can do basic arithmetic, can give you a fairly objective overview of history and can smell the whiff of garlic on a bone from a mile away even when half asleep. What a marvellous creature. A bit like us really.

They don't realize anthropomorphism can work the other way round too. You want to see the qualities of a Mutt in a man? The urge to sniff other people's privates, to pick food from other people's plates, never to think of the universe or how it came into existence and where it's headed, or ask where all the rivers of one's childhood went, but always wondering what's for lunch and can I take this ball and run to the end of the earth. Mutt will stare deep into your soul and smell all the base canine urges.

Momo is sad and scared, and when a man is sad and scared he first takes it out on his own mother, and Momo is irritated with his Mother Dear.

Momo is irritated by her rosary. He thinks it's a godless world and sometimes he gets into debates about God this and God that. I disapprove of these debates about God;

Momo says silly things like *God is dead*, and *who gave birth to God in the first place? And if God is everywhere then why isn't he here? What does he eat? What does he drink? What kind of car does he drive? Is he allowed to go anywhere? Does he also live in a camp that he is allowed to leave but he doesn't because he knows this is home? Is he needed anywhere else in the world? Is he too busy starving his own children on the other side of the planet?*

I try to tell him there's no point in trying to speculate about the moods of your maker. There's no way of telling if we are a manifestation of His despair or if we are His joyous dance or His impossible itch? Little does Momo know that there is no point looking for God in a loaded gun or on the tip of Mother Dear's dagger. No point looking for God in her red flaming hair. God is not done with us yet, and He created this world but He didn't promise us discounts on tinned beef and fresh vegetables – or the safety of our siblings – and there is no point in looking for Him in your foreskin or the design of the womb, or in the tiny arms of a baby when he hangs around your neck.

Look around. He is here. Don't look too hard. He is busy elsewhere.

CHAPTER 43

Momo

These people are not paying us any attention. They are whirling around the Hangar like bad ideas in my head. We need clarity. We need to cover our flanks, I need to marshal my troops. And now Mother Dear steps forward.

Mother Dear is here with her red hair and her pink stone dagger in one hand and now she has raised her other hand and what has she got? The blasted rosary.

'Not the rosary, Mother Dear, not the rosary please,' I say. 'I am sure your rosary has its uses but this is not the place. Do you remember when I was young I used to work that rosary like a crazed-out rosary monster? Look where it has got us.'

We are not gonna sort this mess out with a million-beaded rosary. But she insists on carrying her old-fashioned one with ninety-nine beads, one bead for God's every name. Cheap, plastic beads on a nylon string are not going to win us any victories. What does she recite on it? God this and God that, God up and God down, God above our heads and God under our beds, God in lovers' hearts and God in our enemy's plans, God living and God dying, God writing cooking recipes and God going on a fast, the provider and the taker, God writing travel books and God breeding the fastest horses, God the creator of Mutt and God the creator of his smelly breath, God on long interglacial journeys and God staying home at the speed of light, the most merciful, the most ruthless executioner, God who is gonna free us all, and God with his biggest furnace, the manufacturer of heaviest chains, and God the enabler and the inventor of polio, God who breathes fire and converts our hearts into arctic wastelands, the rosary keeps moving, moving, moving, oh God, the giver of multiple orgasms, and God prolonger of agonies of death, God the provider of reason and the master of sorcery, God the timekeeper, capable of infinities.

She keeps dropping the beads, there are only ninety-nine beads, but she keeps going as if it is her only response to the monster aimed at us, the gun that is gonna fire 330 bullets per minute and bring to an end her silent cries of *oh-god, oh-god, oh-god, help us, help us.*

CHAPTER 44

Mother Dear

Why does Momo think he has to do everything? That he knows everything. Look at what he has brought with him. One look at them and my heart sinks. Can they get my boy back? Between them, they probably can't even make a meal for themselves but they think they can get in a jeep with their guns and their petitions, enter the Hangar and bring my boy back.

Look at the people Momo has got together.

A petty bureaucrat who sold his own son in the hope of job stability. A white soldier who doesn't even know what he is doing here. Momo himself, a teenager who still wets his bed. And that horny little Mutt who humps anything he can hump. He wants to be my son too. Would you like to be rescued by a team as illustrious as this? They need a leader of course. They need a firm hand. They need someone with a cool head.

Do you know how to keep your head cool?

Henna. Put some henna on your head. It will make you a redhead for a few days. I have never understood why anyone would want to be a redhead. I can give up on the looks but I can't give up on my son. So henna in my hair to keep a cool head and a rosary in my hand to keep my heartbeat steady. And with all of God's names on my lips.

CHAPTER 45

Ellie

You can't blame all of Central Command's follies on one man. But you can see all those follies in one man. Say hi to Colonel Slatter, the man who missed the miracle.

Zero-zero ejection seats are the miracle cure in long-distance wars. Here's the guarantee: activate your Martin-Baker zero-zero ejection seat and you'll be fine. Some people do have second thoughts, especially if they are forced to eject over an area where they have just deposited a few tons of the world's finest explosives. But when you got to, you got to. Whatever your misfortune here's the thing: all you get is – and only if you're an unlucky bastard or have bad posture, or just a well-hidden panicky personality – a sprained ankle or a hurt back. But mind your posture and you are as safe as a camel's cunt. Would you rather save your ankles, your back? Do you love your machine so much that you'll sacrifice your life for it? There really wouldn't be any point in that. They wouldn't even be able to show your proud, patriotic face to your beloved family because they know your beloved family wouldn't want to see your face with your eyes melted out of their sockets. These five-hundred-pound bombs don't just go away quietly. They are designed to cause a little inferno. Your fireproof jacket and that twenty-thousand-dollar helmet won't stop you from turning into a lump of twisted coal. Not the kind of coal that lights up your campfires. It would turn you into a piece of coal without any of the positive attributes of coal.

But all that can be avoided if you deploy your Martin-Baker in time. This little beauty will scoop you up like a mother scoops up a baby in his sky-blue sleeping suit. You could be in your sandals and pyjamas and it will still fire you up and bring you down gently. Better to have your boots on because you don't want to break your ankle. If your choice is between getting killed or getting a hairline ankle fracture, you wouldn't think twice. You don't need to go on a survival course to figure out that a cast around your broken ankle is slightly better than your ass in a sealed coffin.

You'd be right to ask how someone like Colonel Slatter, who flew as if there was no gravity and always came home wanting to take off again immediately, made such a basic mistake. Slatter, who dispatched people to the farthest corners of the earth, lost his own way in his own cockpit. *Nature*, he used to say, *and guts, not these blinking screens. The horizon*, he would say, *out there, not on your laser gyros. Turn, pull, bang* – here he would cup his balls – *not on the bloody bang-o-meter; here, feel my bang-o-meter. How can I believe in Oneness when I have a pair?*

And during his self-chosen mission to take out the remotest, the last remaining scum on the earth, this sad-ass bunch, he went on a night mission and he pulled and pulled as if trying to pierce through the mother-ship clouds that had darkened the sky over the desert and then he realized that he was actually pulling towards the desert and not towards the sky. Inverted flight can cause that kind of confusion but what kind of zoomie can't tell between the earth and the sky? Say hullo to Colonel Slatter. He was not an idiot, he tried to eject and it wouldn't eject because the zero-zero ejection seat wants you to be cruising straight, it wants to take you up before it can bring you down, but if you are headed into the ground it tells you to straighten up fast so that it can save your ass.

When they found Colonel Slatter, he was strapped to his ejection seat, burnt to cinders. Mission Barbeque Tonight, is how that night is remembered now.

And here he is now, jolly as fuck, only grumbling about the intruders, telling me to join the party.

Chapter 46

Lady Flowerbody

There is one woman on their side in the Hangar and it has to be her, right? I knew Cath wasn't a cover story, not a shimmer in the desert of his mind. Not an imaginary wife as Momo kept insisting. But someone more substantial, someone who lived and died. Someone mildly famous. I can tell they have slept together. They probably tried to make babies together and then gave up. Sure they had their issues, but why bring her here? He showed me a paper clipping, an old picture of a sickly young girl, more famous in death than in life. Now she has followed him all the way here.

We are no match for this first-world army of ghosts with the finest armoury any military unit can lay its hands on. We don't know what other powers they might have. They are already hovering in the air, floating. And they are motivated. They don't even have to fight to the finish as they are already finished. Time is on their side.

I think we should go back while we can. I can understand a mother's feelings. I don't have to go through breastfeeding, labour, pregnancy and unprotected sex to know how mothers feel. There is a lot of empirical data to tell us about their feelings, there is a lot of literature and poetry and camel-loads of folklore to tell us how mothers feel at any given time. She wants her son back, who wouldn't? But this is a horror show. Will you get all your family killed to save your son? This is tribal thinking; she is a prisoner of her own feudal traditions. She is not evolved enough. This kind of thinking leads to radicalization of young minds. Throw everything you have got at your perceived enemy. Destroy yourself before it destroys you. You become the enemy. In the process of trying to eliminate the other you become the other.

Just because I don't have a child doesn't mean that I am heartless. I understand her dilemma. She has lost a son and she is willing to sacrifice her other son to get him back. I can understand all of that but does she have to dye her hair red? Not only does she look like a witch, she is drawing attention to herself. You go into a battle in camouflage. You try to blend in with your environment. I am wearing grey from head to toe. This woman is going to get us killed. Now there she is standing in front of Momo's big gun. Blocking his sight. Trying to sabotage her own mission. She might be a grieving mother, and she needs proper counselling, but what she needs right now is a slap and I wish I could give it to her.

And I am going to tell these ghosts where to go. I have heard they listen to reason. I should have known that I am the only reasonable person in the Hangar, the others are ghosts or are trying to become one. Doctor is the only man of science here. And he has got a bike and he has got fuel. I should ask him for a lift and ride out of here as soon as I can.

CHAPTER 47

Ellie

Colonel Slatter seems tired. He has the same bravado, his preferred mode of communication still more hand gestures than verbs, but he seems weary of talking to a world that doesn't understand him anymore.

'Remember my parties,' he says, as I sidle up to him. 'Open-door policy. All welcome. Remember when we got those Kandaharis to dance with us. Gave them our guns. And they fired in the air, it's their culture, they fire in the air when they celebrate a birth or a wedding, it's part of their culture. Remember, they sang us a song. And they were our prisoners. And they danced. Fun times. We danced with our prisoners.' Colonel Slatter stares into my eyes as if he wants me to be the official witness to a life well lived.

I have no recollection of that particular party. Sure, I remember being at a party but it was in our bachelors' quarters, not in Kandahar. I do remember I have never set foot in Kandahar; flown over it, sure, who hasn't? 'Yes, good times,' I say.

Slatter grunts. 'Did you have to invite this riff-raff? Gone native, eh? Like those flat breads and even flatter brown bums,' he says. 'Forgotten your own?'

'They are here for the boy,' I say. 'I didn't bring them. They brought me. You have their boy. They want their boy. Give them their boy.'

'Oh that boy was here somewhere. Who do you think brought me down? Who do you think brought you here? That little rascal who fiddled with our comms. The boy has got talent, he is a bit like us. Now he is going to help us out of here. We're teaching him to fly. Stubborn little thing. Says he'd rather eat sand than learn to fly. No aptitude, but we've got to teach him. We've got to pull this shithole out of the Stone Age. We can't be stuck here forever, we need to get out. He wants to get out of here too. We are on the same page, you see.' I study his mouth. The dead don't smile.

'Sir, that's not funny at all,' I say.

'Damn straight, do I look like a joker to you?' he says. 'That boy is going to learn to fly and lead us out of here. Otherwise we're kind of stuck, can't you see? You know the routine or have you forgotten? Think of the children. Always think of the children. They really are our future.'

'Why here?' I ask. 'Why now?'

'Central Command keep up the pretence that we are still around, still on duty, still serving God and country. So these hubs are kept alive, with rotations, rations, pending leaves, a perfect facade. They do it in the hope that we will fade away. The Staff and Command disappears, then the planes disappear. They want to have a cut-price war. They can't be bothered to look for us, let alone take us home. Now we are just slashed budgets. They hope that we'll disappear too. Do you know how love disappears? We slowly erase love from our hearts – don't try too hard because then it'll not dissipate fast enough – it starts with a tiny spot and then it spreads like forgetfulness. Mind you, it's their philosophy not mine. Don't mention the names.'

Colonel Slatter went on a mission before I did. He doesn't know he was found strapped to his seat, burnt to cinders. I am alive, I know it because I have got a headache. He is dead but he doesn't know it. Maybe I can still reason with him.

'Things are still better back home,' I say. 'What do you need that boy for? Let him go. Then we can all go back home.'

'Once you're here, you can't go anywhere.'

Maybe Slatter does know that he is a little bit dead.

'Things have changed now,' I say. 'PTSD counselling, generation-five drugs. Scientific breakthroughs. Retraining. Uni programmes. With all your experience you could probably get a sociology degree.'

Colonel Slatter has nothing but contempt for me. 'Are you here for a hostage exchange? We are no kidnappers. That boy is here of his own accord. Signed a contract. Ask him. Free will. *We* are here because of him. We are giving him a job. We are training him. What else was he going to do in this shithole? He is too sensible to screw sheep and sell bootleg sugar. We are giving him a chance at a better life.'

Colonel Slatter plans to give the boy a better life by taking his life. Where have I heard this before?

'He is only a boy.'

'We were boys once, weren't we? He refuses to fly. Says it makes him airsick. But he'll have to fly, to guide us out of this hellhole and then go home. End of contract. Nobody is going to breach their contract under my command.'

The colour of my own skin is not going to save me. They're not going to spare me. I need to stick by the natives then. There should be an army of red-haired women with daggers and rosaries coming to my rescue. But I know there is only one. And I am not her priority.

I catch a glimpse of Cath, her head sticking out of an armoured car's open latch. What is she doing trying to drive an armoured car? It doesn't surprise me that she is here. I hope she at least knows she's dead?

Nobody seems to have got the memo around here.

CHAPTER 48

Mutt

By the time I have managed to paw my way to the first pile of pancakes, it seems better sense is going to prevail, that peace and goodwill is going to break out like a plague. Someone fires a single shot suddenly, and then it's so silent I can hear myself breathing, panting to be precise, my heart churning. Sometimes excesses are committed in battles, I think I have eaten more pancakes than a Mutt of my stature should have.

Ghosts are trying to scare us away with their firepower. They don't want to talk to us. I always prefer talking. I have spent long nights just talking, warning people not to sleep under those blue plastic roofs. I can hear another sound. There is a little thud over the roof of the Hangar. Then another, then another. The roof is probably made of something sturdy but it sounds like heavy raindrops falling on a tin roof. Something is falling on the roof and we don't know what it is. And they don't care what it is but it's my job as the reconnaissance man – let's say reconnaissance person – to anticipate what is coming. It's a stampede on the roof now. Rainfall gives way to footfalls. Tender at first but it's a stampede now, a playful stampede. Like a bunch of elephants teaching their elephant babies how to do a slow dance.

And down here now they are still busy shouting at people to get out of the way. Mother Dear is standing in the middle, her red hair on fire, she is wielding her dagger. Now I can't decide who is more dangerous here, whatever is on the roof trying to bring it down, or this woman with her sparkly dagger, her red hair flying, her eyes searching for Bro Ali.

And now Lady Flowerbody steps up, she thinks this is the right time to lecture us about relationships. Is anybody asking why we came here in the first place? Where is Bro Ali? They can show off their guns or negotiate all they want, I am going to go and look for him. There are back doors and although all I can smell are stone walls and long, solitary nights, I must go figure it out. Here's what distinguishes us from the human race: when a man has a full stomach he thinks of siestas and sexual activities; when this Mutt has eaten properly, this Mutt goes to work.

CHAPTER 49

Cath

Always the same question. *How are you feeling? Why are you feeling like this? Cath?* I can feel whatever the fuck I am feeling, and why are you even bothering to ask if you are not going to do anything about my feelings? He skulked around as if he had nothing to do with the way I was feeling. And now here he is, back-slapping his mates. They fly toys that cost more than three hundred million dollars apiece and then come home and get headaches. *Think of the children*, they say, *think of all the starving, dying children in the world*, and thinking of the children they go and drop tons of bombs on some godforsaken place and then come home and need some 'me time'. They start a war and after a few millions have died then suddenly remember the young ones. *Think of the children*, they say. All the wars in the world are an afterthought about dead children. No time to think about babies. And when there is a baby on the way, don't call it a baby, because you never know. It'll make you feel worse if something happens. That was the closest he came to feeling my pain. That was the last thing I remember. So I tried not to remember it as a baby, and when it started bleeding, it didn't stop. And he was half a world away, rearranging the geography of some poor country. I try to remember nicer things like the first time we met.

It's quite obvious that he is having fun now. If I was him I wouldn't want to go home either.

This is just like the first time we met.

We met at a party for which the invite said rooftop barbeque. Much later, after Ellie had already bought the ring, I found out that the barbeque bit was an inside joke, military speak for saying we are just checking out the meat on offer. I genuinely believed that it was no big deal if people invited you for dinner and then forgot to give you food. Who goes to these things for food anyway? A party at the rooftop of the Bachelor Officers' Quarters' anterooms is not anybody's idea of a gourmet night. You have to get sloshed and show your support for the boys.

I happened to be there on my Safe Cats commercial shoot and a kindly camera assistant had invited me and now he was sitting in a portly sergeant's lap, whispering in his ear and giggling.

The guy with the bald, shiny head was there, he was pretending to be a priest. He was obviously a senior officer. He was dressed in a maroon dressing gown with a matching beret, and insisted on baptizing everyone. In the dim fairy lights the anterooms looked like a series of interconnected caves. He kept talking very knowledgeably about the divine sanction of man's love for men, especially man's love for younger men. I decided to get baptized because there was a queue. It seemed like the polite thing to do. The priest baptized me with a few drops of absinthe from a plastic bottle. He shouted something in Latin, then poured a few drops of the green liquid into my reluctant mouth. A mock priest at a mock barbeque with real absinthe. My lips stung, my stomach rushed to my mouth, I constricted my throat and managed to keep it down. I did think I was doing it for the country.

After he had baptized everyone, he blessed the barracks then poured the contents of his absinthe bottle into a large plastic bowl full of rum punch. It floated on the surface like a little oil pool. I tried to have a drink from it but felt a wave of nausea churning in my throat. I knew there was always a point when you regretted coming to a party but after you'd stayed past that point you knew it would be OK. I went out onto the wrought-iron balcony and sat on the ledge. I could hear the babble of army brats who, led by the priest, were all chanting something in Latin. It might have been Arabic for all I knew but it did sound like Latin. It was something ancient that people would sing at a small church without knowing the meaning of what they were singing. I felt an ancient loneliness and almost wished, although under any other circumstances I dreaded it, that someone would recognize me as the famous little girl who had died and come back to life. A strange claim to have for my minor fame.

When I was seven years old I got meningitis and died. It wasn't a mistake, all the graphs on the screens surrounding me had gone flat, the doctors had said their regrets and then the machines had started pulsating again and I had come back to life. I was front-page news before I even knew what a newspaper was. Sometimes I felt special, mostly I just felt self-pity. This came over me especially strongly in crowded rooms, in train stations, and in parties like this, where I felt immense loneliness and always wanted to be back home; sometimes the feeling was so intense that I couldn't understand the point of being back from the dead. I looked at the flushed faces around me, a couple kissing tentatively, the officer priest was raising his paper cup again and again and shouting *viva Kandahar, viva Kandahar* and then just *viva viva* as if he was banging his head to some inner music and butting it against some inner wall. I wondered whether Kandahar was a girlfriend who had ditched him or maybe it was a piece of war machinery that he had once been in love with.

I perched on the ledge and looked down and saw a lanky man holding the leashes of five dogs of varying sizes, almost being dragged by them. I smiled. I wasn't sure if it was the absinthe or the fact that all five dogs were jostling for a position around the same pole. I wondered if anyone would notice if I slipped down off the ledge. One of the five dogs looked up from the lamp post and barked at me. I almost barked back, and then felt a hand on my shoulder. I kept looking at the dog instead of looking back at the person whose hand was pressing into my shoulder now. I wanted this moment to last, the hand on my shoulder seemed natural enough, but what if I looked up and saw another soldier with a story of Kandahar? I would definitely puke. I glanced at the dog, which was humping its lanky owner's leg, then I threw my head back, laughing, and looked at him. He wore a T-shirt that said TRIBALS FOR TRIBECA. I sighed.

He bent over to hear, thinking I was whispering something to him. Something metallic grazed my ear. Two metallic discs hanging from a silver chain became entangled with my earrings. I looked up again, throwing my head back; his Adam's apple was gulping air as if he had trouble breathing. I never understood men who wore jewellery. Not that I understood men who had tattoos, moustaches, PhDs in anthropology or those who smoked in bed. I had never known a man in uniform before. How different could it be from your average bank teller or the cab service controller?

Maybe they had real nightmares. I disentangled the metal plates from my earrings and read the inscription. *Ellie*, it said.

What kind of man goes around wearing his own name around his neck? Either a pompous ass, or a brand victim or someone in imminent danger of forgetting their name. Or maybe it wasn't his name at all, maybe it was his wife's name or his mother's. But what kind of man goes around with his mother's name around his neck? I let go of the twin metal plates.

'I died once.' I said it as if telling him a small detail about my small town, like saying that I went to Buffalo Tech, my father left when I was four or my mother died of lung cancer.

'I've seen you in those car insurance ads,' he said.

'Yes, I get that kind of work all the time because I died once and then came back to life. I'm supposed to be the softer face of death.'

'I make a living doing that, I die every day.'

I finally turned around. And looked up at him and found him staring down my neck.

'You're a soldier. You are all soldiers,' I said with a smile, as if I had just been introduced to a room full of friendly hyenas.

'Can I call you Cath?' he said.

'My full name is Catherine Scott Duval,' I said. 'But if you take me out of here, for a little walk maybe, you can call me what you like.'

'I'm a pilot, operational,' he said. 'We give our planes pet names. It's the same thing but slightly different.'

'What's your plane called?' I asked.

'Strike Eagle,' he said. 'SE2.'

I should have known. He liked his weapon more than his wife. He planned, he scammed. It was always easier to bomb some far-off place than stay home and unload the dishwasher.

But all that belongs in another life. It doesn't matter now. If you don't come home, baby, I'll come to you. Now stop fighting and let's go. We're done with this world.

Chapter 50

Lady Flowerbody

What people don't realize is that relationships are sometimes complicated, a bit like international donor-funded projects; you have to work on them because it's work, but you also have to work hard to keep your dignity. It doesn't matter whether you are in a relationship with a local or a foreigner, the basis should be simple; pay me my fees on time, honour my contract, respect my culture, stay out of my physical space unless I invite you in.

The same rules should apply here. You have to tell them to leave. *You have to leave*, I say. I say it politely. You have to say it politely. You can't be aggressive with ghosts. It's easy-peasy. They are not harmful per se, only if you annoy them. You can't be rude. But you have to be clear. I might be a local but I am on a foreign contract. We are equals. I have never worked with these people directly but I know the type. If you tell them to, they will leave. It's my experience that when you tell them to stop, they stop. There are laws, you know.

I don't believe in ghosts but here they are jumping from wall to wall, completely oblivious to local culture and traditions and absolutely no insight into the young Muslim mind.

I did try to make Ellie a man out of a ghost, but it turns out he is a ghost missing another ghost. Now that's an emotional complication I don't want in my life. Relationships can be complicated but you can't allow them to clutter your life. They probably deserve each other. When things get this complicated all you have to do is to say *leave*. You have to say it politely and firmly. *You have to leave*, I say politely and firmly.

Who the hell are you? shouts their leader with the shiny head, waving his gun at my head. *You have to be polite*, I tell him.

CHAPTER 51

Ellie

Mother Dear has her eyes on me. It doesn't look like she wants to rescue me. She's coming at me, I try to hide behind Cath, but I can see through her; she put up with me in life, now she's putting up with me in death. Will there be a reunion, will she finally take me in her arms and forgive me?

Slatter's voice comes over the megaphone. 'We will not shoot unless we are shot at. We respect all women, all children and animals too.'

Suddenly he wants to negotiate. Just like that. People who want to negotiate are always the ones who haven't got anything to offer. 'If you are here to fight, fight. If you are here to take your little boy back, then come and get him.'

CHAPTER 52

Mother Dear

He'll want to negotiate. My man attended a workshop once about hostage negotiation and since then, faced with every situation in life, he starts by saying: *We have two options.* He insists on saying it when he doesn't have even one option. Look at our options: That absconder Ellie who has been eating my food; can you trust a deserter? Somebody who deserts his own motherland, he'll probably desert you for his next meal. Look at him, hiding behind his woman. That Mutt always follows the smell of the bone. Momo is the only brave one in this family. And he has got a gun and he can drive.

I am a bad mother. All the things that mothers fear about their teenaged sons are the things I am finding reassuring. My boy with a gun and a jeep. I have to be cool as ice, like a mother who is on a mission to rescue her first son without losing her second.

Chapter 53

Momo

There he is now, their shiny-headed leader, bouncing off the walls.

He is gonna descend like a bat and I am gonna smash him like a bat should be smashed. He has his arms drawn to the sides, trying to fly like only a dead pilot can, the fucker thinks he can really fly. He is turning now. He has got a glow in his eyes. He is hovering above the floor now. OK, he can hover. But hovering is not flying. That's like a peacock taking off for a fraction of a second.

I am trying to train my gun on him, I am gonna pop his eyes first. And when I pop his eyes, I'll make sure that they gonna stay popped. When I take aim and shoot, he is suddenly not in my sights. He is in my face, he is a whoosh in my ear. Oh, that stings. He just slapped me. *You are dead.* You can't slap Momo and live to tell the tale. What if you go and tell someone that you slapped Momo and he just stood there with his sweet 16 and didn't do nothing?

The spirit goes out of me. You come to fight the fuckers, you bring your troops and you bring your M16. And they slap you in the face. They slap you in the face while everyone is watching.

Chapter 54

Mother Dear

How dare he slap my son, how dare he? You can come here and you can build a Hangar and you can drop a bomb on my house and you can bring your aeroplanes and your dead girlfriends but you touch my son and you see what happens. Now he comes tumbling towards me and there is only one thing to do, plunge the dagger into his heart and plunge it again. You would expect a fountain of blood but the man with the shiny head disappears in a puff of red dust; a red bird comes fluttering out of the dust and flies towards the ceiling. There is already a swarm gathering near the ceiling. With the birds come long-forgotten memories; the boys' insomniac cries in their childhood, piping-hot bread tasted in Kandahar, groping in the back of a yellow bus, dreams of brown beauties dancing in the desert, fat dads cuddling their babies and jumping on trampolines, ball games in the afternoon drizzle.

What are people if not the sum total of their memories?

Instead of running away they are actually coming towards me, in a haphazard queue as if they are lining up at a shrine for a plate of rice and the blessings of a dead saint.

CHAPTER 55

Momo

Mother Dear is using that dagger like a crazy mass murderer, how does she even know where the human heart is? She is gonna be taking them out one by one. One thrust of her dagger and a puff of red dust, no screams, just a flutter of wings and yet another red bird is released into the world. She is the destroyer. She is the liberator. I know what I am gonna do. I am gonna turn her into a one-woman private army and offer her talents to third-world countries, we are gonna become the world's biggest protection racket. We can do coups in small countries, start rebellions in big nation states. We are gonna go global. But first things first. We are gonna find Bro Ali and get the hell out of here. Mutt should be leading the search, showing us the way, but there he is limping away, pretending to be an injured soldier.

CHAPTER 56

Mutt

Ghosts are forever, you can't shoot them with bullets. But does Momo listen? When he shoots their leader with the shiny head and misses, where does the bullet go? A stray bullet is still a bullet, a stray dog is still a dog. It's not the time to make speeches but I do want to say to my fellow countrymen: if you learn to control your libido, if you learn to stand in a queue and if you don't overeat, and don't start shooting at anything that moves, you might achieve something in life.

I know that reckless optimism is harmful for our intellectual health but there are moments when one's defences slip and one is swept up on a crest of triumphalism. Mother Dear was doing a fine job with her dagger but Momo had to do his Momo thing. I have spent half my life asking the question that I am asking now: Why would you do that Momo, why? But it's too late. Even a stray dog is a dog. Even a stray bullet is a bullet. It travels at the speed of 960 metres per second, it doesn't matter if it was intended for me or not, I am certain it didn't have my name on it; it doesn't quite go through my heart but, as Doctor would say, it lodges itself in my chest – as if my chest was a rundown guest house and the 9-mm bullet a weary out-of-towner. In a more just world it could have hit my shoulder, or taken off my useless hind leg. But it's destined to lodge in my chest, three-quarters of an inch away from my heart. God will judge us sinners on our intentions and not our actions and I am sure He'll not judge Momo harshly. But I look at him and want to say: *you son of a bitch.*

Now there's a hush. No shooting, no ghosts butting their heads against the walls. Puffs of red dust everywhere. I think it's the perfect moment to make our exit, say our farewells. Momo thinks it's time for victory celebrations. He's seen Mother Dear dispatch the ghosts, and he launches into a victory speech. *My land, my people.* One day he'll make a fine businessman-politician and I wish I could be by his side. But he has to be careful with these guns. The man who only thinks in dollarized profit margins is suddenly talking about freedom and passion.

'I'm not going to negotiate with my brother's abductors. I am not going to negotiate with the bloodsuckers. I am gonna clean up this land, my land. I am gonna get rid of these ghosts forever. This Hangar will be bulldozed into the ground.'

And my bleeding ass will be buried here. A pair of pale feet scurry past me. Ellie has avoided Mother Dear's dagger as if he has still got one last thing to do. I give a faint yelp to warn Momo.

But Momo is crouching now, his eyes towards the ceiling from where a single drop of blood drips onto his face. He smears it across his forehead. He seems beyond fear.

CHAPTER 57

Momo

Something is gonna happen from above. There is a din on the roof like an army of drunk soldiers jumping up and down. Mother Dear has got rid of the ghosts on the ground but now there is another army on the roof.

Where is my backup? What was I thinking? I am gonna get everyone on my team killed. Why am I here in the first place? Look for him and get out – but what the hell is going on up there on the roof?

I look up in exasperation and there he is. Bro Ali is hanging from the ceiling like a human chandelier, and when I see him my first reaction is thank God, I found my bro. My second thought is what in God's name is he doing up there?

He is in a slightly delicate situation. They have got him tied up from three sides. His arms spread out, they have got him strung up in mid-air through a system of chains and pulleys. Even from seventy feet down below I can tell that he is alive. I hope Mother Dear doesn't look up. I don't want her to see her firstborn in this state of utter helplessness. My first instinct is to take a shot at the chains holding him; OK, maybe I am not such a crack shot, but my sweet 16 has got a telescope. I put my eye to it – I don't look at Bro Ali's face, that would make me lose my concentration – but before I can pull the trigger and set him free from the chains that hold him, my Jeep Cherokee gets airborne. There is a giant metal jaw that descends from above and is clutching it now, the metal jaw is connected to heavy chains, and as I look up, midway between the Hangar's ceiling and my sorry airborne ass is a giant crane and Ellie, sitting in it, is working its metal jaw from above and is pulling me towards him, up, up, up. The jeep is swaying dangerously in the air. Below me all I can see are clouds of red dust. I catch a glimpse of Mutt, hiding in the crane box, yelping madly at a pair of pale feet.

I can expect anything from my best mate, stupidity, greed, definitely greed, all kinds of perversion, but I never thought he had a treacherous bone in his body. After this is over I am gonna teach him a lesson. I am gonna teach him how to be loyal.

But now, suspended in mid-air, I am gonna be learning a lesson or two.

I am going up, up, up. I pass Ellie, he is grinning like a benevolent ghoul and when I pass by him he waves at me as if saying hullo.

On second thoughts he is probably saying goodbye.

Now I am level with Bro Ali's feet. His feet are chapped and dirty as if he hasn't worn shoes for a few months. But his feet are not tied. Now the jeep floats up slowly, so that I can see Bro Ali's face. Doesn't seem he has had much time for showers either. But he seems well fed though. And he seems to have no time for pleasantries. 'Why did you have to bring Mother Dear? And why has she coloured her hair?'

'It's just henna,' I say. 'It'll wear off in a few days.'

'And she has got her rosary,' he says. 'I thought you were going to steal it?'

'I did. She got another one.' Bro Ali is not listening to me. It seems he is talking to himself.

I want to reach out and touch him. He once showed me where the human heart is by taking my hand and putting it on the right side of his chest. I want to reach out and put my hand on his ribcage and feel if it still beats like a drum. 'See, this is the drumbeat that keeps us alive,' he had told me. 'A very subdued thud thud.'

Does he remember the rains; does he remember the first ever frog that we caught and tried to put on a leash and take for a walk; does he remember how I stood up to Mother Dear when he brought a half-dead baby Mutt home; does he remember our races, the races that he always let me win, and later when he couldn't beat me even if he wanted to?

I wonder if Mother Dear can see up from down below. Her two boys perched in mid-air, my palm on Bro Ali's heart. It's still. I wait and wait but there is no beat.

'They think I am one of them. I am not.'

This is what happens when you underestimate your enemy. Who are the people who say *I am not mad*? The mad ones. Who are the people who say *I swear I am not lying*? Those who are lying.

Am I looking at my brother or his ghost? I have had a useless upbringing. I know everything about safe sex, I can feel the pulse of the financial markets, but I know nothing about how to tell a ghost from a not-ghost.

'I am learning to fly, look at my wings. How am I doing? Just a little more time and then I am out of here,' he says.

'Why did they do this to you?' I ask.

'They think I brought down their planes. They think they had to shut down the Hangar. They think I am a traitor.'

'Did you bring down their planes? How did you do that? You can't bring down a plane with a transistor.' I am in awe of him.

'I am a man of peace.' He winks at me and makes a V sign. 'It was human error. I only fiddled with some frequencies. And they came tumbling down.' He flutters his arm like a bird coming down for a landing.

'Does Mother Dear know?' he asks.

I shake my head.

'Does she need to know?'

'She misses you. Every day.'

'She has you.'

He flutters his arm, like an exhausted bird who has flown for days and is about to reach his destination.

'Does it hurt?'

'One gets used to it.'

It seems we'll have to get used to it too.

'Will you do something for me?' he says.

This sounds like one of his trick questions. I nod and grab him around his waist, an awkward hug. He once taught me how to hug and judo-tackle in the same move.

'You have to close my eyes,' he says. I look into his eyes, they are wide open. I can see two Momos reflected in them. 'Do it gently,' he says.

I tighten my grip around his waist. He doesn't judo-tackle me.

On my way down, I notice that Ellie has disappeared and Mutt is sitting by himself in the crane box, whimpering, with one paw raised, as if saying, *be steady, you are carrying a very heavy weight.*

Chapter 58

Mother Dear

He is deserving of all praise, all poetry, because my sons are descending, coming to me. He is the One, the most merciful and the most full of venom, the brilliant author of our life stories and the abrupt ender of them, the creator of the last fish in the ocean, the maker of the largest net to catch it, the creator of coincidence and maker of certainties as big and as frozen as Mount Everest, the most charming of the snake charmers. The saviour. The saviour.

They are hugging each other like two lost brothers meeting, like two angels floating towards me. Ali looks at peace, Momo worried, pained, probably already thinking that when Ali comes home he'll become the younger brother again. My Momo was always a worrier.

He could have given me just one son. But He gave me two. He is the most generous of them all.

CHAPTER 59

Mutt

Sometimes a bullet lodged three-quarters of an inch away from your heart can give you all the clarity you need in life. I can see what is now and I can see what's beyond. Momo has finally seen the light. He has found Bro Ali and is carrying him down to his mother, but he has found him not in any state to go back. This is not the end. Only humans can believe that a boy with a home-made radio brought down their planes. This is their way of keeping the war going.

Right now, I have the urge to put my Momo on a retractable leash and take him for a very long, aimless walk, because he is unbearably sad. He is also scared like a child who has lost his mother's favourite heirloom and goes on pretending that he has put it somewhere safe. The scared child who has failed his exam, doesn't go home because he has lost his school bag as well and is now afraid of going home because he is now also late, and with every single minute that he delays his return he is digging himself into a deeper hole. Shadows are lengthening, birds are going wherever they go at night, and Momo can't move his feet. His heart is a dread multiplier in overdrive. He can't go to Mother Dear and tell her that there's no point looking, let's go back home. He can't even say that Bro Ali is in a better place or we should go home and wait because one day he'll return, like a boy who goes out into the world and returns home fourteen years later, having become a man, same but different. Momo doesn't talk like that. Momo doesn't think like that.

I am up here in the crane box, a heap of red dust at my feet; I can't wield a dagger but my teeth are fine. I am going down now, my stomach in my throat, my heart pumping in slow motion. The lights might be fading now but I know I am going home. I've had a long, eventful life, but only one image sticks: I am a puppy fighting an army of vicious cats and Bro Ali takes me from the street, nestles me in his lap, covers me with a little blanket and feeds me goat milk from a baby bottle. I can smell Momo's own childhood on that baby bottle. I hope we're going home.

CHAPTER 60

Mother Dear

Does anyone have any doubts about the fact that He is the most merciful, the joiner of separated ones? My sons come to me hugging each other. Mutt is walking behind them, a bit slow, a bit thoughtful; it's not like him to not jump up and down and take credit for everything. I take them into my arms. Momo squirms, he was never a big hugger. And I have to laugh at this, Ali is fast asleep. He used to go to sleep in the middle of studying his books, doing his homework, sometimes still chewing his pencil.

When he got his first notebook and first set of pencils with attached erasers he would draw for me, pictures of the places I had never seen. Mostly tall buildings with hundreds of windows and the silhouettes of people stuck in those windows. Sometimes he would draw me oceans, with ships bobbing on the waves and ship-sized fish chasing them. One night before going to bed he wanted to show me a new picture he had drawn for me. I looked and the page in his notebook was blank, all white. *But there is nothing here,* I said. *Look carefully,* he said. *This is the white country. It's made of snow. It's at the end of the earth. It's like a snow desert.* I pretended to look at the picture carefully and then

I asked him: *So what's this country called?* I looked up and he had gone to sleep, still chewing the eraser on his pencil.

He is tired now. I'll let him sleep. I'll sleep with him. What a stupid thing it was when I told him that you are a big boy now, go sleep in your own bed. Momo beta, don't worry, tomorrow it's your turn, tomorrow you can sleep with me. Right now, let me hold him, let me whisper all His names into his ear.

The most merciful, the saviour of humans and Mutts, the punisher of liars and storytellers, the shaper of beauty, the maker of order, the knower of all, the hearer of all, the bestower of honours, the forgiver and hider of faults, the nourisher, the accounter, the rewarder of thankfulness, the resurrector, the originator, the satisfier of all needs, the avenger, the forgiver, the creator of harm, the preventer of harm, the doer of good, the inheritor of all, the creator of all power, the gatherer, the expediter, the delayer, the first, the last.

ACKNOWLEDGEMENTS

Shukria to Juilen Columeau, Akbar Zaidi, Mirza Waheed and Dan Franklin for reading early drafts and giving wise counsel. Hasan Mujtaba and Arif Hasan for their inspirational lines. Alexandra Pringle and her all-star team at Bloomsbury: Angelique Tran Van Sang, Philippa Cotton, Katherine Ailes, Allegra Le Fanu, Greg Heinimann. Habib University and British Council Library Karachi, where some of this was written.

One is lucky to have Faiza Sultan Khan and Clare Alexander, the best readers, editors and collaborators any writer can hope for.

A NOTE ON THE TYPE

The text of this book is set in Minion, a digital typeface designed by Robert Slimbach in 1990 for Adobe Systems. The name comes from the traditional naming system for type sizes, in which minion is between nonpareil and brevier. It is inspired by late Renaissance-era type.